THROW ME TO THE WOLVES

A CRY WOLF NOVEL, BOOK I

LINDY RYAN &
CHRISTOPHER BROOKS

Throw me to the wolves
and I will return leading the pack.

ISBN (print): 978-1-64548-117-1
ISBN (ebook): 978-1-64548-118-8

Cover Design and Interior Formatting
by Qamber Designs and Media

Published by Black Spot Books,
An imprint of Vesuvian Media Group

For my brother, and for H. Warner Munn

You may hear a knock from deep in the house. A series of taps, like a rolling shudder, a dull thump of a fist against walls from inside the center of the place. Well, this house makes all sorts of sounds. Some seem to come from outside, some from upstairs. Most people will say it's just the sort of creaks and gongs you get in any old house settling down.

But that is not what this is.

The house's heart beats. You hear it strongest under the stairs, behind that little closet, on the other side of the ribcage of slatted wood shelves. You'd have to take apart the stairs to get in there, but I tell you, those sounds coming from behind there, that's for certain not the sound of the plumbing.

Because this house, it's not like other houses. It's one of the biggest and oldest in all of Calcasieu Parish, and houses this big and this old are built of more than wood and slab, nails, and grout. Memories soak like blood into the floorboards. They seep underneath paint and wallpaper and they saturate the walls.

You'll leave your stain on it, too.

CHAPTER ONE

I f I blinked I might tear out his throat.

The silence hung, a threat in the air between us, while I stared daggers into the pretty brown eyes of Officer Shiny Badge. Little silver tassels waved from a vent up in the corner behind him—proof the AC worked, though just barely. It pushed the smell of mold at us, which just made me feel more pent up. Still, I inhaled long and deep until the suit jacket squeezed at my chest, and willed my pulse back down. Patience had never been one of my strongest virtues when I was alive, and I hadn't developed any more of a taste for it since—kind of ironic, because now I literally had all the time in the world. Then again, what fun would immortality be if I had to waste it caged up in shitty interrogation rooms like this? Things that go bump in the night have little use for the niceties of the living.

"I am glad that the witch is dead," I told him, without letting the smile part my lips, "but I did not kill her."

The words bit the air with a satisfying crack, and Officer Shiny Badge shifted at the other side of the blond pine table, the legs of his chair scraping the beat-up tile floor. The confident smirk slipped, then fixed itself back in place. I wondered what his arms looked like under the crisp sleeves of his uniform, and watched as he resisted the urge to touch the gun on his hip. Only his eyes betrayed the good cop pretense he struggled to maintain, making a quick dash to the double-sided glass over my shoulder.

I think I'd spooked him.

Good.

I didn't flinch when he reached across the table to shake my Coke can. The little bit of backwash barely made a sound, and he forced a smile. "Let me get you another."

I scowled my consent, the best I could do to appear agreeable.

The cop rapped his knuckles against the door, and when he looked my way his eyes flicked to the two-way glass again. I turned and waved to whoever watched us as the door popped open, and Officer Shiny Badge slipped out.

Alone, I set my eyes on the silver tassels waving from the vent, locked in an interrogation room being questioned about a murder I didn't commit. About a victim I wasn't sorry to hear was dead. I had a right to be grumpy. Pissed, even. Besides, I hadn't been waxing hyperbolic: the dead woman had been an *actual* witch.

I haven't known many practitioners of magic, but I knew enough to tell the bad kind from the wicked. This one had been the worst of them all, and I had the scars to prove it.

The claws too, I thought.

I considered reaching across the table to see what I could learn from the papers stacked there since the start of this meeting. But I didn't. I focused on those little waving tassels, so the men watching through the two-way glass only saw the unmoving back of my head—assuming they hadn't all wandered off in boredom.

A squeal of hinges announced the rookie's return and I snatched the Coke from his paw before he could set it down. If you watch enough cop shows you'd know he planned to fill my bladder 'til I couldn't help but tell him something, anything, just to leave the room. He wanted to make me squirm.

I popped the tab, tipped the can, and guzzled the drink in one draft.

My hosts at the Calcasieu Parish Police Department might be surprised to see how long someone like me could hold her water—or her soda, for that matter.

Officer Shiny Badge cleared his throat. The sound thundered between us, faded into silence.

This was getting old. I'd tried to play nice, but my tête-à-tête with the Calcasieu PD had long since begun to tax the polished, non-threatening persona I'd worn for the occasion. This poor idiot had no idea he was in the presence of a wolf dressed in people's clothing. That of the two of us at opposite sides of the interrogation table, Officer Shiny Badge may be the one wearing the gun, but if there was a big, bad anything in the room, it was most definitely *me*. Big, Bad Britta.

Officer Shiny Badge barely winced when I let out a loud, Coca-Cola-fueled belch. At least it burned away the stink of mold for a second.

Scarlett O'Hara I ain't—sorry, Mom—even if the cop's coif made him a reasonable facsimile of Rhett Butler, minus the 'stache.

I pressed thick heels down into the tiled floor, pounded a fist so hard the empty can hopped in place. "I think," I leaned toward him so the worn edge of the table pressed into my chest, "that the only reason we're sitting here so quietly is because your boss already asked me everything."

Officer Shiny Badge's brow knitted.

He leaned back, crossed his arms over his chest. "Devereaux?" He shook his head and chuckled. "Devereaux's not my boss."

I'd come back to Vinton of my own accord—flown on their dime, of course, but had walked willingly into this so-called informal debriefing with cops who'd never done me any favors. I'd tried my best not to spook the humans, too, even popping in brown contacts to minimize the gleam of my pupils. I'd picked up a cheap skirt suit at an outlet mall on the way to the airport back in Maine, and stuffed my usual all-black clothing into borrowed luggage. Buttoned up in the navy blue suit, my oxblood Doc Martens were the brightest color in the ensemble. I'd shot awake at dawn in my little motel on I-10 and twisted wayward hair into a respectable updo, which seemed to make the silver highlights less pronounced. I had plenty of practice not smiling, so no worries they might glimpse a canine.

Even so, everyone in the station had acted like the devil himself had just come down to Louisiana. Or in my case, the devil *her*self.

So much for trying to fit in. Maybe it was the whole "sole survivor of a triple homicide who let her entire family die" thing that set them on edge, or perhaps I wasn't nearly as good at playing human as I hoped. Two different types of monsters, all stowed away in one woman—lucky me.

I'd barely taken two steps into the station before being corralled into an interview room by crusty old Devereaux, whose sour countenance and rank, coffee-bacon breath I remembered from back in the day. Of course, he'd been Officer Deveraux then. Apparently, *not* solving said triple homicide had earned him the upgrade to detective.

His partner, a reedy, middle-aged bloke whose name I hadn't caught, had taken one look at me and locked the door behind him, hugging a stack of paper to his chest. The brown suit had just a hint of red, and piping on the lapels gave the man a cowboy vibe, but Devereaux wore the boots in this relationship.

The partner gestured to the chair that faced the mirrored wall, its back to the door. "Take a seat, Miss Hall."

"Orchid," I said, and walked around the table to the other chair.

"That's right." Devereaux took the chair his pal had offered me. He wore no coat, shirtsleeves rolled up, jowls lapping over the collar. "Ray Hall was her stepdad."

"Honest mistake." The partner shrugged.

My eyes rolled. So much for Southern hospitality.

Manners don't cost a thing. Those words had been my mother's mantra when she'd been alive. It hadn't worked out so well for either of us, but the lesson had stuck.

Devereaux, as it turned out, was no happier to see me than I was to see him, which was both fine and no big surprise. His mouth formed a tight line, barely visible under the stained mustache that gave him away as a smoker. He tried to set the tone with a compliment, some long-winded way of saying I didn't look any older than the last time he'd seen me. Of course, I didn't, but I shot the remark down right away.

"If I'm just here to ID the body, can we get it over with?"

The question had been met with a sneer, which Devereaux turned into a cough in his fist. "I'm, uh, I'm afraid that isn't gonna be necessary."

"Then why the fuck am I here?"

It came out in a bark. So much for manners.

The reedy guy in the corner bugged his eyes at me, frowned. "We could use your help looking for—"

Devereaux whirled around in his chair like he was the only one allowed to speak to me. He turned back and said, "The murder weapon."

They looked at me with dead eyes, two disapproving dads, but what cut my anger was my own surprise: I hadn't realized how much I'd wanted to see the body. I shifted around trying to get comfortable in the jacket, not wanting to unbutton and expose myself.

"The State of Louisiana is appreciative of your assistance in the matter," Devereaux said and raised a hand. His partner put one thin manila folder in it. "We just wanna review your earlier statement," he looked away, "in light of new events."

I'd laughed, and the sound cut at my throat. "No one had much interest in that statement before."

Devereaux's eyes went round, and he splayed thick sausage fingers over his heart in mock scandal. "It was a possible triple homicide, miss. We were—"

"*Possible?*"

The ill-fitting expression slipped off Devereaux's face and he slapped the skinny, aged folder on the table. He huffed and shook his head, but kept his eyes downcast, looking at the folder, so pale it nearly blended into the table's finish. "We were very interested. I've kept the case open." His eyes shot back to his partner. "It was just such a … a fantastic statement, Miss Orchid, and from such a young kid—"

"I wasn't a kid," I spat at him. "I was already out of college."

"Forgive me." Devereaux's mustache curved up in an unconvincing smile. "Which art school did you go to again …?"

"It wasn't an art school, you yokel." I rolled my eyes. "I got a degree in art from Rice University."

"That's right. Houston." He turned again toward his partner, who grinned and looked at his shoes. "Well, we're grateful you were able to get time off to come help us. What do you do, again?" he asked, snapping his fingers, pretending to forget. "Make apple juice?"

"I don't make the juice." I scowled at him, then at the reedy guy grinning in the corner.

"Know what," Devereaux sneered, "no one really cares about all that, Miss Orchid." He grabbed the file and shook it at me. "See, we're inclined to reconsider that the Hall Murders might have involved some sort of cult activity, given the details of the new crime scene." He slapped the folder on the table and the typed pages I'd signed ten years ago spilled out.

After Devereaux, it had been more of the same for the next two hours—hostile public servants who smelled as poorly as they behaved, trying to be polite about what happened to my family while badgering me about the woman I'd always maintained had done it. One cop slipped and referred to it as the *Hall Murder House,*

and quickly apologized. Another asked about the secret passages in the house, the sealed-off attic door, and it sounded like they'd figured out most of the house's *unusual* features while looking for the murder weapon.

Truth is, they didn't actually have a lot of questions, just hoped that by dragging me through it again I'd blurt out some new revelation, maybe confess to sneaking back into Vinton to off the witch myself. They'd ask me to confirm details from the original statement, then they each asked one question—the same question, worded virtually the same way each time, just filtered through different lips. I'd already wanted to claw my own eyes out when I walked in the door, and my mood hadn't improved any since.

Then, Officer Shiny Badge had come in.

He'd cut straight to that one question, too: if I'd had any contact with the witch in the last ten years? After I'd told the new guy no, we'd faced off silently for the better half of an hour, each of us trying to sort out how to apply the right amount of pressure to make the other crack. Thus far, things were at a stalemate.

At least he smelled nice.

A little *too* nice, actually. I'd spent the afternoon scenting the police force of southwestern Louisiana, and they'd peaked at *eau de beignet rassis*—stale donut—with hints of old cheeseburger. This guy wore the fragrance of freshly tilled earth—all pine needles and moonlight and wet soil—though he looked squeaky-clean. In fact, he looked as if he'd just walked off the cover of *Northwoods Sporting Journal*, put on a policeman's blues, and strolled into the station. He wore the right costume for his character but didn't quite pull it off.

Well, that made two of us. I twitched in my uncomfortable skirt suit, caught another whiff of the officer's musky aroma, and glowered across the table. "Devereaux said you don't need me to identify the body."

Now it was Officer Shiny Badge's turn to grimace like I'd

just stepped in dogshit. "Ah, no, Miss Orchid. That's not why you're—"

"Then why the hell did your department *insist* I come in person?" I shrieked. "Especially," I said, more measured, "if the plan was to stare me to death. It doesn't work." I leaned across the table. "Trust me. I've got a mirror. I've tried."

His eyes flicked to the two-way glass behind me, but he stayed expressionless.

"This could have been handled on the phone. Hell, an email would've been more productive. But this—" I motioned around the room, smiling without showing teeth. "Well, this is a waste of my fucking time."

Sorry, Mom, should've just said *fiddle-dee-dee*.

The cop clicked his teeth and reclined in his chair.

"Let me ask you something," Officer Shiny Badge said, as though his last question hadn't come almost thirty minutes ago. "You gave that statement the day after the murders of Ray, Joan, and Remi Hall."

"That's not a question," I growled.

He flipped open my folder and scanned the statement for the hundredth time. Pretended to scan. "You hadn't planned to tell the police the witchcraft story—had you?"

I grunted. "You mean if that EMT hadn't told them first?"

"Right. You told the paramedic while he dressed your wounds."

"It just came out." Never trust a man in uniform, even the cute ones. "I knew the cops wouldn't believe me."

"The paramedic told Devereaux, who took your full statement at the hospital ..." He waved a hand with *yada yada yada* boredom. "My question is this." He closed the folder. "You weren't a suspect. You were a grieving young adult with no local ties." He interlaced his fingers again, now with the casual look of a guidance counselor rather than a startled avian. "But you didn't leave town right away."

Deep within, my wolf lifted her nose, scenting him. Curious. I glanced at the stack of papers he'd left me alone with when he fetched that second Coke. Perhaps I should have peeked.

"I didn't have family anywhere else," I hissed.

"You did leave three days later, though." He glanced at the file. "The … morning after the full moon?"

"What?" Carbonation from the downed soda bubbled dangerously up my throat. I swallowed, struggled not to fidget in the too-tight suit jacket.

This guy wasn't some unsuspecting rookie, tossed in the hole as a last resort. His brothers-in-blue had been appetizers. He was the main course.

Officer Shiny Badge—the thin, gold bar on his chest said his name was Labaye—attempted a smile as he combed long, tan fingers through his thick shock of shoe-polish black hair. He produced another good cop smile, and this time it reached his eyes, making them warm enough to melt into. My wolf stirred again, tail twitching with interest, but I pushed her down, looked at the tassels hanging limp now from the vent. Sure, Officer Labaye was somewhere on the gratuitous end of attractive, the perfect mix of tall, dark, and handsome that men born and bred near New Orleans often are: lean and broad-shouldered with dark hair, soulful eyes, a rugged jawline, and an accent thick enough to wrap itself around you. But he was also a uniform, and a human and that was a bad combo for someone like me.

"Ms. Orchid," Officer Labaye started in that slow, slightly Southern but mostly Cajun drawl only heard on the Texas-Louisiana line. "We just have a few more questions, so if you'll bear with—"

"*I* didn't kill her." Frustration sharpened the edge of my sigh, made it sound more like a growl. Labaye's smile wilted, and along with it, any preoccupation I'd had with his intoxicating aroma. I crossed my arms high across my chest and took a deep, steadying breath, trying in vain not to inhale the officer's scent as my tenuous hold on patience frayed. "And as I'm sure you're aware, I have a rock-solid alibi up the other end of the Atlantic coast. So, why am I still here?"

I had to grit my teeth on each of the last words to keep from screaming them.

Labaye blinked without responding. The fraying of my hypothalamus quickened.

My wolf grew restless under my skin. The stab of fingernails as they dug into the flesh of my wrists helped to hold back the anger rushing through my veins, but only a little. Managing normal emotions as a wolf was hard with everything—lust, fear, anger—amplified. It would be easy to get lost in emotions, for skin to turn to fur.

But that would be bad.

Good Cop still hadn't said not one damn word. "Would you like to tell me," I spat, "or would you find it easier to speak if I ripped your tongue out of your mouth and worked it for you?"

Manners, Britta. Shit. Normal human girls didn't threaten to rip out a person's tongue.

Labaye's Adam's apple thrust down his neck, then bobbed back up as he cleared his throat. His fingers twittered again, and he busied them shuffling the paperwork that had been lying mostly forgotten on the corner of the table. He no longer seemed so keen on eye contact.

His reaction tempered my anger, splashed serotonin, just enough for me to get the feelings back under control. I gave the cop time to recover while I used the few seconds of quiet and a couple of deep breaths to achieve something that could, in a pinch, pass for inner peace.

The last thing I needed was heat from these people. I wasn't a suspect, had done nothing to warrant being detained. It needed to stay that way.

Forcing my lips into what I hoped was a passably friendly smile, I blinked a few times to wash the glare out of my eyes. "*Why am I still here?*"

Officer Labaye's throat did its little diving routine again, something in there wanting out. With it, what was left of my patience slipped without saying goodbye, and I saw red, slapped both palms on the table hard enough that each finger left a shallow trench in the thin wood, and I almost didn't care if anyone noticed. "*Why,* damn it!"

We stared at each other for a few heartbeats, and Labaye broke first, working hard to get his good cop face back on. "Ms. Orchid ..." he started, taking his time with the words so that his smile carved dimples into his cheeks.

"Look, Labaye," I cut in. "Rookie cops don't get a break, and cute guys don't get my attention."

A dejected expression passed over his face. Either he was sad he'd gotten shut down, or his ego had taken a hit. Labaye looked like the kind of guy who'd be unaccustomed to his million-dollar smile not working on the ladies.

Play nice, Britta.

"Besides ..." I sighed as I passed the olive branch, "you're not enjoying this any more than I am, though you're desperate to convince me otherwise." I relaxed my hands so they stopped pressing into the tabletop, and drummed my fingers, nails clicking a little paradiddle. "You get a gold star for acting, but let's get to the point, okay? We both know I had nothing to do with the witch's murder, so what do you want from me?"

"Okay, Britta," Labaye agreed, his voice less bullshit and more molasses. "I do have a few more questions ..."

"So," I hissed, "ask them."

We were about to talk about *her*—the woman who'd started all this. The woman I owed this furry curse to. I'd run thousands of miles away to forget her, but I'd never be free of her memory.

We needed to talk about her after all these years because she was dead.

And I wasn't the one who'd gotten to kill her.

I dug my nails into the edge of the table so hard I bit my tongue. The taste of blood filled my mouth.

"I know you didn't murder Selena Stone," Labaye said, "but I need your help figuring out who killed her."

Just like that, we had *her* name. I closed my eyes, sucked in Labaye's sweet, distracting scent, and tried to recall what poor, dead Mother had said about manners.

CHAPTER TWO

Selena Stone.

  Selena fucking Stone.

  Selena Stone was the witch responsible for the series of bizarre and disturbing events that had led to my present condition, including the deaths of my entire family—my mother, stepfather, and Remi, my younger brother.

  My fingernails cut little half-moons into my palms, left spidery traces of blood for some latex-gloved cop to clean off the edge of the pine tabletop later. The silver tassels hung limp from the slats of the vent as the temperature in the room soared.

  "Remi was ten," I told Labaye, "the day that woman killed him."

  Poor, sweet, darling Remi. Even now, my heart struggled under the weight of his name. When that goddamned Devereaux had read it off the report a few hours earlier, a swell of tears rushed to my eyes, which I sure as shit hated to show, especially to him. Especially after all this time.

  My brother had been dead now for as long as he'd ever been alive.

  Labaye took my file back off the stack but didn't open it. "You said his death had been the result of a botched exorcism performed by Selena Stone. His death certificate listed—"

  "No, I didn't," I muttered.

  "Pardon?"

  The idea he'd died by exorcism was ridiculous enough, even in the Deep South of the Bible Belt. "I didn't say it had been an exorcism." I sneered and rapped a knuckle next to the closed folder. "The witch said he *needed* an exorcism. Promised an exorcism. But his death," I said, leaning forward so that the cop leaned back, "had been the intended outcome of a spell with an innocent on its ingredient list. Nothing botched, nothing accidental."

Labaye folded those long, tan fingers together, trying to ground the conversation. "Okay, right. Not *really* an exorcism. But you do still maintain that Selena Stone forced your family into some kind of, uh, ritual."

Ritual. If I enunciated sharply enough, my voice barely cracked. "My religious zealot mother and booze-sponge stepfather were all too eager to participate, in the hopes of saving their only son from the demons they'd believed haunted him."

My whole body felt like a knot—my butt barely touched the seat.

Labaye's jaw tightened. "In the interest of clarity, you're saying your parents ... sacrificed him?"

"My parents thought Remi was possessed. Thought that through an 'exorcism' he would be freed of the demons the witch claimed infested him." The little cuts in my palms had run dry, leaving white grooves that would confound palm readers, and I exhaled, sinking back into the chair. "They thought they'd been saving him, not condemning him, when they gave him to her."

"So, you think your parents helped Selena, without understanding the danger to themselves or Remi—and she took advantage of that in a premeditated act of murder."

There was no humor in my smile, no bitterness, just pain. It didn't matter if he needed to believe my version of the events or not, the end result was the same. "No one volunteers to die."

Officer Labaye sat across the table, those long fingers still woven together, and let the statement breathe.

My eyes wandered back to the tassels. I'd tried to save my family. *All* of them.

And then I'd died.

"You're sure the witch is dead?" I asked after a beat, and Labaye nodded. "How?"

"We matched DNA—" Labaye cleared his throat before flipping through a new folder he'd drawn from the stack. "With evidence recovered ten years ago."

I bristled. "Things you recovered from my house?"

"Excuse me?"

"How could you use DNA evidence from my family's murders if you never believed the witch had done it?"

He shook his head. "We'd recovered DNA from Miss Stone's house." His eyes came up to meet mine, then back to a page in the file. "Just, you know, hair pulled from a brush, that sort of thing."

"So, Devereaux didn't totally discount my story."

"Three people died, Miss Orchid," Labaye said without looking at me. "Including a child. My colleagues at the time may not have blamed it on witchcraft, but they were eager to find whoever did it. As for Selena Stone ... she hadn't been seen in Vinton since the night of the murders. Until we found her remains, that is."

"And no one told me she went missing back then, even before I left town?" I grunted. Where had she gone? After me— the world's most undeserving *final girl*? I uncrossed my ankles, clunked the heels of the oxblood Doc Martens—not my ten-hole boots of yore, but just the shoes—and tried not to dwell on those questions any more than Labaye's three-day timeline and worrisome moon comment. "But if you know I didn't kill her, and you don't need me to identify the body, what do you want me to help you with—assuming I even could?"

Or would.

"Well," Labaye said, sucking his bottom teeth and directing his gaze over my shoulder. "I frankly can't imagine who could've done *this*, so I'd be grateful for anything you can tell me."

He pulled a single sheet from the folder, set it down to study for a second, then slid the blurry photograph across the table. The first clue the police had given to the details of the witch's demise.

I snatched the photograph up and resisted the urge to lick my lips.

The line between pain and pleasure is especially blurry for a wolf. Wolves love long-distance runs because euphoria-inducing enzymes flood our system to reduce the perception of pain. The same enzymes kick in to transmute other kinds of pain. It has a lot more to do with bloodlust than plain old *lust* lust. One minute you're in your best fancy-people clothes trying not to cry over human memories, and the next you're hungry enough to *actually* eat a horse—and savor every bite.

The grainy resolution of the printout said it had likely been snapped on someone's smartphone—slightly out of focus, a consequence of a shaky hand. The subject of the shot looked like something out of a gore flick, one of those B-grade "films" with a storyline too shallow to soak up the buckets of red corn syrup dumped all over it and called art.

Blood was smeared, splattered, and sprayed across every surface to gruesome effect. Three tiny yellow rectangles jutted out of the red.

Piet Mondrian meets Jackson Pollock.

I licked my jowls. Lips.

Through the blood, you could just make out the familiar floral pattern on the floor beneath. Mom had fawned over her reproduction Dutch tile to anyone who'd listen. She'd finished laying the parlor floor, with its delft design of cobalt and white, the very day she'd died in our parlor—but this wasn't a photo from that night.

I stammered a bit trying to say, "Lot of DNA, all right."

"Are you ready for this," Labaye said, not without tempting me with another sheet pulled from the file. I nodded and he slid it across.

This shot punched in on one of the yellow evidence markers, and the hairs on the back of my neck tingled. In the blood sat a little pink bundle. An eyeball stared up at an angle, perched on a chunk of meat. A pale cord wound around the eight-ounce steak, knotted beneath the eyeball like a tie under a man's chin. Short, threaded bits of muscle bound the back of the eye to the cord—the optic nerve, I realized, and I guessed that the heart someone had tied it on top of was human. A carefully arranged cairn of human teeth surrounded the two organs.

I set the photo down on the other and met Labaye's eyes. Without extending my arm, I opened the hand, palm up.

He closed the file and folded those long fingers together again. "That's it?" I said.

"This is all we found left of Selena Stone." Labaye nodded at the two sheets in front of me. He leaned in over the close-up. "I think that's an alpine butterfly knot, but even in person it's hard to tell." He squinted. "Tissue's so soft."

I almost laughed out loud, but the sound got lost in a swell of sick on its way up my throat. I swallowed it down. The poetic justice was overwhelming. The scene, and the memories, hit hard. Blood. Pain. Anger.

"Devereaux said you were looking for a murder weapon," I muttered, "but you're missing about a hundred pounds of witch parts."

I spread the two pages out. No wonder they didn't ask me to ID the body. Something stirred just beneath the surface of my skin as my wolf roiled, hungry and curious.

Labaye mistook my silence for something else. He made a soft, grunting noise and eased a tentative hand across the table as if toward a frightened animal with bristled fur and bared teeth. When I didn't respond, he rested his palm flat against the pine, beside my balled-up fist, and cleared his throat.

It must be hard to comfort when you don't know what to

say. I started to like Officer Shiny Badge, despite myself.

"Britta?" His voice sounded oddly emotional. When I didn't look at him, his knuckles brushed against the back of my fist, then tapped the table gently.

"What?"

"I am sorry to have to ask you these questions," Labaye said. "Truly, I am."

"What do you care?" I straightened in the seat and willed my heart to turn to stone. Words formed on my lips, but after all this time, I still couldn't bring myself to speak her name. "I'm fine. That witch"—I spat the word like it started with a different letter—"deserved to die."

I flicked the photographs back across the table and mustered up what cinders still burned under my skin. If I could stoke that flame enough, I could get through the rest of this interview. Later, when no one was around, I could process my emotions in wolfcoat, let them pour over me when I could howl and claw and run out the pain on the service road behind the motel.

But that was later. "Deserved whatever end she got, and worse."

The right side of Labaye's mouth tightened. He patted his palm against the photos, then slipped them into their folder. "Did you know Selena Stone had been murdered?"

He tried to make the question sound offhand, innocent, but it sliced intentionally through the space between us.

"Not before you guys called."

His mouth twitched, but this time it was a grin, and gone just as fast. "Do you know anyone else who might have a motive to kill her?"

He meant, had Selena done to anyone else what she'd done to me? There was no one I could name. "No."

"But you wished Selena Stone dead." Labaye gripped her file in both hands, licked his lips in anticipation of an answer, and cocked an eyebrow. I dared a sniff, hoping for some telltale clue to the emotion behind that quick lick, but all I could scent was pine and musk and whatever expensive-smelling leave-in conditioner he used to seal back his dark hair. The smell tickled low in my body, and I thought I might want to quit breathing.

The red image of Mom's parlor flashed through my mind, and the rage in the pit of my stomach welled back up, spread its familiar spark through each limb. "Yes."

Leaning back in his chair, Labaye opened her file again and lifted it so I couldn't scc. He seemed to search for something specific, the way he scanned the pages.

"So, you haven't been in Vinton for ten years," he started, without eye contact.

"Not since she killed my entire family."

The bluntness of the words seemed to give him pause, and Officer Labaye looked over the top of the file at me.

I let my face go slack and gave him the full weight of my glare.

"And you've been resettled in …" He flipped open a different folder, again just pretending to read. "New England since you left?"

"Maine." I sighed. Somehow we'd taken one step forward, then rewound to the start. Great.

Labaye waved away the snide remarks. "Why Maine? No strings, no roots, you could have gone anywhere."

"Once upon a time, I studied art, wanted to be a painter." I shrugged, deflecting. "Maine holds a lot of natural inspiration. Edward Hopper didn't just paint diners."

He didn't try to hide his smirk. "And you don't know anything about what's happened here since you left? No friends, contacts—nothing?"

"I lived here for one summer. Barely that long." Aside from good ol' Devereaux, I knew one other person in the area, and I wouldn't call her a friend.

"And you never considered coming back, avenging your

family?" Labaye tried to act casual, less concerned with any answer than with lining up the corners of the files stacked in front of him. "Making Selena pay for what she did?"

"I thought about it every day," I replied truthfully.

He rubbed at his jaw and looked at the grid of acoustic ceiling tiles. "So, *why* didn't you kill her? Why didn't you wake up the next morning and come after her for what she'd done?"

The question caught me off guard, rattled me right back to angry, and something ripped in my chest. My wolf was suddenly there, pushing against my insides, her fur tickling the space under my skin. I clenched everything I had and willed her down.

A few days after the witch had murdered my family, I'd woken up naked in icy marsh water, overwhelmed by the mangled remains of my life. I'd come awake slowly, emerging from a dream that mixed gory memories of Remi and Mom, even Ray, with the taste of blood, flesh, and fur. The sensations made no sense. I knew the blood on my hands, face, and throat, was not my own, nor was it theirs, but I had shed it. As I climbed out of the water, I stumbled over a mangled coyote. Flies buzzed around the hollowed-out carcass of a doe on the bank.

The blood I'd shed as a wolf got mixed up in my mind with the blood of my family when I awoke as an orphan. As a monster, in more ways than one. And I fled Vinton, I thought forever.

The truth, then, the unbearable, horrible truthful answer to Labaye's question: I hadn't killed the witch because this was my curse. I'd live forever as the *thing* she'd turned me into—a werewolf, a skin-changer, a *loup garou*—and I'd endure every single day of my existence haunted by the death of people I'd loved and failed to save.

And for that, I hated myself almost as much as I hated her.

"Killing someone is still murder, isn't it?" I finally managed. "Even if you call it revenge."

The disbelieving expression that melted over Labaye's face prickled along the edges of my flesh, tender where my beast's temper had left a bruise. He spoke low as if we sat in a confessional, and the softness in his voice pissed me off.

"I would have killed her," he said.

A tide of wrath and pride, guilt and remorse, washed over me, and the words came out in a snarl that curled into the best fake sneer I could aim at Labaye. My palms were bleeding again. "Oh, you would have, would you?" I snapped. "I'll tell you what, we can compare feelings when someone murders your entire family. Until then, stop pretending you know anything about what it's like to be me, and get back to handing out parking tickets."

Labaye sucked in a deep breath and nodded in a long, drawn-out movement. Something clicked behind his eyes, a flicker behind the curtain of the good cop pretense, and his body language relaxed. "I don't have any more questions, Britta, just a request. The truth is, we need your help. *I* need your help."

I rolled my eyes. "Your murder investigation is not my problem. Even if it—"

"Selena was found in the house."

"Yeah, I picked up on that."

Labaye exhaled with noticeable effort, crossed his arms, and leaned his elbows on the table. "There's more."

He grabbed the file with the new crime scene photos and removed a sheet of paper that had been crumpled, then flattened out. He pushed it across the table and rolled his neck.

I looked at the paper and jerked a hand to my mouth, a gasp catching in my throat.

On the paper were the unmistakable, bold lines of a child's illustration, sketched roughly in beginner charcoal. The drawing was unfamiliar, but I knew the artist instantly—knew the slant of the shading lines and the way they tracked in alternating depths with each stroke.

It wasn't one of Remi's drawings I'd ever seen before, but it was undeniably his work.

On the page, a smiling young boy with disheveled hair stood, fingers curled in the fur of a large wolf with eyes colored in with neon yellow highlighter.

I stared at the wolf.

I stared at … me.

CHAPTER THREE

Officer Aaron Labaye had flinched when Britta insisted they ride out to the crime scene, but he'd agreed. Before starting the car, he handed her the drawing of the boy and the wolf. She stammered a few words of faint protest, but he assured her that if the drawing was evidence of anything, it had no place in a police report.

Aaron had done his homework on Britta Orchid. Pulled all the old case records, ran the database to build a profile. There wasn't much to find online about the woman, either before or since the Hall Murders. Her family had been killed before social media had taken off when people left only the faintest of digital footprints. If Britta had made her mark on the Internet since, he couldn't find so much as a Facebook profile.

In the end, Aaron wasn't sure what he could've dug up online that would have prepared him for the woman he met in the interrogation room that morning. Throughout the interview, he struggled to pinpoint that feeling in his gut, figure out what was personal reaction as opposed to professional opinion. Luckily, she'd taken a while to warm up, and the time Britta spent defrosting had given him a chance to reclaim his senses and remember why he'd asked her to come back to Louisiana in the first place.

Selena Stone.

Aaron hadn't counted on Britta being so eager to see her old homestead again. So, he'd baited her, using the photographs of Selena's remains to pique her interest. When she'd reacted more blithely than he'd anticipated, he played the last card he had—the

23

bizarre portrait, apparently in her brother's hand. It hadn't mattered how much she'd distanced herself from the events of ten years earlier, how much anger she had stored in her girlish frame, no one could have seen that without a million questions banging around inside her head, demanding answers.

Britta had stared at that drawing for a full minute before she bolted out of her chair. "We're going to the house," she'd said.

Aaron exhaled and gave a quick thumbs up to the two-way mirror, shuffled the papers on the desk, and hoped no one would stop them on their way out. Britta knocked on the door, which the officer outside opened, startled as she brushed past. Aaron nodded at the man and followed.

Of course, this meant he'd have to go back, too. He'd seen his share of horrors in the Hall Murder House, but Britta had lived them. If she wanted to go, he couldn't very well sit this part out. Not if he wanted her help.

And he didn't just want her help. He *needed* it.

"I'll drive," Aaron had managed to say, patting his pockets and shouting at her back as she shot out into the parking lot and thumbed the fob for her rental car, a Prius bearing Texas plates. He thought for sure she'd slip behind the wheel and drive away in a rush of exhaust before he could catch up with her, but she pulled a small carry-on and a totally unseasonable leather jacket from the backseat, stalked back into the station, and vanished into the ladies' room without so much as a second glance at him.

He grabbed a couple of things including the keys to his cruiser and stood by his desk, one eye on the ladies' room door. Britta probably wouldn't bolt, but he couldn't take the chance. He needed to be with her when she saw the crime scene for the first time—he couldn't afford to miss anything. Not now.

"You're setting yourself up for trouble," a voice drawled as Aaron waited for Britta to reemerge from the generally ignored women's room. Devereaux leaned over the partition, his hip pushing against an unused desk. An unlit Marlboro bobbed between his lips.

"Trouble?" Aaron watched in his peripheral vision as Devereaux tucked the cigarette behind his ear and sipped at his coffee mug. The man sucked the center of his mustache and exhaled noisily with each swallow.

"If she knew anything, we woulda got it, Labaye," Devereaux said. "Taking her back to the crime scene? She got a screw loose, kid. Traumatizing her won't crack the case. You're gonna be babysitting a signal twenty." The older man tipped back his mug, swallowing what was left of the coffee in a greedy gulp. He chuckled on the exhale and shook his jowls. "Been there."

Aaron never much cared for Devereaux, and what little respect he had for the man was waning. He folded up the crude child's drawing and slipped it in his pocket. "After the murders," Aaron said, "you never told her Selena Stone went missing?"

Devereaux banged the coffee cup down on the empty desk and puffed out his chest. "It was a fucked up time. We didn't have any contact with her—by *her* choice," he emphasized, "until she called to say she'd left town." He clamped one white-knuckled hand on the top of the partition.

Aaron had read the file. A slip from the coroner's office noted the cremation of the Hall bodies—well, the two that still needed it—a week after they'd been recovered from the house, which would've been just after Britta left town. She hadn't even been given the courtesy of burying her family. No wonder she was bitter.

Before his colleague could dole out any more useful advice, the door to the ladies' room swung open and Britta emerged, having shed the cheap, polyester skirt suit, looking much more comfortable in head-to-toe black-on-black. She'd let her neatly coiled hair loose around the frames of her dark sunglasses, and Aaron could just make out the strands of silver interwoven through her brunette locks—distinctly gray, despite otherwise looking like a college student. The dark red shoes had looked dressy enough with a fitted suit, but under the black jeans and leather jacket, Aaron couldn't decide if the look was more punk or metal. He snatched a pair of standard-issue cop aviators from his desk and hooked them in his breast pocket.

Something in his stomach twisted. It felt like hunger, but he'd lost his appetite.

No, he reconsidered, *not hunger.* As she zipped closed her luggage, Aaron recognized desire coiling in his stomach—the type of which he'd never known before. There was something he had not expected in Britta Orchid.

Devereaux clapped a sausage-fingered hand on Aaron's shoulder, startling him back into focus. The man's voice dropped to a harsh, coffee-stained whisper. "Look, Labaye, you can think of her as a witness or a victim, but if you think of her as anything else, know what's gonna happen?"

Across the room, Britta waved an impatient hand and Aaron jerked forward, stumbling over his first step. He didn't hear the rest of what Devereaux said, and he didn't care.

Britta and Aaron drove in silence through the slums of Calcasieu Parish, paying too much attention to the lazy willows and empty lots blurring past to bother with conversation. Early evening settled in as the sky faded from cloudless blue to a murky orange over the western horizon, giving Aaron's dilapidated hometown a hazy glow.

"You doing okay over there?" he asked when the silence in the cruiser had grown stale.

Britta scoffed beside him. Her leather sleeves creaked, arms locked high over her chest as she scowled out the window, face half-hidden behind her shades. Protocol mandated civilians ride in back, but she'd clomped across the parking lot to his cruiser and slid into the passenger seat despite his protests.

"Oh, sure," she spat at the windshield. "Not only has Selena Stone exited this world minus an eye, some teeth, and her goddamned heart, but my dead brother marked the occasion with a self-portrait with a … some dog. So, yeah, I'm great."

Whatever Aaron had planned to say died on his lips. Pleasantries weren't easy en route to a murder scene, even less so while ferrying a former victim. Or witness. Or whatever.

He cleared his throat and tried again. "Aren't you hot in that jacket?"

She tilted her head to shoot a glare over her Ray-Bans, which scorched down to his bones, then she turned back to face the window without responding.

The uneasy feeling thickening the air inside the car said Britta's cooperation was tenuous at best.

"We don't have to do the small-talk thing," she snapped. "Just drive."

Aaron nodded and drummed his long fingers on the steering wheel. Would turning on the radio be unprofessional? Would she even notice? The drive to her old house was only a couple of miles, but Aaron felt every inch pass under the wheels of the cruiser.

The silence grew stale again, and Britta sighed, letting her arms fall into her lap with visible effort. She shuffled in her seat, pulled at the seatbelt, then let it settle back against her breasts.

"This place hasn't improved much since the last time I was here," she said.

Aaron cast an apologetic glance in her direction, hoping it would read through his mirrored sunglasses. "After Hurricane Katrina, then Rita, we got a chunk of government money, enough to fix some of the older buildings and repave Center Street, fight off the mold. But the storms kept coming and the government money dried up."

The hard set of Britta's jaw loosened as more rundown

homes bumped by. "My mother used to say a natural disaster was God's way of punishing us, but Remi liked the thunder. He always liked the rain." She fell quiet and shifted again. "Modern-day Sodom and Gomorrah, that's what Mom called New Orleans. Probably would've said it was too bad the whole place didn't wash into the sea."

Aaron bit down and took a slow breath. "People started moving away," he went on before silence could fill the car again. "Walked out of town using what FEMA gave 'em to rebuild. Hardly anyone's moving here, and more folks trickle out every year."

"But not you?"

He shook his head, feeling Britta's eyes burn pleasantly into his profile. He tapped his thumbs against the steering wheel. When she faced front, he could breathe again. "Not much left here now, but it's home."

Aaron brought the cruiser to a stop at a red light next to a small brick building. The sloped roof sagged, mostly caved in at the middle; the windows had no glass, not even boarded up.

"That was a DVD place." Britta surprised him by jabbing a finger at the building. "JD's Video or Frankie's Films or something."

Aaron eyed the crumbling storefront and laughed. "That place was about five different rental places, including Frankie's, I think," he nodded. "Then a bakery for a little bit. The Daily Bread."

Britta pulled off the sunglasses and stared through the windshield, seeing something Aaron couldn't. Whatever it was, she didn't share. Her voice was husky when she spoke again. "It was a dump then and it's a dump now."

"Well, it's like they say, isn't it?" Aaron tugged down his aviators to wink over the frame. "If it ain't broke, don't fix it."

Britta glared at him for half a second, then the ghost of a laugh slipped out before she bit down to hold her scowl in place.

"Yeah, I remember that being on the town charter," she said, "right below the part about open season on metalheads and goths—art-school kids included." Her body language relaxed a fraction as she sank into the seat, then she nodded at the street ahead. "Light's green, Officer."

He pushed his sunglasses up the bridge of his nose and rolled through the intersection. "We can't all be as endearing as Devereaux. Would ruin the charm of the community."

She crossed her arms over her chest and gripped the elbows of the leather jacket. "I thought you'd called me down here to ID the body." She'd brought it up more than once, but having shown her the photos, Aaron didn't know what else to say. "Whatever I told myself," she went on, "whatever I told Alec, or Malakh, that was the only reason I came." She slid the sunglasses back on using both hands. "To see her," Britta said. "Really dead." She turned to the window again so all he saw were silvery black locks when she said, "I don't even get to do that."

Aaron wanted to ask about those two names, one of which was definitely a man, but she'd brought an abrupt end to any levity they'd pretended might exist in the cruiser.

With one hand on the wheel, he swung the front of the car around a sharp turn and came to a full stop.

A low rumble issued from Britta's throat, half-growl, half-groan.

Aaron's pulse quickened and a bead of sweat ran down the back of his neck.

He put the car in park and killed the engine. They stared up at the off-white columns topped by a huge, triangular pediment that stretched back to the house like some ruined antebellum temple, and summoned every bit of collective courage they had.

CHAPTER FOUR

TEN YEARS EARLIER

"You're going to love it, Britta, honey," Mom said. "This house is a gift from the Lord—a reward for our faith and trust in Him!" She preached over the rumble of the engine. "Everything is going to be so different now."

My book fell out of my hands, and I stopped listening as my mother rattled off the virtues of the new house, real-estate agent-style, her itemized list clogging the inside of the truck cab like too much tissue in the bowl of an old toilet with bad pipes. She spoke in the same fast, excitable way she always did when on some new kick, amped up about three octaves on moving day to our miracle house.

I slouched in the passenger side of the rickety Ford F150, hauling a literal truckload of cleaning supplies to the new house in the hottest part of the afternoon—the hottest part of the *year*—and picked at the lacings of my ten-hole leather boots. Mom had dressed appropriately for moving day in summer, in her denim shorts, cross bouncing around in the V-neck of her T-shirt, but my whole wardrobe came in *black* and *long*. I might melt before we crossed the bridge at the Texas-Louisiana line. Ray and Remi had left earlier in the day with the U-Haul, my Mazda hatchback hitched behind it. I'd wanted to drive Remi in my car, but Mom had recognized us as a flight risk, so it was the twenty footer for Remi, and Mom's old Ford for me. Otherwise, the kid and I might have made it to Mexico right about now, parents and college debt be damned.

Moving back in with my family the summer I'd graduated from Rice had to be the stupidest thing I'd ever done—though that's not saying much, since I hadn't screwed up too badly in my twenty-three years so far. And as the recipient of a brand-new college degree and a brand-new student loan payment, I'd found myself unemployed and unmarketable in Houston, with no better luck in San Antonio, Austin, or all the way to Dallas. Fat lot of good a degree in Art History had done, other than give me a lot of strong opinions on contemporary artists and watercolor toxicity.

That's the Catch 22 of the American Dream, isn't it? *Work hard, get an education.* Well, that's all fair and good, but no one tells you that once you've received said degree you can expect to work twice as hard to pay back the money you borrowed. Of course, no one told you, since no previous generation of students faced such a steep debt-to-income disparity—and this is assuming you're lucky enough to get a job in your field of study. In reality, nobody wanted to pay *real* money for the thing I'd *borrowed* all that money to learn. The whole "starving artist" thing applied as much to summa cum laudes who only just *studied* art.

I'd thought art history was the prudent choice. Had I considered how much cheaper it would've been to actually *be* an artist, I might have skipped college altogether. I'd still be unemployed, but at least I'd have been less bitter about being broke.

I also couldn't paint worth a damn, but art was all pretty subjective. One person's scribblings were another's Kandinsky.

Broke, in debt, freshly kicked out of my dorm with no prospects, I didn't exactly have an abundance of options. I didn't even have *options*. I had one. Move in with Joan and Ray until I could figure out how to put my useless, expensive art degree to work.

There was an upside to moving back home, though, to make the whole ordeal totally worth it.

Remi. I got to be with Remi again.

I loved my little brother. More than loved, I *adored* the

kid. The truth of it was, though he was my younger brother—half-brother, if we're splitting hairs—Remi might as well have been my own son.

My father had died in the line of duty when I'd been too young to appreciate the loss. Lonely, heartbroken, and not impressed with single parenthood, Mom found salvation in the early days of online dating. She'd sit me down in front of her Magnavox desktop unit and praise the wonders of Web Personals while we waited for the next profile to load. To her credit, Mom got into online dating way ahead of other people her age, but that made appropriate options slim. She settled quickly on Ray, a former body-builder who'd become a pudgy, mean-spirited, desperate drunk she thought ready for rehabilitation in the hands of a good woman.

Talk about romance.

We moved in with Ray, and one year into marital disaster and already on the other side of forty, Mom had birthed Remi as a second-marriage-saver baby. Once the kid had crowned from womb to world, she passed the torch of motherhood on to me and did not look back. Only thirteen at the time, I stepped right up into night feedings, diaper changes, all of it. As soon as I got us through potty-training, I'd taken a part-time job, spending most of my pay from the grocery store where I worked so Remi and I could eat what we wanted without having to lean on Joan and Ray for cash.

It was never a question of whether Mom and Ray loved us, just that they'd been too preoccupied to raise one more kid, let alone worry about the one that was nearly out of the house.

Ray already had two kids from a previous marriage he didn't speak to—by court order—and he'd never quite figured out how to hold down a job. Mom found her new *joie de vivre* selling cosmetics door-to-door while moonlighting at a boutique that sold anything and everything you could cover in rhinestones and sequins.

Poor Remi never had a chance, with his warm brown eyes and wide, curious smile. Being a de facto teen mom made my adolescence a little unconventional, sure, but it probably saved me a lot of heartache and drama, too. Who could fret about boys and pimples when you had a kid to take care of?

I missed extracurriculars and skipped prom, but I wouldn't have traded a minute of it.

Leaving Remi behind while I spent four years at college had been hard, but he'd started Lumberton Primary, and if I wanted any sort of future for us, I had to start paving the road to take us there. I hadn't gone far, just a hundred miles away to Houston, and I'd driven that beat-up Mazda back to visit every chance I could, regardless of how many times I had to scrape the bottom of my piggy jar for gas money. Still, I felt guilty for abandoning the little guy.

He was turning out just like I had been as a kid, sullen and isolated, and he deserved something better than a drunk dad and bedazzled mom in a little southeast Texas town. At ten years old, he'd already developed worry lines in his forehead, and every time I saw him, I thought he looked a little sadder.

It was an odd look for a kid. Little kids were supposed to be happy.

I figured once I graduated, I'd land some great gallery job, somewhere like New York City or Los Angeles. I'd put Remi in private school, get him a puppy—which Ray strictly forbade—so he didn't have to depend on flaky imaginary friends. I couldn't wait to start over—get free of our shitty parents and hot, shitty Texas, too.

So far, things hadn't worked out quite how I'd hoped.

I'd graduated just in time, though. Mom and Ray had found Jesus, and evidently the good Lord lived on the other side of the Texas-Louisiana border. By the time I got my diploma, they'd put the family three-bed, two-bath on the market and signed papers for some half-dilapidated colonial in southwest Louisiana, in what had once been a larger plantation plot. After a decade of shoddy domestic life, one heavenly vision would deliver what a few go-arounds with Alcoholics Anonymous could not.

A goddamned, God-blessed miracle.

And today, it was all coming true.

My mother, whom I loved dearly despite the woman's best efforts to cure me of such affections, took no pleasure in the quiet companionship of silence and tried to fill every second of the drive to Vinton with noise. She'd flipped through every East Texas radio station—a lot of Bible stuff, and Alan Jackson, Tracy Byrd, Chesney and Paisley and Keith—and made it through a couple of stations out of Lake Charles before starting in with my old enemy.

Babbling.

I didn't have much to say and stared at the flat scrub zipping past as Mom prattled on about how all the work the new house needed was a blessing, since diligent hands bring riches while the other kind do the devil's work, and I thought, *You better be talking about Ray right now.*

I'd spent the last week asking a million questions about the house and the move and the unfair timing, questions she'd deflected at every turn. Eventually, frustrated with my constant inquiry, Joan Hall had defaulted to "God works in mysterious ways"—parent code for: *This is happening, so you need to get over it, Britta.*

Mom might have been happy about the move, but she hadn't been the one who'd lain next to Remi every night for the past week while he'd cried himself to sleep. The poor kid would start his last year of elementary school trying to make new friends. Being the new kid was bad enough. Being the new kid in a school the size of a thimble, even worse.

I crossed my arms and tucked my body as tightly against the truck door as I could. Sure, families moved, but people didn't typically go from vision-from-God to new-home-purchase within in the space of four weeks while ignoring the consequences on their elementary school-aged child. They'd quit their jobs—well, Mom had, because Ray, of course, hadn't had one—and driven off into the sunset to a house they'd yet to set foot in, convinced they'd survive on the currency of prayer if nothing else. I was barely an adult, and even I knew impulsive when I saw it.

Had I only gone into a boring paralegal program at the community college right there in Beaumont, instead of spending four years trying to tell the difference between a Loiseau and a Monet, I would've graduated long ago with a guaranteed job and could've moved Remi and me into a sensible townhome in the good school zone on the other side of town. Mom and Ray and religion could have moved to the moon and it wouldn't have mattered one iota.

"Just think about how much fun you'll have as a young woman in a big plantation house. Honey—" Mom gasped like she'd just remembered something. "You can sweep down the stairs into the parlor when your dates come to call," she said. Her bare knee jumped as she let go of the clutch and cranked the wheel, taking us off the interstate by the Love's truck stop onto rough, uneven pavement.

"You'll be just like Scarlett O'Hara!"

"Perfect," I scoffed from my side of the cab. The selfish, simpering southern belle was *exactly* who I wanted to emulate. Not to mention it was 2002, not 1868, and sweeping down the stairs had fallen out of fashion, not to mention romanticizing Civil War-era plantations and all the nasty social norms of the time. Besides, Mom didn't know Scarlett, had probably never seen *Gone with the Wind*, much less read the book, or devoted any critical thought to how the heroine relied on seducing married men, unable to tell the difference between love and lust. Then again, what did I know? I'd majored in art, not comparative lit.

"Mom, did you think, *really* think, this through?" Sure, Britta, try this again, ten miles from the new house. "You're leaving behind everything—family, friends, your *job*—and moving to some house you've only seen in pictures."

"I may not have been to the *physical* house, but I *have* seen it, Britta." My mother tapped a polished fingernail to her temple before wagging it toward my side of the cab, emphasizing key words with the bluster of a campaigning politician. "Everything from my vision matches *exactly* with the photos from the realtor. You've got to have more faith, honey, and stop being so caught up in 'evidence.'" She added one-handed air quotes to the last word and veered onto the main drive that snaked through town.

My mother, who'd recently fought the teaching of evolution in Lumberton Primary, had little use for science or other pesky details of logic. Joan Hall *believed*.

With a heavy sigh, I squirmed against the door, trying to find a comfortable position without the handle jabbing into my spine or the broken seatbelt buckle stabbing my backside. I reached under the seat for the paperback I'd brought along for the ride. The nausea I'd get from reading in the car would still be better than wasting another sentence in this conversation.

"It's like they say, Mom," I started, making sure Mom got a good view of the book cover—Carl Sagan's *The Demon-Haunted World*. I deepened my voice in my best Rhett Butler impression. "*Never pass up new experiences—they enrich the mind.*"

"What on earth are you talking about, Britta?"

I flipped the book over in my lap. "Nothing, Mother." I could make out the steep triangle point of a large, white house looming above the trees in the distance.

Mom waggled her finger again and trumped Margaret Mitchell with the Bible. "'The thing that hath been, it is that which shall be, and that which is done is that which shall be done, and there is no new thing under the sun.'"

I wanted to respond to her ecclesiastical gibberish with something from *Oh, the Places You'll Go*, but she stopped the pick-up in front of a rundown rural home, built in the Greek Revival style adored by slave owners. Four Doric pillars rose fat and plain from their square bases to disappear up into the overhang. Shutters hung crookedly from the first-floor windows, were mostly absent from the second story.

Hugging his favorite stuffed animal to his chest, Remi sat in the open gate of the moving van, from which not a stick of furniture had been removed. He looked up at us, but he didn't smile, his mouth as straight as that line in his forehead.

.

CHAPTER FIVE

I knocked the heels of my Docs together three times and vainly tried to wish myself anywhere else. But my shoes weren't ruby slippers, and this wasn't Oz. So, I sucked up my fear, choked it down like the monster I was, and opened the passenger door of Labaye's cruiser. He had wanted me to ride in the back, as per protocol, where I would've had to wait for him to get the door—but I'd rather walk than be hauled to the scene of my own family's murders like a suspect.

Today wasn't the day for perpetuating monster stereotypes.

The air-cushioned PVC soles sank into the marshy, unkempt front lawn, bringing me face-to-face with an old enemy. The front doors, flanked by the remains of an iron gate, stared like two soulless black eyes. Most of the front windows had been boarded long ago, but the transom over the doors and the window up in the pediment stood open without glass. The four columns grinned like tall, hungry teeth, discolored by a thin, crawling layer of silky green mildew plaque. Pale ribbons twisted like crypt moss around the bases, remnants of police tape bleached by the sun, the words *Do Not Cross* hard to make out. Was this faded warning a leftover from the night my family had died—a warning to keep others away? The only good thing about the state of the house was it said no one currently lived in the place.

It had never occurred to me to ask.

A flash of orange drew my eyes to the second story, and I thought someone had replaced the balcony railing I'd helped Mom install over the entrance, but the wrought iron had just rusted so badly I'd be scared to walk out there. Just as well. The last woman who'd done so had thrown herself from the railing in a makeshift gallows, after all.

Labaye grunted at my side. I hadn't heard him get out of the car, much less settle so close that his arm nearly brushed against mine. Either I was losing my touch, or the house was already affecting me.

I needed to stay focused. Whoever or whatever left that drawing in this house meant I could not afford to be off my game. I'd seen how that played out once; I didn't have it in me to go through it again.

If any bit of Remi *was* still here, I would find him. I would save him this time. It wasn't like I could die trying twice. Well, it was *unlikely*.

The metallic jingle startled me as Labaye slid a keyring from his belt. He tapped them against his thigh then took a step forward, looking over his shoulder to scan the yard. His training had kicked in. His gaze swept past me without landing. Perhaps he struggled with his decision not to treat me like a civilian. He'd had a hard time with eye contact since we'd gotten in the car.

"The crime scene guys took care of most of the cleanup," he said. "But the house has been vacant since your family ..."

I stared back with one brow lifted and arms crossed high over my chest, curious as to what word he'd choose.

"Left," he decided. He shrugged apologetically.

"Nice save," I growled. I shook out my arms to get the blood back into my fingers, maneuvered around him toward the broken porcelain of the driveway.

My mother had loved the ridiculous tiled driveway along the side of the house—had been quick to mention it every single time she had an excuse, and plenty of times when she didn't. She'd been so impressed that a previous owner had put such effort into something people normally paved. It had been chipped and in disrepair when Joan and Ray had bought the place, once brilliant colors dimmed by the heat and humidity of the bayou until it looked like an asteroid had hit. She'd restored it, honing her skills before tackling the parlor floor, but now most of the small squares had once again come loose from the grout, shifted like shaken puzzle pieces, some reduced to powder, the rest bleached white as old bone. My eyes skipped quickly past the magnolia tree. I never let my gaze linger too long on the dark spots hidden behind the waxy green leaves. The backyard that Mom had spent that summer carefully planting and tending now showed bare patches but was mostly overgrown with bramble and weeds.

What would my mother have said about all her hard work now?

Oh, Britta, this tile would make a lovely mosaic piece.

I shook the echoes of her voice from my mind and savored the crunch as I stepped over broken bits of porcelain. My mother and I had disagreed on a *lot*, especially about all things aesthetic.

A peculiar mixture of rage and regret surged and might have overwhelmed me had I looked into those parlor windows, which had never been boarded up. I resisted the urge to give the finger to whatever miserable old spirits watched from inside, as it probably wouldn't make me feel any better anyway. The pale haint blue still clung to the bottom of the overhang, better preserved than the rest of the paint. Southerners use that shade of blue above external doors. Even though she'd clucked about it being a silly old superstition, Mom had still applied it to the narrow soffit under the eaves all the way around the house. Fat lot of good it had done.

"We go through the back," I barked at Labaye, who, having briefly mastered one step forward, now stood with his black tactical boots rooted in place, staring up at the house.

I snapped my fingers. "Hey, Officer." He started like a spooked cat, the good cop act lost to jumpy rookie. "Let's get this over with."

"I won't tell you no, Britta, but that place should have no hold over you."

Shirtless, hands on his hips and bare feet shoulder-width apart on his front porch, Malakh betrayed no emotion—as always—as a man, that is. I could tell from the slight head-to-toe flush that shaded his dusky flesh scarlet, he'd just been in his other, more expressive form. Maybe he'd only slipped on those faded jeans when I'd knocked at his door. The older ones often slept in wolf form. The alpha musk that hung in the air would recede as the sun climbed to coax the scent from the evergreens around us.

"No, of course, you know I don't care," I said, though I did. "But won't it attract attention if I turn down a chance to identify her body?"

"Tell them you can't get away from work." Malakh's mane of pure silver dreadlocks swung as his eyes shot to his porch swing. That he didn't sit said he wanted my visit to end fast.

"Can't get away for one day to testify against the woman I claimed killed my family?" I squinted as if to say, *Preposterous!*

"They want you to testify?" he asked. "Or to identify her?"

"I'm not sure, Malakh." The leather jacket creaked as I crossed my arms high across my chest. The Calcasieu Parish Police Department had reached me at work, and I'd only agreed to come so that fucking Corinne, the other dispatcher, wouldn't overhear anything I couldn't wave away. "If I don't go, I'm afraid they'll suspect me. I'll endanger the whole pack."

"Suspect you of killing this witch?" He scratched at his bare chest, then slipped his hands into his pockets. "You've been here. With us."

"Or, you know," I stammered, "of killing my family way back."

"Were you ever a suspect?"

"How could I not have been, since I was the only one who

walked out of that house?" I almost ended the question with *alive* but changed my mind. I hugged myself tighter in the chilly shade. "So, if the witch didn't do it—if I don't care enough to, you know, see this through when they're going to pay for the flight and everything."

Malakh frowned at the words *see this through*, but his face went slack again just before I heard the voice behind me. "You're flying somewhere?"

Even in his wide-toed cowboy boots, Alec didn't leave a mark on the leafy pussytoe along the edge of Malakh's driveway. His peacoat and black leather pants cut a crisp silhouette against the bright forest, like a figure in some Caspar David Friedrich landscape.

I hadn't seen Malakh move, but his feet seemed a little wider apart, fists on his hips again. He grunted, or maybe it was a bark. Alec addressed our alpha by name with the slightest bow of his head, fists clenched at his sides, and no bend in his knee.

Malakh accepted it. "The witch who tore her has died and the police want her to go down there ..." he said, "for something."

"Interesting." Alec gave me a slow nod. I'd seen him close a distance of ten feet in an instant. I took half a step away—a gesture subtle enough to get him to stop without pissing him off. "If the police contacted you," Alec said, "I'm guessing—"

"Someone killed her," I said.

"Well, that's got to stir something in you, Britta," Alec growled. One corner of his mouth kicked up, as much smile as you ever got out of him. "You never really got over all that."

"Never got over her cursing me and killing my family?" I said. "Yeah, I suppose it stirs—"

"There you go, 'the *Curse.*'" Alec made quotation marks in the air, an unusually human gesture for someone generally happy to pretend he'd always been damned. "It's like I can't teach her anything." Alec smirked at Malakh and tapped a finger against his high, sharp cheekbone. "The witch chose you for this gift," he told me, and I fought the urge to roll my eyes, "with which you will live forever—"

"Not now, Alec," Malakh said.

I should've thanked him.

Alec's shrug managed to look graceful. "The job is never done. But that was your *human* family, Britta. To hell with that." The smirk had turned downright derisive. "Besides, your former home is plague-ridden after those hurricanes. Louisiana," he snarled, "home of the Saffron Scourge."

"For Christ's sake, Alec," I said, "Katrina did not bring back the Yellow Fever."

"Last outbreak in the States hit Louisiana less than a hundred years ago."

Actually, just *over* a hundred years, which Alec goddamned well knew, but if I said so it'd prove I'd been listening to his rants after all.

"Does anyone else in our pack even know about your past? Well, Malakh, of course." Alec waved his hand to our alpha, who hadn't so much as shifted his weight, knuckles gone as white as his hair. "You wouldn't go with her, would you?" Whenever Alec tried to show deference, it seldom worked. "If she needs it, I can go—if you think it's a good idea, of course."

"I'm not asking for anyone's help, Alec." I kept my voice even. "I came to tell Malakh what was up, so could you—"

"Then you're not asking permission," Malakh said.

"I am." I kicked my oxblood Docs through dry pine needles when I really wanted to curl up on that porch swing and hide behind him. "Sorry, yes, Malakh." My deference came without thinking, instinctive, natural—literally my second nature.

"Obviously this isn't a good idea," Alec started, but Malakh shot him a stern look.

The male of the species emits a sharper scent right before he marks his territory, and now it was Alec's turn to study his boots.

He rubbed his jawline against the high collar of his peacoat. I could feel the heat come off him from ten feet away.

Malakh moved to the top stair. "Alec will stay with the pack," he said, eyes locked on me. "Do what you have to do and get back up here, little sister. Then you're done with your past."

I turned down the driveway without another word.

And I didn't hear anything until the end of the driveway when Alec's voice came again from just over my shoulder. "He's right."

My thick rubber heels spun on the soft needles. Back at the porch, Malakh had slipped inside.

Alec's golden eyes flicked back there too, then he looked at me more confidently. "You'll get closure." Both corners of his mouth went up in that rarest of genuine smiles. "Finally start seeing us for what we are."

I snarled when his fingers reached for my hair.

He didn't push it, only said, "Your future." He held the smile. "And a very long one at that." His scent took on a thick bass note as he withdrew the hand, clapped it to the other, and turned into the woods with a spring in his step.

While Labaye fumbled with the locks at the back door, I tapped the toe of my Doc Martens on rotted steps. The stench of bleach singed the hairs in my nose, wafting out through the cracks in the windows and the widening gaps where the casing around the doorjamb had pulled away from the siding to reveal decayed insulation. It didn't take heightened senses to understand a stink of bleach this heavy masked something else, but it couldn't quite hide the metallic smell of blood and bitter mildew. It might have been simpler to just bust out all the windows and doors and let the wind rinse the place out.

Putting a hand over my nose didn't help. "I have a pretty

strong shoulder," I said through my fingers. "Want me to push the door open?"

"The house has seen enough," Labaye said, too busy hunting for the right key to play. "Don't think we need to add a B&E to the list."

When he finally swung the door open, it creaked on rusty hinges to reveal a dark, dank, musty old mudroom. My throat contracted as I took in the kitchen beyond. Our furniture had all gone to charity, but other than a bit more dust and signs of simple neglect, the inside of the house itself looked more or less the same.

Labaye let the keys dangle from the lock. He fidgeted on the narrow deck beside me, either stalling or nervous. I didn't care.

He gave me a big doe-eyed stare, eyelids pushed wide with questions.

"I'm fine," I snapped.

I stepped past him and my vision adjusted immediately to the gloom. The thick layer of dust and grime on the windowpanes muted the fading glow of the late afternoon sun, though the house had never benefited from a lot of natural light, despite its many windows. The lines of the interior architecture sharpened into focus, revealing claw marks on a kitchen cabinet, the darker patch where blood had seeped through the carpet, stained the boards below.

For once, I would've been okay with bumbling human vision, because I doubted Labaye could see the things I saw.

His presence at my back wasn't terrible and helped me move through the den into the dining room, toward the grand double entry behind the front doors—away from the parlor where Mom had died, and Selena's teeth had been found. Fresh, bright yellow evidence tape sealed the French doors to that room, which was fine by me. Even with the bleach competing for attention in my nostrils, I could smell what was once on the other side, and the scene of the witch's death wasn't what had drawn me back here.

My eyes roamed across torn wallpaper and frayed carpet, barely logging the scant evidence of human habitation in the corners. An empty Styrofoam cup. The yellowed pages of an old newspaper. Even a murder house wasn't scary enough to keep out squatters. A panel popped open in the wainscoting said that the cops had found the servant's passage between the kitchen and the dining room, and I wondered if they'd found them all. There were so many places to hide in this house. Even more if you didn't mind a little suffering.

I stopped at the foot of the stairs and looked up into the belly of the beast. The enclosed stairwell tunneled between the floors. I steadied my hand on the banister and took a breath. The bedrooms wrapped around to the left, I remembered, branched off around the attic door that had been painted shut. A small sunroom hung above the driveway.

I needed a minute to prepare myself for what waited upstairs. I turned back to face the front doors.

Hairs rose on my arms, but not from my wolf. A tremor ran across every inch of my skin. The first time I'd met Selena Stone, she'd stood exactly where I stood now.

Behind me, Labaye stepped where I'd stepped, straining to be quiet, his woodsy scent comforting as his fingers reached around me for the heavy deadbolt inside of the front doors. Had the police put that there ten years ago, or had they done it after finding Selena? The bolt made a sharp sound when he threw it, then he reached for the faux crystal doorknob. The brass keyhole plate Mom had cleaned with salt, vinegar, and flour had turned dull and brown again. Labaye opened the doors wide, but the afternoon light was no longer strong enough to fill the room, as the sky melted into purple wax.

We'd been in the house longer than I'd thought. The moon called over the horizon.

It would have to wait.

I gulped a warm lungful of stale air, turned my back to the evening, and stepped up to the stairway. Nineteen stairs. Nineteen stairs separated me from the place where everything had started.

No, *ended.* I gripped the banister and lifted a heavy foot to step number one.

"Don't you want to see where I found, well," Labaye called over my shoulder, surprised I was intentionally overlooking the parlor's grizzly crime scene, "what was left of her?"

"Didn't you already get everything there was to find in there," I grumbled, and Labaye's brow scrunched up. "Besides, the witch isn't who I came here for."

Midway up the stairs, the empty sunroom came into view, and I'd stopped shaking and started to sweat. The little hairs on the back of my neck had resumed tingling, and now my wolf stalked the lengths of my limbs, adding to my discomfort.

I did not turn back. I did not run screaming from the house. But how goddamned stupid could I be to believe any part of Remi lingered here?

Nevertheless, if something—or *someone*—still haunted the place, I needed to find it. Them. If not, well, Selena was still dead and the boy-and-his-wolf drawing could be some kind of terrible prank.

Over the past decade, I'd gotten fairly good at talking myself back into the realm of the rational despite the evidence of my circumstances.

Still, I would've felt safer if I could have shifted right then, and my wolf knew it. Wearing my fur felt like wearing armor, if armor came in the form of an extinct species of *caninae* whose jaw could snap bone like twigs. The only thing holding me back was Labaye. Didn't figure it would sit well with the authorities if I suddenly turned furry and dropped down onto four paws.

No shifting in front of humans, Britta. Alec's words, not Mom's. There was a reason monsters didn't make the best bedtime stories.

Besides, Labaye had started to grow on me, and it was a relief to pretend things like curses and girls-turned-beasts didn't exist in this version of the real world, even if only for a day. He followed up the stairs so closely his sweet scent cut through the fetid odors of the house, his sweat mixed with pine, musk, and … what?

"Are you sure you don't want me to go first?" he asked in a shaky voice, probably mistaking my sharp inhale for anxiety. His fear added an extra layer to his scent, but that wasn't the mystery note.

"No offense, Labaye, but I got this."

"Suit yourself." His tone indicated an expected level of umbrage. Frankly, I didn't care.

My thick rubber heels squeaked as I turned at the top of the stairs, and pressed my back against the open doorjamb of the little sunroom. The steps didn't even creak under Labaye's black boots as he came up behind me.

Down the long empty hallway, all the bedroom doors were closed, the mismatched door to the attic still sealed. One last blade stuck out from the ceiling fan.

Underneath Labaye's musk and the acrid scent of bleach, something else hung in the air, with a sweet, warm bottom note, like vanilla. Baking smells might please humans but could bode ill for things that existed on the other side of living. Cryptids, like all animals, rely on the bacteria and other microorganisms in our gut to help digest the food we eat. A dose of sugar can upset the balance of those microorganisms and wreak havoc on our insides, which essentially meant we got to go eternity without so much as a birthday cake.

The scent seemed strongest near Remi's room, at the end past the attic door.

Maybe it was in one of the chemical cleaners.

Sure. *Make those floors shine with lavender, fresh linen, and black magic vanilla!*

Labaye had stopped one step behind me. Standard tactical positioning, but I'd be lying if I said the closeness didn't bring a flutter to my stomach.

"Remi's bedroom," he whispered.

I caught his nod in my peripheral vision, motioning down the hall as if I didn't know. Labaye knew whose room had been whose because the Hall Murders had made this house the stuff of urban legend. Weirdos from New Orleans to Austin could probably spout off the entire story from crap they'd read online or seen on that episode of *48 Hours*—I had declined their invitation. It might even be right. Hell, for all I knew, the Vinton Chamber of Commerce might run ghost tours at Halloween. Maybe those pranksters had left some dog parts and a primitive drawing for Labaye to find, hoping to churn up interest for this coming fall.

Wishful thinking.

Labaye locked eyes on Remi's door. He'd drawn his pistol in both hands, blocky muzzle toward the floor. "That's where I found the drawing."

I figured the flick of his thumb across the back of the barrel said the safety was off, but I'm no expert.

I nodded, swallowed, and with a deep breath began the long, slow walk down the hallway, clenching my hands so tight my nails reopened the little crescents in my palms.

CHAPTER SIX

When my hand wrapped around the tarnished doorknob to Remi's bedroom, Labaye gave me one of those deliberate nods meant to signify readiness. His Adam's apple bobbed, while I silently counted to ten to take my mind off the corpse-like clamminess of the doorknob under my palm. When I reached ten, I twisted the knob, remembered it stuck, and pulled up to give the brass orb a little shake. Finally, the latch gave way and the door creaked open, the piercing sound shrill enough to unhinge my heart from my chest along with the wood from the frame. The breath caught in my throat as my brother's old bedroom came into view through the opening—the dark hardwood floors, dirty windows obscuring the street view, broken ceiling fan.

Remi's furniture and belongings had been packed up and carted away back in the day, but evidence a sweet little boy had once lived in this room remained if you knew where to look.

A permanent glue smear on the windowpane where he'd tried to peel off a sticker of the Ninja Turtle Raphael, named for the sixteenth-century Vatican muralist. A swipe of blue watercolor over the windows and above the door to the Jack-and-Jill bathroom between Remi's room and my suite. I never understood what he'd been trying to do up there … When I'd suggested we repaint his room, he'd selected a fresh mint green from a thick stack of color swatches at the home improvement store, but heat and humidity had sickened his bedroom walls to a sallow olive.

Actually, the entire room felt sick, and I froze in the doorway. The air, musty from disuse, carried the strange, medicinal vanilla scent that suggested old magic. Dust as thick and gray as dryer lint clung to every surface, a little too reminiscent of ash for my liking.

"Okay?" Labaye whispered, and it chased away a memory of Ray. He'd relaxed his grip on his gun, aimed at the hardwood between his shoes.

No words came. I returned one of those confirming nods.

All combined, the sights and scents of the last home from my real life made me nauseous and lightheaded. I covered my nose with one hand, mostly to hide the tremble in my lips.

Labaye breathed out loud in the threshold beside me, and the fear—or maybe anticipation—made those big eyes glisten. He licked at his lower lip, which made something like hunger twist deep in my stomach despite the lump of unease in my throat. I didn't want to step into the room, but if I stayed this close to Labaye I'd burst into flames.

To be simultaneously torn between terror and lust was a strange sensation, and I didn't care for the thoughts raging inside of my head. No time for distractions. Whatever I felt toward the handsome rookie would have to be sorted out later, preferably back up north with my pack. I didn't fit in there any better than I did here, but at least *there* was far away from my dead brother's goddamned bedroom.

Labaye nodded, signaling me forward. I shoved the door with such force it slammed into the wall, plaster puffing into the air, the thud of sheetrock falling to the floor.

I moved only far enough into Remi's room for Labaye to step in behind me, and closed my eyes, letting the weight of the space roll off my shoulders. I breathed in, listening to the silence, and half-hoped I might wake from the nightmare of the past ten years, everything back the way it should be: Remi, wide-eyed and alive, showing off his newest drawing and asking to drive out to the Dairy Queen for ice cream, or maybe a walk to the library.

Holding my breath, I opened my eyes to nothing, to the empty space where my little brother had once been.

I had to laugh. What a silly pup. Remi was dead, and that Britta had died, too. Nothing remained for either of us here, no part *of* either of us. This place was just bones. I glanced at the fireplace, and sure enough, it was undisturbed.

"Everything okay?" The cop felt the need to ask again, this time at normal volume.

"Just peachy," I mumbled back.

"There's nothing here."

"You're kidding." Sarcasm sharpened the edges of my words.

Labaye slipped around me to walk the perimeter of the empty room, and I made my way toward its center. When my Docs hit the spot directly under the broken ceiling fan, I shivered in the heat of the second story. I rubbed my hands against the sleeves of my jacket for the tactile comfort alone. Only fur and the feel of dirt under my paws would get me warm again.

"You're cold?" Labaye holstered his gun.

I rolled my eyes. "It's drafty," I said, though it wasn't. I turned my back to him and leaned on the narrow fireplace mantel. Remi had found it kind of cool to have a fireplace in the new bedroom, even if he never got the chance to light it. Probably no one had cleaned the flue in decades. The novelty had been short-lived, however, when he insisted he heard voices coming from within the wall. I hadn't believed him. No one had, at least not until it was too late. Ray had, not so helpfully, said they never heard a thing from their bedroom on the other side of the wall, as if that was definitive proof.

Despite all Selena's ghost stories—maybe *to spite* Selena herself—I'd waved off Remi's fears. He'd come for help and I'd told him he'd only heard the wind tickling the chimney. Echoes from elsewhere in the house. His imagination. Something logical. Explainable. But they'd been the tipping point, those voices.

If I'd just believed him, so much might have been different.

I squatted as if to warm myself in front of the fireplace's mound of undisturbed dust, listening for the voices that had haunted my brother but heard nothing. If anything of Remi remained in this room besides smudges of color and adhesive, I knew where to find it. With the witch dead, I was the only one still alive who'd know where to look.

"Where'd you find the picture?" I asked without turning around.

Labaye's boots echoed against the bare floorboards. "Here," he said, voice uncertain.

He took another step, then stopped short, and tapped his foot. "No, here." The vibrations shuddered up my spine. "Right in the middle of the floor. Like it was waiting to be found."

He'd stopped right under the light fixture, where I'd felt the chill.

The hint of vanilla. Cold spots. "Imagine that," I muttered, and reached into the fireplace.

Any hope of a Halloween prank had faded fast.

My fingertip found the hidden groove below one end of the lintel, barely wider than fishing line, tracing a square path through blackened brick. That hairline crack separated Remi's bedroom from a place no one ever should have been able to find.

Yet Remi had found it, somehow. That night.

Closing my eyes, I inhaled that odd, medicinal vanilla, flattened my palm against the crack, and pushed. The bricks gave way easily, sliding over just enough for a grown man—certainly a small boy—to crawl through. The shadows, pitch-black even to me, made the dank passage still less inviting. Wolves could see in the dark, but this was not just the absence of light. It was a hungry darkness, the type that chewed you up before it swallowed you.

"Whoa." Labaye squatted beside me, his voice thick with wonder. "I had no idea ..."

"Don't sound so impressed," I said, tilting forward onto my

knees and grimacing at the dust that turned my black pants gray. "It's not fucking Narnia."

Actually part of the attic, the odd space snaked between rooms from one of the old house's many remodels. Remi and I had discovered other hidden pockets in the house together, but this one had gone unnoticed. We hadn't found it until the very end, and now I only cared about this leftover from a time when the house's servants—and even more often its masters—had used secret spaces to practice rituals unwelcome in any church.

Considering the evil shit they got up to in the daylight of the Old South, this was saying something.

I dipped my head into the fireplace, but Labaye grabbed my arm. I turned to face him, fury and surprise widening my eyes.

His tan fingers dropped away, settled on his holster. "Shouldn't I, you know …?" He motioned awkwardly toward the crawlspace.

"What happened to ladies first?" I growled. "Is your chivalry failing you, Officer Labaye?"

The rookie stuttered, tried to figure out a safe way to respond, and for half a second I wondered what it felt like for him when he touched me. His hand on my arm had felt warm, even through the thick leather sleeve, like bathwater I could drown in. Part of me wanted to look away, but my wolf glared at him.

"I just …" he said, "I …"

"Think it's in there?" I asked him, and when the confusion on his face deepened I said, "The rest of the witch?" I didn't wait for a response.

I moved one black denim knee into the dust, then the other, and didn't exhale as I shifted my gaze from Labaye into the looming darkness, the musk and vanilla now so strong it burned my eyes like sulfur. Black magic, all right.

"Follow if you want," I spat as I ducked my head through the small opening. "But grab me like that again and you'll lose a hand."

Guided by memory, I slid forward on my knees about five feet into the darkness of the crawlspace, then rose to my feet. Labaye pushed into the small chamber and stood at my side, his chest to my shoulder, hip to hip. He ran his hand along the wall, traced a finger along the mortar, and I thought of Remi learning to render brick in charcoal that summer.

Exposed rafters crossed just above our heads. Labaye couldn't have guessed the size of the room we'd come into, but I didn't repeat the earlier threat and focused on steadying my breath. It reeked of vanilla and other herbs I couldn't name. The foul funk of black magic occluded the smell of bleach and suffocated the air in the dark space, pushing inside me, poisoning me. Even my wolf buried her head from the stench. Exactly zero of my paranormal qualities reassured me right now. Not in this place. Not in this dark.

"What is that?" Labaye said in disgust, the scent apparently just as nauseating to humans.

"It's magic. Magic and death." I breathed in deeper. "But not a corpse."

He coughed to clear his lungs. "Can you see anything?" I couldn't smell his fear over the other odor, but it crept around the edges of his voice. A clinking sound near his hip said he'd found his flashlight.

The old Britta would've reached for Labaye's hand in the darkness and held on for dear life. But I wasn't that Britta anymore. I listened for the click of the flashlight and hoped it would be bright enough to outshine the black in that brick-lined room.

A brilliant beam of light reflected off a white, powdery scribble on the unfinished floorboards. The light tipped as Labaye traced the rough edges of a witch's circle, etched in chalk. The echo of pain flooded my senses—sharp, stringent, unyielding—and just the memory of stepping over those thin white lines was enough to bend my knees, twist my throat. When the spasm passed, I recognized the symbols, sharp angles, curves, pointed and horned, drawn around the outside—I'd seen them the day I died—though I didn't know exactly what they meant. Just outside of the circle, a large, black mirror hung on a tall wooden easel.

The wolf scratched against the inside of my skin. The plain, round mirror's presence, paired with the circle, was bad. *Bad* bad. Beside it, an old-fashioned rocking chair tilted back, angled to face the circle. I shivered again.

"What is that?" Labaye whispered. His light bounced off the black face of the glass.

I reached out for his forearm and pushed the light away from the mirror, back to the circle. The rafters cast moving shadows across the ceiling above.

"A scrying mirror." I had never seen one with my own eyes. "It's used to communicate with the dead, whose spirits haven't found peace." The beam inched back toward the mirror and I pushed it more forcefully this time. "Don't," I barked, louder than I had intended.

Patience is a virtue, Britta.

I sighed and tried to speak more evenly. "Don't look into it," I warned. "Never know what you'll see, or what will see you."

Labaye's fear beat against my skin in waves, but he kept the flashlight on the circle.

"That way." I directed with the flat palm of a traffic cop, and he obeyed. "But don't move. Stay out of the circle." In the small chamber, the chalk line fell just inches from our toes. "They're made to keep things in or to keep things away. I don't know which kind this is, and with that mirror around I don't want to find out."

Labaye's beam wandered, tracing concentric circles in a tightening loop within the witch's circle. My body was a balloon, the capacity of my preternatural lungs measured in tight puffs of air once each ring was complete.

By the fourth ring, the pain in my chest was nearly gone. On the fifth, whatever air was left inside my body turned to ice. A mound waited in the bullseye of the circle. Twisted gray head poking out from under, ears lying flat to either side. Two eyes stared back at us, black as the mirror but without the shine. One hung low against the cheek, above a twisted pink mouth. Instinct raised my hand, but it stopped short, frozen midway between my stomach and mouth, fingers gripped in a shocked fist of fleshy talon. In the center of that face, gray felt skin pulled away to reveal white batting inside. Rothko, my brother's beloved, battered, stuffed elephant, had lost his trunk.

I sank onto both knees, thought that if I did melt into the floor, I would pool all on this side of the chalk line. The dust would burn like acid against my flesh, and only the threat of agony kept me upright—but just barely.

Remi *had* been here. Whatever was left of him, his real body long since gone. Rothko had disappeared the night of Remi's death. I couldn't remember if Remi had left him in the parlor or not, but Devereaux swore they hadn't found him. The old elephant hadn't been in this room, of that I was certain. When they didn't find Selena's body, I'd wondered if she'd taken Rothko, but all I knew was that the toy had been as gone as Mom, and Ray, and Remi—and now he was back.

My focus drifted up to the mirror. Why resist? Had it pulled Remi's spirit from the other side, trapped him within this circle, endlessly and alone, with no company other than whoever had placed the mirror here, and watched his suffering from the rocking chair? Had Rothko acted as a tether, to bind him between one world and the next?

Only one person could be so cruel.

Breath shuddered across my lips, and Labaye twitched at the sound, the beam of his flashlight jerking abruptly. Something stirred as the light brushed against the outer edge of the circle.

Footsteps shuffling toward us echoed in the black.

The head of a stark white rat poked over the chalk line of the circle, followed by another. I reached for Labaye's forearm despite myself, and as I pulled myself up, the beam flicked to the side. He gasped, and his fear rocketed from terror to panic. His hand shook as he brought the light back to the circle's edge to find not a mouse, but the pale feet of a child, small, delicate, little-boy ankles. Shins. All white, all so unnaturally, unbelievably white.

The unsteady beam of Labaye's flashlight climbed until the full ghastly specter of my dead baby brother stood across from me. His mouth gaped under blank, hollow eyes fixed over my head, on the man whose sleeve I still clutched. I didn't hear Remi's name tear from my throat but felt it the same time my knees gave way.

If I had called his name aloud, Remi gave no sign he heard it. The line across his forehead that used to indicate worry just looked like a wound.

"Britta—" Labaye started, then stumbled over the line into the sealing circle.

With a banshee's shriek, the apparition flung itself at Labaye, while the flashlight rolled toward the mostly unstuffed elephant.

CHAPTER SEVEN

I could only stare as the specter of my beloved little brother tore with hands that looked like claws, and dragged the rookie into the circle. Labaye screamed and flailed, tried to fight back, his fear so thick it filled my mouth in the brick-lined chamber. He tried to hold off something—someone?—not entirely solid with one hand, while his other floundered to unholster his gun.

The flashlight rolled to a stop, its head across Rothko's flat torso, and cast a wavering spotlight on a gruesome scene I could only watch, anchored in place outside of the white-hot circle. My wolf pressed against my skin and the tickle of wolfcoat raced over my limbs, but the sensation was too dull and far away to grab, to wrap around myself. To turn.

I thought I'd known horror before, but this ... I couldn't have prepared myself for this sight if I'd had a thousand years to do it, instead of only ten.

The thing attacking Labaye looked like Remi, but my brother had never been so cold, detached, never so violent. The figure wasn't translucent, nor was it opaque, and its eyes, two black holes like the defaced stuffie, sucked the life out of me. I tried to look away, tried to stop grunting his name in time with my own pounding heart. Every time I caught a glimpse of those inhuman eyes, they pulled me in, as if they could steal my soul while his claws ripped at the rookie's flesh.

Labaye's leg shot out of the circle—knocked over the easel and splintered the scrying mirror, jagged shards crashing across the floor.

"Britta, help!" His panicked voice, tight with terror and pain, shattered my mute shock.

When he screamed my name again it spurred me to get up, though I had no idea what I should—or could—do. Breaking through the circle hadn't been a simple thing ten years ago, and I didn't think I'd get so lucky again, even if I could stomach the pain. But I had to do something, or Labaye wouldn't leave the room alive—or maybe at all.

I reached for whatever part of Labaye I could grab without crossing the bounds of the ring of chalk.

"Remi," I shouted, climbing to my feet. "Remi, let him go! *Remi!*"

Remi, or his grisly doppelgänger, paused over Labaye, now covered in welting, angry scratches, and blotchy with bruises. The thing turned on me, the seam in his forehead deeper than ever. Though the black eyes looked nothing liked my brother's, his face like one of Rodin's rough plaster studies. I knew as he pushed me back from the chalk line, mouthing my name, that this was really him.

Labaye screamed out when the hand that had so gently shoved me away tore through his shirt, down to the flesh. The cop struggled, weak against a foe who appeared to get stronger with every attack. Remi's form knitted together, a sketchy figure refined, detail becoming denser. As the ghostly shape of my little brother grew solid, Labaye's eyes dimmed. He threw a sluggish punch that never connected and faced my brother, his jaw slack, losing consciousness—or worse.

Crouching on the rough floorboards, I screamed for Remi until my voice gave out and my mouth hung open, silent. Even Remi's movements slowed, the brick walls falling away, leaving only the noises of the shuffle and my ragged breathing.

Labaye made one last breathy plea. "Britta." His eyes slipped closed, mouth slackened, and something inside my chest seized up.

I would not watch another person die because of dark magic—even at the hands of my brother. Even a human I barely knew.

I scrambled to my feet and turned my mind inward to the place no living mortal had. I shrugged off my leather jacket, and it slid down my bare arms, fell to the floor.

Come, wolf, I called.

And she came.

I fumbled with the laces of my oxblood Docs and threw them behind me as my wolf barreled against the bounds of my body to force her way out. The sensation danced between pain and pleasure as bone and muscle twisted, stretched, reshaped into something more powerful, more primal, a form not seen in the wild for tens of thousands of years. Fur tipped in starlight silver wrapped itself around muscle, coursed over skin to move in the air like a living thing unto itself. When my hands touched the floor again, they were paws, razor-sharp claws piercing the hardwood. I inhaled the potent scent of every bead of sweat and blood trickling down Labaye's body.

Something else, too. That unique note in his scent. To the woman, to Britta, it smelled like musk and man. To the wolf, scent is one of the most important ways to communicate—glands in our tails, our paws, give precise signals—and Labaye called as strong as fresh pie pulled from the oven, so sweet and delicious my tongue ran wet with desire—in a way which had nothing to do with the urge to feed.

My lips curled into a snarl, and my ears slid back in warning. *Mine,* my wolf growled.

The rush of instinct, part protective, part possessive, surprised me. What was Labaye to me?

His scent took on another note, and my stomach knotted. I could smell him dying.

The chalk line at my feet shimmered as I leaped over it, a razor-thin tremor slicing its way into muscle and meat. Someone had designed the circle to hold something, but not to hold me— not this time.

My growl cracked the air like thunder as I landed at the center of the circle between Labaye, barely conscious, and Remi's strange form, strengthened by the life it drained from its prey.

My brother blinked at me, and the recognition in those eyes lent them something that resembled life.

I positioned myself on all fours over Labaye, fangs bared. *You will not harm him.*

Remi backed away, staring at me as his figure faded to spectral mist. The harsh lines of his face and forehead slackened, his black eyes dimmed to soft shadow, and the cruel set of its lips softened into a familiar, crooked smile. What stood before me was no demonic apparition, but Remi as I had known him. As I had loved him. The boy who I'd failed to save in this very room ten years earlier.

"Britta." His voice rang out clear and curious, though he seemed somehow far away, and a very human grief panged in my chest.

A shadow in Remi's eye glistened. A tear.

I wanted to respond, but couldn't—not in this form. Wolves' mouths weren't made for human words.

"You shouldn't have come," Remi said. The light animating him faded, pulling him farther into the shadow. "Britta, save me," my brother pleaded.

I could only stand over Labaye, panting like some stupid animal.

For a moment, Remi's face hung like smoke before me, then he dissipated into the dark around him and was gone.

CHAPTER EIGHT

When Aaron came to, he was staring into the yellow eyes of the largest wolf he'd ever seen.

On instinct he threw himself back, his shoulder crashing into the fireplace, yanked the pistol free from the holster on his hip, and leveled the barrel at the great animal before him. The wolf shuffled back on long, stout forelegs, larger than any domestic canine. The huge head bowed to show it meant no harm, though the lips on the broad muzzle trembled. It resettled on its haunches, claws clicking across the floorboards as Aaron gasped and coughed his way back to consciousness. Searing pain shot from head to toe. The surge of adrenaline receded, and the gun swayed with each heave and shudder—but he left the safety off.

When he could breathe again, Aaron struggled into a sitting position and brought his knees to his chest. He filled his lungs with as much air as possible and blinked until he got his bearings, passing his free hand over his body to check for injury. Every inch of him hurt, but he found no wounds. No blood, his clothes disheveled and dusty but not torn. No marks to explain the pain radiating through him.

What the hell just—? The pain numbed as memory flooded in.

He'd scouted the house with Britta as planned, the downstairs, then up into the bedroom at the end of the hall. He'd followed her into the hidden chamber behind the fireplace, and he'd been attacked by a ghost—not *a* ghost, but what appeared to be the ghost of Remi Hall. There had been screaming—Aaron's own shouts, Britta's, maybe even the apparition's. There had been pain. Then darkness, the soft brush of fur.

Now he lay in the center of the dead boy's empty bedroom staring at a wolf.

A wolf with Britta Orchid's eyes.

His pulse slowed. Not quite normal, but not so fast its reverberations sounded in his head.

Aaron was not afraid, although emotions swept through him, and he felt each pass across his face in rapid succession and hoped the wolf could not read them all. He lowered his arm and held the pistol out as he clicked the safety on, as though the wolf might understand, and he laid the piece by his knee on the hardwood.

"Britta?" he asked, stretching and then crossing his legs to sit comfortably on the floor. He looked up at the broken ceiling fan, remembered it having some significance before, but could not remember why.

The wolf made a grumbling, noncommittal noise in its throat and bobbed its huge head.

No. *She* made a grumbling noise. *She* bobbed *her* head.

"You're ..." Aaron searched for the right word. "Y-you're a ... werewolf." He shook his head, forcing out a sigh, then ran his tan fingers through his disheveled hair, dragged them along the line of his jaw. He stopped at his mouth, wrapping his palm flat over his lips as his gaze tracked up from the giant paws over the midnight fur, tipped with silver, to the firefly eyes.

The great creature in the room with him was unlike anything he'd ever seen before—not the monster he'd expected from grainy horror films depicting half-man, half-beast mutations, but an enormous canine with distinctly human intelligence in its gold eyes. The fear that should have flooded him shuddered in his chest, quieted.

Britta the wolf looked back at him, and Aaron realized he'd been staring a long time. But how would she expect him to react to seeing this? She cocked her head to the side, blinked, and grumbled again. It was not quite a growl. Though she apparently could not speak, Aaron imagined what sort of snide remark she meant to shoot at him. He laughed, put his hands up in front of him, then wiped at his brow.

"Sorry," he apologized. "First time."

Her ears flattened, then rose in what he could only interpret as impatience.

"Can you—?" he floundered for the right words, clicked his teeth. "Can you shift back? I don't know, uh, how long it takes."

She wagged her head from side to side. A clear no. He'd never have thought it, but communicating with a wolf was oddly natural.

He clenched his fists in his lap to resist the urge to touch her. It tugged at him from deep inside.

Britta's fur bristled as Aaron shifted onto his knees, then pulled himself across the floor to close the distance between them. As he brushed past his gun, it turned on the rough floorboards, a lazy Russian roulette spin. He didn't hurry, and stopped just within touching distance, adjusting his butt onto the heels of his boots. She stiffened as he approached, shifting side to side on her front paws. Her grumble deepened into a growl when he reached out a hand, but she stayed still.

Her ears flattened, eyes narrowed, and Aaron could almost hear Britta's rebuke. *Don't you dare try to pet me.*

He wiggled the fingers on his outstretched hand and forced a laugh. "Not without your permission, I swear. I'd like to keep all my appendages." He didn't know if he'd meant to pet her, scratch an ear, or offer his hand to sniff like you might with any unfamiliar dog.

The closer he came to her, the stronger the pull. The air between them felt alive. Britta's nose twitched, but she didn't move as he settled in front of her, his knees pulled to his chest and arms wrapped around them.

When it was evident he would keep his promise not to touch her, she lowered her head onto her forelegs on the hardwood floor beside him. They both stared into the empty fireplace.

Aaron wiped at the sweat that had collected around his nose. "It must have been awful seeing Remi like that," he said.

Britta grumbled beside him. Her head bobbed again, and Labaye imagined she was glad to be in her wolf's form and not to have to talk about it.

"He's in this damn house. After all this time," he said. "Or what's left of him. Trapped in that circle. And he's angry." His voice flattened into a mumble. "Hell, I'd be angry, too."

Britta growled and shifted in place.

"I'm sorry," he said. "I'm not trying to upset you, just thinking out loud. Bad habit."

He reached out without thinking, the same way he'd brushed her hand back in the station, but stopped just short of touching her. His hand hung in the air between them. In a trick of the light that filtered in through the dirty windows, Britta's fur fluttered, like it reached back to him. She rose into a sitting position on her haunches and pulled back to face him, the canine expression unreadable.

Aaron looked up at the broken ceiling fan, and the pain, the screaming from moments ago flashed in a shiver through him. He remembered the brush of fur against his skin.

"You saved me," he whispered. "You knew the circle was dangerous, not to mention … not to mention the thing attacking me. But you—you let me see this." He ran his eyes over the huge wolf. "You came in after me, even if it meant facing off against your brother."

Britta dropped her head.

"Thank you, Britta. I am in your debt." Then lower, more to himself than her, he said, "And are you staying like this because you want to, or because you need to?" He clenched and unclenched his hand, then shifted into a cross-legged position on the hardwood floor. "You deserve to know what happened here, to help your brother, and I promise to do everything in my power to help you."

Britta gazed at him with a softness he hadn't seen in her human eyes. She hesitated for a moment and then, as if only just deciding, she let out an agreeable huff and slid her head onto his crossed ankles in silent agreement.

CHAPTER NINE

TEN YEARS EARLIER

The belt buckle had managed to sneak back under my hip and leave a dent in the softer part of my left butt cheek, and the humid air filtering in through the unrolled window left a sweaty sheen on my skin. As soon as the truck squealed to a stop, I unclipped the belt and pushed open the passenger side door, leaving the window down. When I hopped out of the pickup, Remi dangled his legs from the gate of the moving truck, but didn't jump off, didn't smile, just made Rothko, the little stuffed animal I'd given him when I started college, wave his trunk at us.

My book fell onto the floorboard of the pickup as I got out and I left it there, blasphemous paraphernalia contaminating Mom's hallelujah-on-wheels as I gaped at the sight before me.

My little 1990 powder-blue two-door sat on the crumbling tile drive next to the U-Haul—Ray had unhitched my car, so you couldn't say he hadn't done anything. He appeared from between two of the fat white Greek pillars and waved, tethered to the side of an older woman with cracked olive skin and shaggy hair so blond it appeared almost white.

When Mom told me we were moving to the bayou, my brain, in an attempt to soften the blow, had queued up visions of *Steel Magnolias*, and other garden-variety, feel-good Southern movies I'd watched as a kid. As Mom's pickup had rumbled into the sleepy little Louisiana town of Vinton, I'd anticipated graceful magnolia trees, thick with white blooms, shading the porches of columned homes where old women sat in rocking chairs waving at passing cars. Sally Fields and Dolly Parton would be working on Easter eggs for the church's annual egg hunt, even though it was summer, while Olympia Dukakis argued with Shirley MacLaine.

Instead, we'd passed empty, rundown homes with wild grasses growing around rusted stumps of old pickups abandoned on empty gravel roads, vestiges of a crumbling town forgotten by time. A crooked sign read *Welcome to Vinton. Population 3,217.* A dump of epic proportions. *This* was where Mom's visions had led her—seriously?

I patted Remi's thigh, forcing a smile out of him. One of my old sketchbooks that he'd pilfered from my art bag sat next to him on the edge of the U-Haul, alongside a tray of oil pastels.

"Hey, buddy. How was the ride?"

Remi shrugged without looking up. "Long."

In truth, the ride had only been a hair over an hour, but *long* had a way of meaning so many more things than time.

While I hunted for something encouraging to say, Ray trotted off the house's front porch wearing one of his smarmy showman smiles, heading toward the U-Haul and Mom's pickup. Remi hopped down and took his things to find a spot on the front lawn, but when his sneakers squished through soggy grass, he rerouted back to sit at the edge of the tiled drive. He flopped Rothko at his side and buried his nose in the sketchbook with an expression of deep concentration, the tray of pastels open beside him.

"That the realtor?" I asked through the window as Mom rummaged around in the truck's cab, gathering her Big Gulp and Bible. Something about the way the platinum-haired woman waited between the columns made my skin itch. "I would have thought she'd have cashed her commission check and skipped town by now."

Brown dust swirled in the pickup's final exhale and settled

like a dirty rag over the hood as Mom flung herself out of the old Ford, squinted past the moving truck and the huge wraparound driveway. "I don't know who that is." She dismissed the stranger with a flick of her wrist and turned to the bed of her pickup. "But, Britta, just *look* at the house. Isn't it beautiful?"

The house did have all the hallmarks of classic Greek Revival architecture—four huge pillars, a balcony that ran along the entirety of the second floor, large windows, even a big center entrance beneath a huge pediment—but the grace had long since deteriorated, leaving behind rows of broken windows, two and a half sprawling stories of dust and peeling paint surrounded by an unkempt lawn. Only snarling weeds remained of the gardens, and untended vines peeked in the dark first-floor windows and crept up the walls. Even the porcelain tile of the driveway had begun to dissolve with years of neglect.

"Maybe beautiful a hundred years ago, but this place is a disaster," I said, providing the smug opinion of a recent art school grad. "Seriously, Mom, the place is going to crumble any second. Seems awfully unsafe for a vision house. Didn't God take a peek at the home inspection?"

Ray joined us at the back of the pickup, and I turned away as they sorted through the army of cleaning supplies. My mother didn't have time to waste on my snarky comments anyway. She danced in place, round bottom jiggling in her denim shorts, and even Ray managed a half-smile that the rest of his face didn't seem to know what to do with.

I walked over to Remi.

"Welcome to the Overlook," I teased, squatting down on the crumbling tile beside him. I'd read him some of the tamer parts of *The Shining* the past holiday break when we'd wished we were snowed in with Jack Torrance instead of sweating out a Texan Christmas with our folks. He'd had a couple of nightmares after the topiary animals came to life for the first time, but had asked me to read more.

I ran my fingers through Remi's soft brown hair, several shades lighter than my own, and pulled the long locks away from the worry line on his forehead. The kid hadn't outgrown his fuzzy duckling hair stage yet, though he'd lost every single one of his baby teeth. I kept waiting for his hair to turn black like mine, but it stayed light. Besides the hair, Remi had the same pale skin and green eyes Mom and I shared, and looked virtually nothing like his big and blond and bulgy father, while I looked a lot like mine.

"Latino blood is strong blood," my father used to tell me. "Makes us better lovers and better fighters."

I wasn't sure about the former, but so far the latter rang true.

"Wanna go take a look around?" I asked Remi. "See what the fuss is all about?"

Remi scrunched up his mouth, gave me a sidelong glance as he closed the book. "Not really." His fingers were stained brown from the pastel in his hand. He'd been sketching the willow tree in the front yard and doing a fair job of it, even if he did overshadow the spaces between the leaves. Still, our drawing lessons were paying off. He'd be ready to upgrade to charcoal soon.

"I can't believe we have to live in this stupid old house," he grumbled. "Dad talked about it the whole way here. I pretended I was carsick just so he'd stop."

Kid learned all his best moves from his big sis.

"It's not so bad," I lied, trying to sound reassuring as I studied the house again. Mom and Ray, each with a milk crate filled with bottles and brushes, stood in the shadows behind the Doric columns talking to the shaggy-haired woman. "You can tell your friends back home it's haunted." I grinned at Remi. He loved to spook people almost as much as I did. This sense of humor had not fared well against the newfound religiosity of our parents, who had confiscated Remi's collection of magic tricks, his crystal ball—an old glass doorknob I'd bought at a junk store—and other ersatz supernatural bric-a-brac, then ceremoniously barbequed it all in the backyard, while I studied away in Houston.

A mischievous smile twitched across Remi's lips. "It sure looks like it. Landon Daniels would probably be really into it."

"Yeah?" I asked, hugging Rothko in my lap. Remi had been wringing the poor thing's trunk again. A nervous habit. A tear had opened where the trunk met the face, and the stitches all around had come loose. "What does Rothko think?"

"Rothko's head is full of fluff like Winnie-the-Pooh." Remi shrugged, but he grabbed the elephant by the trunk and tucked him under his arm just the same.

He stood up, wiped porcelain dust from the seat of his jeans, and took my hand as we trudged up the yard to the front door, leaving the sketchbook behind. Our parents stood at the side of the house with the white-haired woman, who stretched both arms to indicate the brown, weeded corners of the yard as though giving a tour of Singer Sargent's Corfu gardens. A pair of thick, wooden doors loomed behind heavy wrought-iron gates. Remi let go of my hand and tried to wrap his fingers around one of the rusty rods. He looked up at the overhang above the entrance.

"Hey, Britta, look—it's painted blue so you think you're seeing the sky."

"It's called *haint* blue," I told him. "People in the Deep South used to paint blue over their front doors and windows to stop evil spirits from passing through, ward off bad omens … that kind of thing. Like throwing salt over your shoulder."

Remi returned to my side, lacing his fingers in mine, rusty grit from the gate sticking to his skin. "What if they're already in?" The way he asked suggested he'd already given it a good amount of thought and didn't like where it got him. "I mean, if they painted the ceiling *after* the bad already got in the house, it'd be stuck in there, right?"

"I wouldn't worry about it." I gave his hand a gentle squeeze.

"Scary stuff is for books and movies. This is just a gross old house. It only looks bad because it's been neglected for so long."

I pushed against the front doors, but they'd swollen shut in the summer heat and wouldn't budge. Instead, we went the way Mom and Ray had, up the crumbling drive to the back door, walking in blissful quiet. Remi's eyes bugged at what he saw inside. He looked at me like he had something else to say, but when I met his gaze, he only shook his head and stepped into the house.

Like the exterior, the house's insides had all the classic antebellum trappings—an enormous foyer, a sweeping stairwell, a window-lined parlor, and a grand dining room—all featuring intricate glass and woodwork. And, like the exterior, all in a depressing state of disrepair. The den looked like it could be cozy, with full-length bookshelves built into one wall and plenty of space for seating. The den's faded brown carpet squished ominously when I stepped on it, sending a shudder up my spine. I leaned down and pulled the tops of my socks up above the edges of my ten-holes, pretending the sour-smelling fluid soaking through the carpet was just rancid water from the ancient window unit. I didn't want to think about other possibilities.

Opposite the den, past a wide countertop, dark cabinets lined the kitchen walls over an ancient sink and stove. Two gaping holes stared back from where a pair of refrigerators had stood at the far end of the room—maybe one had been a stand-alone freezer. The pantry could probably hold enough food to feed the entire town. Even Ray, who chowed down with such voracity his face contorted with the effort, couldn't eat enough to warrant this kind of storage space. His laugh floated down to us from upstairs, though I didn't hear my mother's voice or the white-haired woman's. Remi and I walked silently through the kitchen, tracking muddy footprints on the dusty hardwoods.

A drooping chandelier greeted us in the dining room where the green wallpaper might have been pretty three decades earlier. Faded curtains, which bunched at the ends of a pair of filthy windows lining the eastern wall of the room, had long since been washed nearly to white by the blazing Southern sun. I couldn't very well make a gown of the stuff if I had to go call directly upon Rhett Butler for help.

A less faded rectangle of the green paisley wallpaper suggested a picture, or maybe a mirror, had once hung on the wall, and I reached up to run a finger over the dot where a nail had been pulled out. I steered Remi past the marble fireplace, filled with lumps of old ashes and something I suspected might have been the carcass of a rat.

The dining room opened into an empty parlor—the kind reserved for teatime—which I suspected we would use even less than the dining room. The backside of the front doors provided a piece of punctuation between the two rooms as the front of the house. I flipped open the little brass door on the peephole and peered through to see my mother standing next to the U-Haul with Ray. Had some auditory trick of the old architecture bounced his laugh down from upstairs? He and Mom stood with their heads back, their arms raised toward the sky, lost in prayer.

Remi pointed to the glass doorknobs and said, "Crystal balls."

The doors opened easily from the inside. The fresh air relieved the dank pressure inside the old house. Remi started to walk out, but I turned him toward the stairs up to the second floor, leaving the door open behind us.

"We haven't seen the bedrooms yet," I said.

Remi's gaze darted nervously up the stairwell. He chewed at his lip. "Up there?" The worry line deepened. He hugged the stuffed elephant to his chest, the trunk flopped over his arm.

"We should check out the whole place." I pulled him in

against my hip where I tried to rub the tremors from his tiny shoulders. From Mom's many lectures about the magnificence of her vision house, I'd pictured a wide open staircase with a polished banister one might slide down on the way to the ball. But walls pressed tight on either side, so that the stairs spilled toward us like the tongue in the throat of some animal, and disappeared around a corner above a landing.

I shouldn't have teased Remi about the house being haunted. I didn't give ghost stories any more weight than my mother did to science, or book learning, but this place might just make a believer out of me.

"Mom said each bedroom has its own bathroom," I said when Remi's shoulders had stilled. But his shoes stayed anchored to the squishy carpet. "And most of the rooms have a fireplace, too."

Dark, curious eyes met mine, eyebrows scrunched into an incredulous scribble. "Fireplaces?"

I nodded, crossed my heart. "This house has been around for a *long* time, before stuff like central air and heat. Old-timey slave owners probably didn't know how to respond when temperatures fell below one hundred degrees, so they put in fireplaces to keep the drafts out."

The upstairs also had a sunroom and a small alcove above the driveway with a sunroof. An attic, as I recalled from another lecture, had been blocked after a previous owner's small son had gotten locked up there. The front balcony had also been closed off, but I'd forgotten why, along with the details of a long list of other remodels.

The little hairs on the back of my neck trembled as I peered up the unlit stairwell. When my hand found Remi, I rubbed his arm for my own reassurance as much as his. The South was full of secrets and pain and ghosts—how many lived here?

"Boo!" Mom giggled from over my shoulder.

Remi yelped and I spun around, shoving him behind my

back while I tried not to pee in my favorite jeans.

"What the f—" I started to yell at my mother, but realized we had company. *Still* had company.

The shaggy-haired woman stood beside her, wearing an oversized amethyst necklace and a smile so saccharine sweet it gave me cavities. A handsome woman of indeterminate age, she cradled a basket in her arm, silver rings flashing on each of her fingers and a nest of dull, faded scarves wrung about her slender neck. Pale eyes, the same haint blue I'd explained to Remi, swept from my head to my feet, pausing to wink at the boy peeking from behind my back. She might be a younger woman trapped in an older woman's body, or vice versa, and she had an easy elegance that made me think maybe we'd found the Olympia Dukakis or Shirley MacLaine character I'd hoped we'd meet.

Her basket hung lightly from her fingertips, brimming with an assortment of odd items—a bottle of unlabeled wine that might have been home-brewed, a copy of the local phone book, cornbread, incense, and a jar of what looked like pickled pigs' feet, which my mother would be too polite to complain about.

The white-haired woman reached out, bracelets clinking from her wrist, and clasped cold fingers around a hand I hadn't offered.

"It's a pleasure to meet you, Britta," she said in a heavy Creole drawl as sweet as her toothy smile. "I'm Selena—Selena Stone—and I am so, *so* glad you're here."

It was not the first house built in town, but among the first, and it's the oldest still standing today. A man named Lemieux made his fortune in North Carolina and had the place constructed around 1802. Took courage for those early men settling the area, because the French, Spanish, and Mexicans still fought over it, even though Louisiana had been a state almost twenty years by then.

The magnolia tree alongside the house only stood about twenty feet high when Mr. Lemieux bought the land. However old it was then, by rights it should be long dead by now, but the leaves still grow waxy and green in summer, and the blooms are still white. That's because it's not just birds and squirrels making their homes in those branches.

When he brought his wife and children out from the Carolinas, Mrs. Lemieux made a little altar at the base of the tree with a wooden Christ statue, but every morning she'd come out to find it knocked over. She worried Choctaw Indians did it, as they still lived all around these parts, so she hired a man to stand watch, but he took off after that first night and wouldn't return.

By then Mr. and Mrs. Lemieux had begun hearing knocks on the windows and the back door. But the knocking would come at upstairs windows as well, and not just the ones nearest the magnolia branches.

After the hired man ran off, Mr. Lemieux staked out the backyard one night. That was the first time he saw them, the eyes in the trees. Dark little creatures with wild hair and teeth flashing in the moonlight. Mr. Lemieux, he instructed his wife to move the statue to the front yard, and he sawed off the branches closest to the house. That was when they painted the overhangs haint blue. Mr. Lemieux decided to leave the things in the tree alone. Mrs. Lemieux would sometimes catch eyes peering in a window from between the branches. When their daughter Michelle was a girl, she claimed to play with the little phantoms, but her parents insisted she made it up.

Some years later another man named Giraud owned the house and decided he'd had enough of knocking and peeping. He sat waiting late into the night for whatever hid in those branches, and they taunted him so bad he climbed up that tree, and when the little hands and feet came at him he nearly fell to his death. Giraud was never the same afterward, but he and everyone who's owned the house since has left the magnolia tree alone.

CHAPTER TEN

L abaye left the scene of the Hall Murders on four wheels, and I left on paws.

I hadn't bothered to shift back, in case Labaye had wanted to talk about his feelings—and of course, he had. Fortunately, the cop took the hint and allowed time to pass in companionable quiet as night fell and we each digested the events of the evening, sprawled on the floor in my brother's room. The fact that Labaye stopped talking was almost enough to make me forgive the number of times I'd caught him staring. Almost. His attention had started to make me cranky. If he'd been afraid I'd snap and chew him up for dinner, I'd understand—wasn't that what one would expect when they saw an actual, honest-to-God *werewolf*? But he looked at me with more interest than fear. Nobody looked at my wolf like that, not even other wolves.

It *was* nice to not have someone run away screaming, but I didn't love being fawned over either. Whatever the hell had possessed me to lay my head in his lap, I didn't need him getting all weird about it.

We'd sat like that on the floor in Remi's bedroom for a while. When Labaye felt strong enough to walk again, we'd taken one last tour of the house, still avoiding the parlor. Without a word, Labaye lay a hand on one faux crystal doorknob and I growled, short and soft. He smiled and grunted, "Yeah, back door's probably better?"

Labaye threw the deadbolt on those front doors but didn't

bother to make sure the back door locked behind us. Not like anybody would walk willingly into the place—nobody without a death wish. That hellhole had gone from crime scene to derelict and back again, and had seen its share of witches and ghosts and wolves, and who knew what other living dead things.

Home sweet home.

I darted past the magnolia tree and skulked along the shadows at the edge of the front lawn, as Labaye crunched across porcelain tiles to the driver's side of his cruiser. He stopped and turned.

"Your eyes," he said and sucked in his breath.

The contact lenses had popped out when I changed, and the nocturnal gleam was unsettling, particularly to prey, but the way Labaye stared made it feel like I was the one being stalked. My wolf looked up, intrigued, but I moved deeper into the shadows.

"It's kind of …" He shrugged. "Beautiful, in a way. I just wasn't expecting it. Didn't know they did that. It's like …" He shrugged again, sheepish in the dark. "Well, kind of like fireflies …"

It is most assuredly not *like fireflies, Officer Labaye.*

"I meant what I said earlier, Britta. I'll do whatever I can to help you get to the bottom of this," he said. "Scout's honor." He held three long, tan fingers to his temple.

Of course, he was a boy scout. I blinked, wishing I could roll my eyes—a gesture that lost its effect in wolf form.

You'd think after being pulled into a circle and beat up by a dead kid, he'd have had enough of the paranormal, and could go back to patrolling safe rural highways or something. Perhaps he felt indebted to the person—or monster—who'd saved his life. Or maybe he just didn't want a cold case this early in his career and needed to close the loop on Selena's demise.

"There's a coffee shop on West Street, the Coffee Stain," he said. "It's no Starbucks, but it's better than meeting at the station. Seven a.m.?"

Blink.

I took another look at the house, then turned and stalked into the darkness of the weeds and bramble, not bothering to even flick my ears when Labaye called my name twice. I hadn't yet decided if I wanted to deal with him again or not, and I wasn't going to give him the satisfaction of wagging my tail goodbye.

But I knew I hadn't seen the last of the house.

By the time I'd run far enough to rid my snout of any traces of bleach, magic, and Labaye, the moon hung high in an indigo canvas dotted with stars, which meant midnight was approaching. I scrambled down a gravel ditch for a drink, then followed the shallow stream behind the houses into the large wedge of land that sprawled between West Street and Highway 90. Though there'd been some development, I still found plenty of ground to light my nervous system up with a runner's high that's far more powerful than any human has ever felt. I shot across I-10 so fast any driver who even caught a glimpse would just marvel at the fastest deer he'd ever seen.

When I'd originally gone to the northeast, I'd avoided the more crowded areas for rural Maine, where, as in the bayou, you didn't have to go far to see the stars.

The shimmering sky brought a deep comfort.

Pack animals by nature, wolves—my kind or otherwise—long for company when slipping silently through the darkness. So-called lone wolves are more likely to be male, though female loners aren't unheard of. As a mortal, I'd been the odd man out, my best friend the brother that I raised. Even as a wolf, I remained a black sheep. I never hunted with the pack in Maine, and I'd be damned if I'd cuddle up in their dogpile. Not my style. But, in the decade I'd spent as a wolf—eight years in my current pack—I'd never felt the urge to belong as much as in this moment, a thousand miles from my den. Had Remi's ghost brought this out? Was it the endocannabinoids flooding my nervous systems with bliss? Or something else …

Not that the other wolves of my pack would have understood anyway. Malakh had accepted me into his pack, but the alpha didn't babysit needy new pups. Alec, my one companion and a fellow newcomer to the pack, accused me of being too tied up in my mortal past, so I'd stopped talking to him about Remi or Selena years ago. The rest of the pack had all long since lost whatever remained of their mortal families to time. None of them, as far as I knew, had survived what I had, though they all had their own stories—some equally terrible, just no witches. Alec refused to tell me how he'd been torn. Malakh's tale, I knew, went back to the shores of Ancient Egypt, and featured the old gods. Still, in all this time, he said he'd never met another wolf who'd been cursed by a mambo.

My stomach growled. I should feed, but food held no interest. I paced under the starlight, trotting out of the farmland south of town, back among rundown single-family homes and rusted trailer parks, making sure to keep in the shadows.

Every time I blinked, Remi's face—or the face of Remi's ghost, to be more accurate—waited behind my eyelids. For ten years, I had grieved my brother's murder, my family's death. I'd hated Selena but clung to my guilt and shame for not coming back to the swamps of southwestern Louisiana and tearing her limbs from her body while she begged for mercy. Now, in the space of one night, everything had changed.

I could've followed the farmlands to the motel the cops had booked me, but by the time I got tired of walking, I'd returned to the place I'd left. The place I'd been trying for years to get away from.

I nosed my way through the back door of my family's old house, grateful Labaye had left the door unlatched. I padded up the stairs to Remi's bedroom, laid in front of the fireplace, and closed my eyes to sleep.

"I wasn't sure you'd show up," Labaye said, peering over the tops of his aviator sunglasses.

I slid into the chair across from him at a lopsided table in the Coffee Stain, which might have been named for its grimy décor rather than any clever pun. His brow cocked, Labaye tried not to let me see his eyes wander over me as he closed the file he'd been looking at, but he did a bad job of hiding his inspection. He pulled my carry-on bag out from under his seat and slid it across the table without comment.

"Yeah, well, that makes two of us." I hooked my bag over the back of my chair. Of course, I didn't exactly blend in. Scarlett O'Hara never arrived to meet a gentleman with the waistband of her black jeans split in the back. The fact I'd arrived in the sleepy, backwoods Louisiana town, where the dress code options were camouflage and/or dungarees, decked out head-to-toe in black didn't help, but I hadn't planned on sticking around long enough to worry over my wardrobe.

Officer Aaron Labaye, as clean-cut in his civilian dress shirt, cuffs buttoned at the wrists, dark wash denim, and boots as he'd been in uniform, pulled his sunglasses off and smiled. What looked like a five o'clock shadow had crept down the sides of his jaw. He set down his coffee mug, and a little splashed over the rim. The stubble made Labaye look like a hardened man of the law, rather than a shiny new rookie. He tucked one aviator arm in the pocket of his shirt, and the weight of the glasses pulled his collar open to expose chest hair as dark as the coif he'd left untamed, going for a casual look today.

It was working. My wolf grumbled. I stopped breathing.

Labaye folded his napkin into a neat square the size of a credit card. "Your rental was still parked at the station this morning," he said and went down on one knee. Rather than propose, the cop slid the folded napkin under one foot of the table. "Guess you weren't in any condition to drive," he grinned, tested the tabletop for steadiness.

I'd woken, naked and human, when ambient dawn crept through my brother's bedroom window. After I fetched my clothes from the scene of the fight and scurried back out of there, I'd gotten dressed and tied my Docs before noticing I'd missed my leather jacket, but it was already too warm to bother crawling behind in the fireplace again. This resulted in me showing a lot more skin than I normally would have. This far south you didn't get my kind of pale among the living.

Rather than dignify Labaye's last comment, I scanned the other patrons, trying to be more subtle than my cop sidekick. I'd taken Remi to the Coffee Stain a time or two back in the day. The heavy sweet scent in the air reminded me they made their own bread pudding—from scratch, like somebody's mama had made it, probably.

The thing about not aging meant I looked *exactly* the same as I had the one summer we'd lived in Vinton—but would that make it more likely I'd be recognized, or less? Did Marty McFly's parents ever think, *Gosh, doesn't our teenaged son look almost exactly like that Calvin Klein fellow who crashed our prom?* Or are our synapses just a little too spongey to make a connection so counterintuitive? I recognized the owner, watching us from behind the counter with a dishtowel draped over her shoulder, but I bet she just wondered what the cop wanted with this pale weirdo. Being a stranger was scary enough in a town this size, let alone the thought of being recognized as the girl who'd let her whole family die. The other faces in the café, none of them familiar, glanced over with only the mild interest any out-of-towner might attract.

"Nice to see you as *you* again," Labaye said, then lowered his voice. "How long does it take to shift back?" He leaned forward, elbows on the folder. "I kind of missed it when you changed, what with your brother …" He indicated a bruise on his collarbone, the only mark Remi's phantom had left. "Do you change back at will, or do you have to wait …?" The smile made him look younger than ever, as though the bruise were the result of some playground skirmish with another kid. "Does it hurt?" His voice dropped with each bullet until he whispered across the small table, "What does it feel like?"

"What the hell, Labaye." I scraped my chair back, earning a sharp shriek from the tiled floor. "Buy a girl a drink first. Jesus."

Heads turned toward us. He had the grace to look embarrassed.

"I'm sorry," he said in a hush. "I've just never, you know, met one before."

"Curiosity killed the cat." I hadn't meant it as a threat, and my words didn't have any bite—or at least not much.

"Don't worry." He winked. "I know you're the big, bad wolf and I'm the little piggy, puns intended."

That earned a smile. "The bigger question," I said, "might be how you rolled with it so easily. If the word *werewolf* isn't scary enough, surely seeing the monster is."

"You caught me at the right moment." His voice dropped back down. "I mean, at the moment of the, whatever you call it … the shift, your brother's ghost had his claws in my throat." He tugged his collar. "I had one second to register," he waved his hand vaguely across the table, "*you*, then I passed out."

Offering a raised eyebrow, I sighed and shook my head. I hadn't slept worth a damn and still hadn't bothered to feed. I had no spare energy in my already diminished reserves to riddle Labaye's interest in my wolf. Everything needed to go into helping Remi.

When the teenage waitress finally appeared at the edge of our table, I ordered black coffee, to go. She nodded at Labaye's half-empty mug before walking away.

He raised an eyebrow. "So you take yours without sugar?"

"We normally just drink the blood of our victims," I explained, my voice as deadpan as I could make it in a whisper. His Adam's apple bobbed and one of his eyes twitched. I'd decided to cut him some slack but couldn't go too easy. If I kept him just scared enough, maybe he wouldn't ask so many questions. Or at least stop staring.

"Kidding." I smirked as the waitress breezed by, handing me a to-go cup and splashing a warmup in Labaye's mug.

He cleared his throat and coughed out a laugh. "I guess I didn't actually stop to think if you even drink coffee."

"I rather like coffee." I shrugged, ignoring the rumble in my empty stomach. I took a sip, the warmth spreading through my body. I'd expected Folgers to be the juice of the day, but this stuff had a kick, wasn't even bitter. "It's normal food that's the problem. Doesn't sit well." I owed him something after making him sweat. "So, you offered to help."

He folded his fingers together and lay them on the folder. "If we can figure out why Selena was in that house, and if your brother, uh, returned *before* she was killed—"

"I know what she was doing," I blurted out before I could stop myself. I'd intended to keep this part a secret, at least for now. I set the cup back on the table and pushed it away like curdled milk. Something about Labaye made me a little too goddamned loose-lipped. Usually, I found it hard to open up and tell anyone anything. Maybe he'd paid that girl to slip something in my coffee. "And, by the way, I don't appreciate your implication."

He seemed torn between which question to ask first. After a concentrated sip of his coffee, he settled on, "'Implication'?"

My skin prickled as patience abandoned my serotonin-deprived nerves, and my wolf growled. "That Remi had something to do with Sel—with *her* death."

Labaye stiffened. "You don't think he did?" He'd looked at me the same way yesterday, from his side of the interrogation table. So much had happened since then I could almost forget he was a cop—until I caught a glimpse of the pistol on his hip. I'd saved him, and he'd offered to help, but solving a crime was his top priority. That, and we had different ideas of which murder deserved a solution.

"Do I think the ghost of my ten-year-old brother," I hissed, "who died at Selena's hand, yanked out her eye, her teeth, and her heart to decorate my mother's tea parlor?" The witch's name felt like poison on my tongue. "Do *you*?"

"I don't think we're ready to rule out any options at this point." Labaye's diplomatic tone made me cringe.

"The dead don't generally kill the living," I snapped back.

He sputtered and looked frantically around the room. When he spoke again he'd lowered his voice so much I had to read his lips. "Do you know that for sure?"

I didn't. "I know my brother ... dead or alive. He wouldn't hurt anyone. Even her."

Now it was Labaye's turn deadpan. He clicked his teeth and tugged at his top button again to show off the bruised collarbone.

I narrowed my eyes and tried to control my pulse. I squeezed the edges of the table to stay seated and not walk out.

Labaye came to help, I reminded myself.

And he was human: stupid, predictable, linear. Especially cops, who always assigned a good guy and a bad guy, and rarely took the time to look past the black and white.

But Labaye had to be different, didn't he? Out consorting with a dead girl in daylight, one he now knew to be an actual monster. He'd even bought me coffee.

Gritting my teeth, I tried again. "I know what she was doing. She tried it before. None of this was ever Remi's fault." I bit back on the tremble in my voice. "Isn't ruling out *illogical* options part of the detective process?"

"Okay." Labaye leaned in and asked, "So, what *was* she doing?" He used his good cop smile, and it occurred to me he'd never said how he'd found Selena's remains. Judging by the faded police tape in the front lawn, no one had set foot in the house for years.

"Well, what do you have to go on?" I let my voice trail as if rolling his question around. "Did someone report noise from the house?"

He dropped the smile and his brow knitted together.

"What made you go in there?" I asked. "When you found her? Her remains."

The smile came back, patient, the kind that begged to be ripped off.

Manners, Britta, Mom called from the grave.

Labaye pushed the paper cup toward me like a bargaining chip. "You first."

"What is this," I barked, "middle school?"

He sighed. "What do you think she was doing there, before she was," he spoke carefully and low, "before she died?"

Something didn't smell right, and I didn't think it was my trust issues.

I ignored the coffee and crossed my pale, bare arms high over my chest. "Selena was working magic in that house. You saw, and I'm telling you it was just like the one she'd made in the parlor. That's all I am saying for now. *Your* turn."

Frustration passed over his face, but his smile didn't falter. "So, what *did* you see before," he asked. "What did she do to you and your brother?"

He dropped the smile and I blinked hard. "This feels a lot more like an interrogation than a conversation. Are we on record?"

"I think we're past that, Britta." Labaye laughed, and even though I'd been holding my breath I caught the nervous sweat beading on the back of his neck, noticed his fingers brush the holster on his hip. Whatever he was holding back, it scared him. "Officially off the record. I promised to help, and I intend to do it."

My sigh sounded more like a growl. "Look. I wasted hours in your station yesterday, and all I learned was that Selena is dead.

All you showed me was a grainy photo of maybe five ounces of her remains and a kid's drawing. Then you saw me shift—and I saved *your* ass." I snarled. "You've learned a fuck of a lot more from me than I've even had the opportunity to ask you." He floated both hands, palms just over the folder, and I reined in the volume. "If we're in this together, start sharing, Labaye. What are you hiding?" I picked up my cup but thought better of pouring caffeine on top of all that agitation. I drank it anyway.

Labaye tightened his smile and put his hands down firmly on the top of the file he'd kept closed. "Please call me Aaron."

I growled, biting my lip. This guy had used up all his brownie points and had started to piss me off. "What were you doing in my goddamned house, *Aaron*?"

"Entering an abandoned property doesn't require reasonable suspicion, much less a search warrant, Britta," he said flatly. "Now meet me halfway. Please."

I stood, kicking the chair back, and pulled my carry-on bag over my shoulder. "Let me know when you're ready to open that folder, Officer Labaye."

He eased back in his chair, as though he couldn't care less about the file on the table.

"I have my own business to attend to," I said, "and it's time I get some real help."

CHAPTER ELEVEN

I knew what Alec would say before his face even appeared on my laptop, so I braced myself as best I could.

To hell with Labaye. It'd been silly to think I could count on a human for help. Even sillier to think he might be … different.

"Britta." Alec greeted me with his usual growl. He did not suffer pleasantries, and even on the dim screen of my five-year-old Dell, his image conveyed the usual degree of severity. You got the sense he'd prepared for membership in the spooky things club since the day he'd been born into mortal life—whenever that was. He looked the part, all cheekbones and angles, the trademark high-collared peacoat worn with the flair of a nineteenth-century gentleman, even indoors. A preternatural poster boy.

My nerves—and hunger—were getting the better of me. I could still taste the coffee, too, though I'd forgotten the cup when I stormed out of the café. A wolf can go a long way on a big enough feeding, but otherwise hunger can be a deadly Achilles' heel.

I grunted Alec's name, glad he couldn't smell my nerves. Asking for help was only slightly worse than needing it to begin with.

"I take it things are not going according to plan in—" Alec curled the side of his mouth, expressing contempt rather than joy. "Louisiana." He said the word like it tasted bad. I got it. He'd made clear his feelings about my trip. Alec relished his status as werewolf—as lycanthrope, *loup garou*—whereas he thought I'd barely sniffed around the edges of my new identity, too wrapped up in my own past.

Still, as soon as his face appeared on-screen, it brought me a measurable amount of relief.

Alec wasn't just another member of the pack. He'd found me, tail between my legs, and introduced me to Malakh, made a place for me in a den that welcomed me with open arms *and* open paws, even if I did not reciprocate. Malakh encouraged me to con nect with the rest of our wolves, but I didn't *bond* ... not anymore. This morning in the café had served as a good reminder why.

Everyone always wanted something, and I'd lost anything I could give.

"Things here are ... complicated," I admitted. "But it's nothing to discuss over Skype."

Alec gave me that blank expression he'd perfected with decades of practice. "Are you asking for my help, Britta?"

I sighed. The ass, he had to make me say it, didn't he? "I am."

The left side of his mouth darted up again. Curled and released. This smugness should've set me off, but at least he didn't dole out an *I told you so.*

"I'm always at your call," he said, "but it's a long flight. Perhaps we can resolve your problem without me coming there in person."

His way of saying yes while still saying no. "Alec, it's not. Believe me."

"Short version, then."

"The woman who cursed me is dead." Alec rolled his eyes, and I fought back the edge of whine in my voice. "Murdered, maybe. Probably. The police found her remains. That's it."

Alec sneered. "*Remains,*" he said. "Humans love their euphemisms."

I shrugged. "I found something else." I thought my screen might have frozen until he finally blinked. "Her crafting room, in my old house."

"You're sure no one can hear you, Britta?"

I spun the laptop to show him the dark curtains drawn

across the long window beside the door. "I'm in my motel room," I said, hoping the walls weren't as paper-thin as they looked. "There was an active circle, and," I said more quietly, "my brother. Trapped there. Or his spirit. It attacked Labaye, and I had to," my voice cracked, "fight Remi off to save him."

The screen—or maybe Alec—glitched. His brow arched, carving a deep question mark into his smooth forehead. "Who is *Labaye*?"

Trust a man to fixate on what he perceives as competition, instead of the actual problem. "Well, I told you, the police found—"

Alec's eyebrow lowered, hard, forcing his yellow eyes into slits, and he rubbed his chin against the popped collar of the peacoat. "Britta," he snapped. "What did you look like," he said, his voice the perfect cadence of disdain, "when you saved this mortal cop?"

I winced. Across the mattress of the motel bed, Alec's heat pulsed through the laptop. In his view, wolves sat at the top of the food chain. Supreme beings. If I confessed I'd let Labaye touch me in wolf form, the keyboard may very well burst into flames.

"Britta," he warned through gritted teeth, "that was reckless, and—"

"I know, Alec," I said to ward off a lecture. "But he would've been killed—"

"And so what if he had?" Alec barked, and the screen flicked to black for a second. "What's the life of one mortal?"

On this, Alec and I had never agreed.

"Never trust them, Britta." He shook his head, mustering up his wizened sage mode. "Mortals fear us, but they also envy us. You know firsthand what desire for the *loup garou*'s power can do. There can be grave consequences."

"Like being cursed to spend immortality as a dog?" I said, all caution about who might be listening through the walls forgotten. The growl came from my stomach, not my wolf. "Yeah, that's nothing I'd like to pass on, trust me. I know how to keep the claws of my wolf in, Alec."

"There you go, 'curse,' '*my* wolf'!" He rolled his eyes, the favorite of his few remaining human gestures. "It isn't a curse, and you didn't die—you *became* the wolf!"

I tapped the volume down. Somewhere over near the manager's office, water flushed through pipes for a moment then stopped, but otherwise all I heard was the highway. Alec had stepped away from his desk, and paced in front of a closed door, in the house he shared with two other members of the pack. For a moment, I mostly just saw leather pants crossing back and forth.

Beyond Alec and Malakh, I hadn't told anyone about my past—not Selena, or the life I'd lost down here. With Malakh's permission, Alec became my own private *loup "guru." He'd* taught me to hunt, to control my shifts, how to fight on four legs. We'd grown inseparable, as much a function of our special brand of friendship—the sort that wasn't really all that friendly—as the fact that I never quite fit in with the rest of the pack, and he'd never wanted to.

"We're not transmitting the common cold, Britta." He sat again and shifted the laptop on his desk so he fit better in frame. "Passing on our gift is one possibility, but it can come with other … entanglements."

"What do you mean?"

Normally, Alec loved it if I asked questions. He'd compliment my curiosity, when really he just liked an invitation to go on. But now he shifted in the chair, one knee bumping the desk so he had to straighten the screen again. He showed teeth when he spoke. "These are things you would see for yourself—*important* things—if you'd stop thinking of this as a curse," he said, "but as something sacred. A gift."

He folded his arms on the desk and actually smiled. "Britta, you've been given an opportunity to live forever. You are part of the earth in a way no mere *man* could dream. It is not something to turn your nose up at, not unless it is toward the moon in thanks."

"Fine," I said. "I'll be more grateful about being undead. Now, if there's something I need to know to help my brother, save the sermon for when I'm home."

The corner of his mouth tightened again. Letting out our perfectly nasty selves had kept us close the past several years. No games, no bullshit. It was refreshing, even if I wanted to strangle him sometimes.

A shiver ran through him as he settled in the chair. "What I am trying to say is that if, gods forbid, you'd torn this policeman, there are three potential outcomes." Alec took on the misty-eyed expression that always overcame him when he found the opportunity to educate me on the finer points of damnation. Most of the pack referred to a wolf breaking mortal skin in a non-life-threatening way as a *tear*—like slicing skin with a blade's edge, a superficial wound, rather than stabbing it. A "tearing" between the human world and ours.

"One," he went on, "obviously, is death." Even if the tooth or claw doesn't go deep enough to kill, most human blood can't support the change, and the marked spends a few months shifting between man and wolf, then dies. "A mortal who receives the tear must have magic in them already," Alec said, "or the gift will not bloom. I have no doubt your witch marked you with that in mind—even as a mortal you possessed some magic, as did I, and all of our pack."

Alec had, in fact, constantly tried to convince me of that— Selena had chosen me knowing what I could become. *A wolf in the thrall of a witch could be a powerful weapon*, he'd told me more than once.

I waved my hand at the screen to hurry him along. "Okay, three options," I said. "A deep enough wound kills you, or a wound that doesn't kill you … kills you. What's behind door number three, Alec?" Humans weren't the only ones who could try my patience.

"Allow me to phrase this delicately," Alec said, managing to look sinister and sardonic at the same time on the pixelated screen. "If you turn him, he's yours. Forever."

"Like, a child?" Alec had told me about wolves building packs by hunting down humans they deemed worthy of our "gift," but Malakh didn't believe in it, and our pack had not grown since my arrival.

"Not like a child," Alec said. "*Yours*, Britta. Your mate."

I swallowed. The idea seemed preposterous at first but then struck me as something I should have guessed. What better irony than being partnered for eternity with someone who'd almost killed you? "So our idea of marriage is a bizarre *you bite it, you bought it* sort of thing?"

Alec's lips thinned into a line. "It is part of the magic which animates us. We either select a suitable mate, or the moon chooses one for us." He bunched up his mouth and I realized this was the first part of the gift he didn't seem to feel kindly about. "A lone wolf is a weak wolf. A partner makes us stronger. Makes us whole."

"Which is why wolves mate for life." Finding a mate hadn't been on my list of priorities, not even when I'd been alive, with Remi to take care of. "So, what, the magic just selects your spouse, and bam, they get cut and we're stuck?"

"It's a little more involved than that, Britta." Alec's gaze wandered up thoughtfully. "Mated pairs ... are a team. They both live, or they both die."

Well, that sounded unpleasant—an ambiguous gothic love story I liked even less than modern romances. At least in those everyone lived happily ever after. This sounded like a wolfish version of *Romeo and Juliet*.

I hated when he was cryptic. "This feels like something I should have known about earlier, Alec."

For once, there was doubt in Alec's golden eyes. I remembered Remi's drawing, that yellow-highlighter eye of the wolf, and stuck the tips of my fingers into my jeans' pocket. "It ... it's not something I've experienced." His brow screwed itself up in a knot, but he shook it off. "Dally with this policeman and it's on you, Britta."

Not gonna bite. "How … how could Selena have known if I had magic in me? She didn't fill me in on that part." I couldn't help countering Alec's sarcasm with a little of my own. "And how do we know the difference between a tear that'll turn and one that saddles you with a furry ball and chain?"

"How do we know anything, Britta?" His tone carried that tight patience one used when a toddler had asked a question they should've already known the answer to.

"Smell," I said. "We smell it on them."

I shuddered as the scent of Remi's secret room invaded my memory, followed by Labaye's musky pine. "I know what magic smells like. Labaye doesn't have it."

Alec's tone was hard, his eyes skeptical. "You say this like it's a bad thing."

"I said it like it's a fact."

"Anyway," he continued, crossing his arms and leaning back, "I will come, Britta. On the next flight. And we will deal with your former home together." He shifted in the chair and flashed a sincere smile for just a moment. "Your human friend can return to patrolling the swamps of southwestern Louisiana, or whatever it is he does, and leave us to our business."

A breath I hadn't known I'd been holding escaped my lips. "Thank you, Alec."

"On one condition," he added after a pause.

A lump rose in my throat. Always a cost for his help. Usually, it just meant putting up with Alec himself. This time I sensed it would carry a higher price tag.

"I would have preferred to discuss this in person, but given present circumstances, I do not think either of us can afford such a luxury." He shifted stiffly and cleared his throat, in an uncharacteristic display of discomfort.

I'd often wondered what Alec had been like as a mortal—or *when* he'd been mortal, for that matter. After all our three a.m. heart-to-hearts and the secrets we'd shared, the details of his past remained a mystery, beyond the fact that he'd been a wolf longer than I'd ever been alive. He showed an interest in macabre history and talked at length about the Bubonic Plague, the last stretch of the Yellow Fever outbreak that made its way from Africa to America. I wasn't sure if his fascination was personal or academic. Between his sort of over-the-top distaste for rats, an unrelenting hatred for the American Southwest, and a peculiar clip to his speech, my best guess was that though he had the appearance of a young man, Alec had spent time amongst the French settlers down in this part of the country.

However long he'd been a wolf, time hadn't softened him— he'd only grown more cynical.

"You and I have always shared a proclivity to spend our time under the moon in quiet solitude. Although we are in many ways dissimilar, we are cut from a cloth quite different from the rest of our pack."

When Alec waxed poetic, bad things were upon me, and the current lecture had started off a little Shakespearean, even for him. He settled forward and folded his hands together in front of his laptop in a gesture that reminded me of Labaye, when maybe Labaye should have reminded me of Alec. "For many years now," he went on, "you have been my trusted companion, and if you would grant me the honor, I would have you as my mate. Not by predestination," he said, raising a hand, "but by choice."

Alec stopped and gave what may have been his most genuine smile, and for a split second, he'd never looked less like an animal, but more like a man. "I grant the timing might seem suspicious, but I'd already decided to ask upon your return." He said something else, but I lost the thread, consumed by my thoughts.

I snapped back when he promised, "I will help you in this, without question or complaint. In return, I ask your hand as my Luna, and I do commit my soul to yours, for as long as we share the same moon."

The lump that had lodged in my throat swelled to the size of a wrecking ball. I gaped at the image on my screen. How had this gone from a plea for help to a lesson in lycanthropy, to a fucking marriage proposal?

"Alec," I said. "I duh-don't know …"

His countenance hardened to stone, and his voice turned cold. "You are not required to accept, Britta. Nor are you required to answer at this moment." A banging sound came through the laptop speaker, the feet of his chair as he shifted around. "I'll be here when you've made up your mind."

What a crappy way to barter yourself into a mate. I didn't need his help badly enough to say yes.

"That's messed up, Alec," I sneered. "I need to figure things out here, and you've literally made it the least important aspect of the whole call. You want to use it to negotiate a … a mate?" I crossed my arms and squeezed the air out in one big breath to try to calm myself. "That's bullshit."

Alec's image flickered, and he winced at my use of profanity. I bet he loved those old-timey southern belles like Miss Scarlett.

"The witch is dead," he shrugged, "and you remain as you were. I can help you put your brother's spirit to peace." I flinched when his hands shot forward, the image shook, and he pulled the screen closer to his face. "But do not reprimand me over *timing*. Britta Orchid will always find a reason to be angry, and a reason to resist allowing someone a space in her heart."

Well, he wasn't wrong, but even for him, that last bit was a whole new level of melodrama.

"Thanks for nothing," I snapped.

The corner of his mouth twitched. "I will be here if you should change your mind. But do promise me one thing."

I just stared, arms covering my breasts.

The image bounced as he dropped both fists onto the desk in front of his laptop, so I met his yellow eyes over big thumbs in forced perspective. "The next opportunity you get to intervene in the matters of man, do not try to be a hero. It is not in our nature, and it is not our business what happens in the world of men. Either walk away or, if you take a side, make sure it is on the side of your kind." He rose slowly, only so far that his eyes came to the top of the screen. "Make sure he's dead."

Alec's hand shot out, and the screen went black.

.

CHAPTER TWELVE

The early morning meeting hadn't gone at all the way he'd wanted.

"You have reached two-oh-seven, seven-four—"

Aaron tapped *End* to cut off Britta's tinny, automatic voicemail greeting and set his phone back on top of the folder, face up—not that she'd return his calls, not this soon, anyway. The first couple of times, he'd popped outside to make the call, but every attempt had gone to voicemail after five rings, so it didn't seem like too much of a faux pas to try from inside the Coffee Stain. Did it ring unanswered because she'd tucked the phone away so she could cool off—or did she sit in her motel looking at the screen, knowing it was him? Probably the latter.

Aaron stretched his legs beneath the table and leaned back in his chair with a groan, his hands over his eyes to ward off the mid-morning light filtering in through the Coffee Stain window. He hadn't slept well the night before, less preoccupied with his minor injuries than with what lay ahead.

He popped the last bit of bread pudding into his mouth and pushed the empty plate away. When he'd asked Britta to meet him early this morning, he'd thought they'd have a little breakfast together, that he could build a bridge—not push her off it. But he'd miscalculated, that much was clear—mistaken comradery for trust. Problem was, he couldn't pinpoint where he'd gone wrong. One step forward, two steps back.

Is it possible to tame a wolf?

For this to work, he'd need to earn her trust. He just had to figure out how. And to stop thinking about her firefly eyes, and the weird tremble in his stomach whenever she crossed his mind.

"How's everything for you this morning, darlin'?" The voice from over his shoulder sent Aaron shooting up in his chair. He wrapped his fingers around the mug in front of him, resisting the urge to touch the gun tucked in his shoulder holster. He couldn't afford to look spooked.

"Just fine, thank you, ma'am." The words cracked on his tongue and Aaron cleared his throat with a swallow of cold coffee.

Mabel Landry, the Coffee Stain's matronly owner and resident town gossip, set Britta's half full to-go cup on the empty plate and wiped the spot where Britta had sat with one hand, a pot of coffee in her other. Aaron had breakfasted at the little corner coffee shop nearly every morning since he'd been hired by the Calcasieu Parish PD, and not once had Mabel appeared to refill his coffee, much less clear his table. She'd undoubtedly seen the entire exchange with Britta from behind the counter, so the fact that she'd waited to come over until he'd finished eating could only be attributed to her good southern upbringing.

"Thanks, Mrs. Landry," he said, pushing his mug toward her.

"I don't think your—" Mabel's voice broke off as she made a small show of fumbling for the right word. "Friend's coming back." Her eyes darted to the window and back, and the coffee pot and the saggy flesh of her arm floated over the table as she waited for Labaye to respond.

"Probably not," was the only answer he gave, and she made no move to fill the mug.

Gossip was a valuable currency in small towns, and even police matters made the rounds at the local watering holes. No doubt Mabel would tell every customer who came through her doors for the next week about the stranger who'd stormed out on a member of local law enforcement—so she'd want to get as much detail as she could.

"Awful pale to be from around here," Mabel said. "Something about her looks familiar though." The older woman squinted as she flipped through a mental Rolodex of residents and patrons, setting the coffee pot next to the to-go cup and empty plate. Aaron prayed a decade-old memory didn't slither out from the crypts of her mind. Few people in town might have made the connection to the Hall Murders, but Mabel sat at the top of the list—something Aaron had overlooked when he'd picked the morning's meeting spot.

"She got family around here?" Mabel asked.

Aaron almost said *Not anymore*, but adjusted and just said, "No."

Mabel's brow pinched low as she cataloged names or faces, a mass of wrinkles lining her forehead.

"She's from out of town," he said, fixing on the smile that made women like Mabel Landry swoon. "Just passing through."

She planted a hand on her hip and glared down at him. "She wouldn't be passing through to talk about what you boys found at the Hall Murder House?"

Aaron hid his frustration behind another sip of cold coffee and screwed up his face to feign confusion. "Mrs. Landry," he said, "what the heck have your customers been telling you?"

She scoffed and flapped her dishtowel at him as if scolding a petulant child. "Don't sass me, Aaron Labaye. Ernest came in here just the other day, going on about how the Hall Murder House ought to be torn down. You're a cop now, but you probably don't remember how hard that was on Vinton. I do." She tapped her temple with one long pink fingernail, then dropped the towel on her shoulder.

"I remember, Mrs. Landry," Aaron said, feeling all of twelve years old. *Ernest Devereaux*. The veteran cop's loose lips had a bad habit of fluttering among civilians like a sail in stiff wind, almost as bad as Mabel herself, who kept right on like Aaron hadn't said a word.

"House has been cursed since the first nail went in," she said, "a history of tragedy and death."

"All houses have history," Aaron said, hoping to push her well-placed suspicions in another direction. "You name one old building that doesn't, especially in these parts."

"Now I'm not talking about old ghost stories, Aaron," she said, leaning in and lowering her voice. "I hear you boys found another body in that house. Is that what this is about?"

And Mabel reached right in front of Aaron and placed a hand on the folder—something even Britta hadn't had the nerve to do.

Aaron slapped both his hands on top of the folder. "Hey," he said. "This is CPPD property." He took his eyes off her long enough to check the folder, relieved to see he'd left it face down so she couldn't read the name on the tab. "Now don't worry, Mrs. Landry. Everything's under control, I assure you."

Mabel huffed, one chubby hand pressed to her breast where the towel hung. "I'm a taxpayer, and I go to town hall meetings. I have a right to know if there's someone dangerous coming into my restaurant." She picked up the empty plate with Britta's abandoned cup as though presenting evidence. "What did you want with that girl?"

"I promise you, there's nothing to worry about there," he said, remembering Devereaux's unsavory remarks from the day before, and the secret he learned in the attic last night. "And she won't be in town long." Whatever Devereaux had blabbed about at the Coffee Stain, it didn't seem like he'd mention the witness they'd called back to the crime scene.

The old woman cast a disbelieving eye in Aaron's direction, then exhaled and let her hand fall away from her chest as she cleared the table.

"I'll take a to-go cup when you get a chance," Aaron said through his best smile.

Mabel looked like she might tell him to get his own coffee, then popped the lid off Britta's cup, poured the cold contents of his mug on top, and handed it to Aaron, who had to laugh as she walked away.

Not Officer Labaye's best morning with the ladies.

He picked up his phone and dialed Britta's number again.

CHAPTER THIRTEEN

After disconnecting the call with Alec, I closed the laptop, leaned my head back against the headrest, and exhaled until my lungs hurt. As Scarlett O'Hara herself had said, "If he thought I'd marry him just to pay for the bonnet, I won't."

I pulled Remi's drawing from my pocket, unfolded it, then grabbed my cell and popped my headphones in. Labaye had continued to blow up my phone with a long series of calls I would not return.

My coworker had recommended a true-crime podcast. Some rich young bloke had taken his fiancée for a yacht ride, but he fell overboard, and police recovered his body after it washed up on Monhegan Island. They arrested the fiancée, who couldn't explain the perimortem blunt force trauma to the yachtsman's cranium. In soothing tones, my trusted podcaster followed a widowed aunt's quest to vindicate her niece—but I couldn't concentrate, and tossed the phone to the foot of the bed.

The human I'd stupidly begun to trust had insisted on keeping his own secrets, so I'd be double-dog-damned if I'd share mine, and the one wolf I thought I could count on had made it clear reinforcements weren't coming unless I agreed to marry him.

Men. Alive or dead, they were nothing but a complete pain in the ass. I should've known. Asking a dude for help was like playing with fire. Or magic. It always came with a price, and I had no intention of paying either Labaye's or Alec's, happier to tell them both right where they could shove their motives, too.

Well, to hell with them. I had my own crack team of three—me, myself, and I.

And there was Remi if I could figure out a way to talk to him. But which Britta would he want to talk to—the sister he once knew, or the wolf he'd drawn in his circle? I found the fact that Remi also wasn't exactly the way I remembered him mildly reassuring.

Did ghosts suffer from identity issues, too?

I pushed out another heavy, wounded breath. What a freaking bizarre reunion. Both dearly departed, though only one of us had gotten to die. I'd crossed into the world of the undead, leaving my brother's phantom trapped in between.

I didn't want another brawl with Remi's restless spirit, so just violating that circle again—even if it didn't hurt as bad as the one back in the day—would not do. The scrying mirror presented a far more promising option, but it had been smashed to pieces in the struggle with Labaye. Not that I knew how to use the thing, anyway. I could've tried a simple *Mirror, mirror, on the wall* sort of incantation, but seeing as how this was no fairytale, I doubted it would do the trick. Maybe Alec had it right, and I should've spent more time exploring my new world of magic and curses after all.

Fortunately, one person in this backward bayou town would know how to talk to the dead—and unlike Labaye, she didn't have a case to solve. No doubt she already knew I'd returned, and awaited my visit—maybe hoping it never came. I wouldn't go to her if I had any other choice, and only hoped she didn't kill me on sight.

I should've taken the damn coffee. Or thrown it in Labaye's smug face, I thought as I drove past the Coffee Stain, cursing the cop under my breath. Either would have been more satisfying than leaving it on the table. My stomach stirred, and with it, my wolf.

I put the rental car in park and killed the engine. Immediately, the air grew stale and the familiar weight of loneliness and dread set in. Had I really let that man *pet* me? I was seriously losing it.

With a deep breath, I shoved the driver's side door open,

slamming it behind me as I flipped my cell to silent and slid it into my bag. I didn't bother to lock the car. There was nowhere in this little town I couldn't get to on two feet—four if I felt adventurous—and I didn't know or care about the current crime stats. At this point, I'd be more than happy for an excuse to hunt down some would-be car thief. Might improve my mood. Could definitely do something about my hunger.

I chased the thought away. Rumors of *loup garou*s were all too common in the bayou, and one man had already come face to snout with the beast. Labaye was keeping his mouth shut about my monster, but the last thing I needed were superstitious good ol' boys loading their guns with silver bullets. Even if no one found me out, the grapevine would undoubtedly reach all the way back to Maine, and Malakh would have something to say about it. Or, worse, Alec.

Pairs of railroad tracks that hadn't seen any action in decades bookended a two-block length of mom-and-pop businesses. Between those two blocks, a road crossed West Street and led directly back to my old house. The police station was a short walk to my left, beyond which sat a tiny playground contained within a rickety chain-link fence, connected to the pitiful excuse for the town's library to my right.

I headed to the latter.

The rusted entry bell announced my arrival as I slid smoothly between the dirty glass-paned doors of the Calcasieu Parish Public Library. The withering, steady gaze of a dark-skinned older woman at the desk snared me from behind black cat eyeglasses. Immediate recognition with no hint of surprise, followed by a quick scan of the few patrons seated in the main room. The intricate knot of ash-colored braids tumbled out from her headdress onto a bright gold and green scarf draped over her shoulder, forming a collar up to her chin. Her lips curled into a familiar, tight scowl. Other than a slight hardening around the eyes, Edmée

Byrdie looked the same as the last time I'd seen her. In her turban and caftan, she looked even more out of place in Calcasieu Parish than me, but everyone in Vinton knew and respected her.

A tremor—the kind imperceptible to mortals—shimmered through the floorboards up through the thick Doc Martens soles, as her power flicked out to touch me. I lowered my face in a show of submission, directing my gaze at her thumb and three fingers, at the empty space where her ring finger should be. Heady vanilla and rose perfumed the air as she stepped out from behind the desk.

"Good afternoon, Mam Byrdie." I greeted the woman by her formal title, keeping my voice low enough not to be overheard by ears curious as to what the odd stranger might say to the kindly old librarian.

Looks could be so deceiving, and never mind little pitchers—small towns had big noses.

The mambo didn't blink. "I wondered when I'd see you again, *sha.*" Her voice carried the lilting notes of a creole accent, but the kindness in her tone did not match the set of her mouth. Or her scent. Anger boiled, hot and hungry, beneath her skin—anger, and disgust. "You left without saying goodbye."

Her voice dropped to a dangerous whisper and she stepped so close her power beat in angry bursts against me. "I know what you are now, Britta Orchid," she hissed. "A cursed thing, no longer welcome here."

There was no love lost between the resident mambo and the wolves that had once called Calcasieu Parish home. That pack had long since left the swamp—driven out, I'd come to find out, by the woman in front of me. Once upon a time, I'd come to the local Vaudun priestess with questions about haunted houses and black magic—something she referred to as Hoodoo. Of course, I hadn't known what she was then. If I had, I might never have trusted one witch to advise me on handling another. But the strange librarian had been my friend, and Selena had not, and Mam Byrdie had a soft spot for the wide-eyed little boy who had listened enrapt at my side to her tales. Now, I'd come back with more of the same questions. This time, I not only believed her horror stories, I'd become one of them.

"I need your help," I replied before she could cast me out— or worse. "Selena is dead." I glanced around the room again and whispered, "Someone left pieces of her in my mother's parlor."

Mam Byrdie clicked her teeth to say I hadn't told her anything she didn't already know. Neither of us grieved Selena's demise.

"I found an active circle in the attic, with something—*someone*—in it. She trapped my brother, trapped Remi in her circle—or his spirit, I don't know. I recognized her writing around the circle." I waited in the hush of the library for her to say anything. "Would she have tried to cast another spell?" I asked when the silence thickened, but she just kept staring.

"It doesn't matter now," I finally said, switching my bag to the other shoulder. "I just need to make sure Remi is free, and …" My voice trailed off. "And the witch is gone for good. You're the only one who can help me. Who can help Remi."

Mam Byrdie raised a brow behind the cat-eye frames, the scowl on her lips relaxed, and something inside her reached out like it had back in the day. A gentle probe, tender but not shy.

Without waiting to make sure I followed, she turned and walked through a passageway topped with an ornately carved lintel. Above it hung a copy of an old Flemish painting of two figures playing chess. Not a print, but a copy—someone's best imitation of Van Huys. I'd turned my nose up at it that summer I lived here, but really it combined a touch of international culture with well-intentioned local effort, so maybe I had been a brat to judge.

I followed the old mambo past a row of bookshelves toward the back of the library. As I hurried to keep up behind her, her gold scarf shifted. Four vertical lines of long, pale scars raked down the back of her neck, disappeared beneath the collar of her blouse. Old scars, with a pink edge like they hadn't healed completely. I hadn't known what they meant ten years ago.

As if coming here for help hadn't been nerve-wracking enough. Only one type of claw scarred like that, and it didn't come from any strictly *natural* animal. Mam Byrdie had never said why she hated wolves so much.

Now I knew.

She'd been attacked by one of us. Marked, it would seem, but not torn. I'd been too timid to ask where she lost the finger, but a werewolf? *Wonderful.* With the razor-thin line between white magic and black magic, usually things ended up somewhere in the shades of gray. I'd always known Mam Byrdie walked in the light, could be counted on to stand against someone like Selena Stone, but if she wanted revenge against my kind for some past injustice, she could take it now—on me, and extinguish both of our problems.

Mam Byrdie passed through the back office of the library, colorful caftan billowing behind her, then into a small room where books lay scattered about a dingy carpet, among a mess of candles. I looked back over my shoulder half expecting the library to have vanished, to find myself transported into some kind of subterranean temple, or a tomb.

At the center of the room stood an altar surrounded by mismatched shelves and tables pushed together, piled high with dried herbs, books, and bottles, half-burned candles arranged at the feet of faceless saints—no marble figures, these idols had been carved from wood, cast in cement. A little bundle of dry roses sat atop the altar.

Her *humfo*. She'd taught me the word for the sacred temple or altar of the Vaudun, but I'd never entered one.

As she rounded on me in front of the strange display, any illusion that Mam Byrdie was a simple parish librarian evaporated. Her hand stabbed through the air, and her power dug into my skin where the four fingernails landed. My wolf jerked within me, resisting the pull of her call, but unable to ignore it.

"What evil do you bring to my doorstep, wolf?" she demanded, her stare hard and unblinking. "I thought the witch's death would end it. But now *you* are here."

My wolf stretched, pushing against its human bounds, and away from her hold. If she kept this up, she'd force me to shift. She could force me to do a lot of things. Her power was too strong, and I'd let myself get weak with hunger.

"Please," I managed through gritted teeth. "I don't mean you any harm."

The old woman snorted, but her hold slackened as her fingers went limp in the air before me. "You cannot harm Mam Byrdie," she sneered before dropping her voice to a low hiss. "Where is the rest of your pack, wolf? One wolf means one thing—more will come. How many lurk in the shadows of my parish?"

"I'm alone." My voice caught in my throat, and Mam's chin lifted. "The rest of my pack will not come."

"Name your alpha," she demanded.

"Malakh."

As abruptly as it had struck me, the force of her power receded. I dropped my bag to the floor between my feet, and she studied me for the space of a few minutes, keen, dark eyes searching for deception, her steady gaze inside me, surveying the uneasy beast within, which had long since quit being human. Satisfied with her inspection, she softened.

"Britta, *sha*," she cooed, "you should not have come back," more disappointed *for* me than *in* me. "There is nothing left for you here."

My stomach clenched, but not from hunger. "I can't leave until I know ... until I know Remi's okay."

A sharp jerk of her head and the glimmer behind her glasses said she would help—not for my sake, I imagined, but for the little boy she'd once adored.

"Tell me what you saw," she said, reaching for a small table near her humfo. "Leave out nothing." She pushed a couple of books out of the way, revealing a shelf of small, clear bottles filled with fluids and herbs whose names I didn't know. The smell of magic hit my nose, but lighter, less bitter than the scent in my house, with that strong rose flavor—Mam Byrdie's light craft, as opposed to Selena's dark. Still, just in case, I covered my nose to ward off the odor.

Witches, good or bad, were like men in uniform: not to be trusted blindly.

"She had a circle in the old chamber," I said. "A scrying mirror. I need to know what Selena was doing before she died, and what it has to do with my brother."

"Does anyone else know of this place?" Mam Byrdie's handed fluttered over one of the tables and plucked a small white mortar and pestle she might have gotten at Williams Sonoma.

"There's a human cop, Aaron Labaye. He found Selena's body—uh, her remains—and took me to the house. When we went into the chamber, Remi—" I tried to force the image out of my mind. "Remi's spirit attacked Labaye. Pulled him into the circle. It wanted … it tried to kill him. I had no choice but to cross the line and save the cop. I broke the circle, and the mirror shattered, so with nothing to hold Remi—or whatever it was—he vanished."

"Did *you* save this policeman," she asked, dropping a pinch of herbs into the little white mortar, "or did your wolf?"

Not another lecture. "My wolf, but I didn't tear him."

Mam gave me her profile, silhouetted in the pale candlelight, and returned to her work fussing with the little jars as she crushed and mixed herbs. "Aaron Labaye," she said. "He was just a boy when you lived here. His family is old blood in this town. Old blood."

"Is that good or bad?"

"Neither," she said and grinned at the powder she'd made in the white cup. "Blood will out." She turned to lock eyes with me, and my wolf started under my skin. "I see only one reason Selena would cast a circle to hold your brother's spirit, and it has little to do with the poor child."

"Then what?" The whole thing made me feel cornered, the cluttered, dim room tight around me. "Why'd she cast the circle, that mirror—Why now? None of it makes sense."

Mam Byrdie's sudden smile, more of a grimace, offered no comfort, and my insides twisted up with her lips. All she said was, "It is time."

"Time?"

"*Wi.*"

I recognized the word as Haitian Creole but didn't know the meaning.

Her four-fingered hand rose. In one fluid movement, she spun to one of the tables, then back, brandishing a cluster of herbs at me. "Have you learned the ways of your kind, Britta Orchid?" she asked. "Just because you might live forever does not mean you should ignore the years that pass. Even an immortal curse does not ignore time." She drew the last word out, ending with a soft laugh in the back of her throat. "It has been ten years since the night your brother died." Then she whispered, so close to my face that the rank of pinto beans and coffee masked the vanilla and rose for a moment. "The time has come for the witch to claim you ... if she can."

There had been ten plagues of Egypt. Ten Commandments. Of course, there'd be a ten-year expiration on me, too.

"*Wi,* ten is the number of completion, of law. To someone like Selena, it is the number of infinite opportunities—when her magic inside of you will be at its strongest." She waved a bouquet of herbs in my direction, then ground them into the mortar with the rest. "If she could claim you now, you would be hers forever. The blackest magic is patient. It waits, grows hungry. Then, it consumes." She set the white bowl between two candles and searched the tabletops. "The circle you found was not for Remi. Selena kept your brother as bait."

"Bait?" I echoed. Flinched. "For what?"

"For you, Britta."

A wolf in the thrall of a witch would be a powerful weapon. My blood froze despite the sweat turning the back of my neck tacky. All this time I'd been too scared to consider what Mam Byrdie had just confirmed. Now I had no doubt.

Selena's spell had always been about me. Not only had I failed to save my family—they'd died *because* of me.

Mam slid her glasses down her nose to study a bottle that couldn't hold more than half a pint. Empty if not clean, it met her approval. She stuck an old tin funnel in the neck, then poured the contents of the mortar in, tapping the bowl with the pestle to knock out the last of the powder.

"But ... but something killed her," I said. "Interrupted her?"

Mam Byrdie nodded as she poured the contents of a small vial down the funnel, corked the half-pint bottle, shook it. "So, does her killer think he can make you his?" She handed me the bottle, the contents now milky and green.

"What is this?" I couldn't help but wince as I held the bottle in one outstretched hand. The stuff looked like it would stink if I pulled the cork. I was no fan of magic, even in liquid form.

The old woman narrowed her hard eyes, and power rattled the boards beneath my feet. A few candles blew out. My wolf responded, uneasy, and I pushed my bag behind me with one foot. "I will help," she said, "because I knew you once, and I loved that little boy, but this will be the only help I give, Wolf." Mam Byrdie's voice was tight as she nodded at the bottle I held. "Pour that over a shard of the mirror to speak with your brother. Find your answers, and end this."

Be still, I begged my wolf. "Thank you." I jammed the bottle into the tiny pocket of my jeans, where it stuck up against my bladder.

I grabbed my bag and turned to go, but the mambo called me back.

"Britta." She said my name with a new tenderness. "If Selena is truly gone from this world, she will have left a piece of her behind. A way back. You free your brother, set him to rest, and you go away from here … and don't come back."

The lights dimmed some more, and I walked away from her humfo, past the long shelves, into the main room of the library.

The inside of the house isn't all that's changed over the years. There used to be several smaller buildings out back, but over time they got torn down by storms and age. The slab way behind the magnolia is all that remains of an old carriage house. Problem was they could not house an animal in there without it going bad. Crazy, I mean. When they gave up on keeping horses, they tried cows, and it might go a month or so without incident, but eventually you'd be replacing a wall and putting the animal down. Well, they got tired of rebuilding it, so all that's left is that slab. Even the owners before you, their little boy had a dog, and you don't want to know what happened to that poor thing. I was just a little girl then, so I don't remember it very well.

CHAPTER FOURTEEN

TEN YEARS EARLIER

Time passed slowly once we'd moved into the crumbling old plantation house, and Mom worked me pretty hard, if not Ray and Remi. Selena had come to visit every day.

Every. Single. Damn. Day.

The shaggy-haired woman with nosy blue eyes had been there so much and so often it seemed Joan and Ray had purchased her along with the peeling paint and broken fixtures, like a part of the house herself.

As we unloaded that first day, no sooner had I set down my first box from the truck than she appeared beside me in the kitchen, scarves aflutter, tearing the box open to tell me when the countertop had been replaced, and complimenting us on our serving ware and asking if it had been a wedding gift for Ray and Mom. In the days following, she ignored my protests and assisted Remi and me with spackling and repainting the downstairs rooms and replanting the outside gardens, plastic work gloves pulled carefully over her ringed fingers. I tried to ignore her, but Remi hardly got anything done thanks to her babbling. One night she led a prayer circle with our parents and opened with the story of a priest who'd lived in the house. She seemed to know everything about the place and was determined to find out everything about us, too. If she disappeared in the afternoon, she'd return with a casserole, so she never missed family dinners around our table, a perfect time to quiz all of us at once. Any time I tried to maintain the least little bit of privacy, Ray would accuse me of being rude, and Mom would echo her refrain about manners.

Sometimes, I admit, Ray was right.

Her incessant questions weren't the only intrusive thing about Selena. The way she stared at Remi and me soon passed from unsettling to downright nightmarish. She watched us the way a predator studied prey—scrutinizing every move, always with a lazy half-smile. As she found ways to wriggle herself into every aspect of our lives, her watching never ended.

All the while, she displayed her bizarre fascination with our new home, desperate to ensure we saw it the same way she did: flawless and worthy of adoration, the perfect home. She never missed an opportunity to share some comment about the unique history or architecture.

"You know this place was just up for sale," I reminded her as I lay on the bathroom floor trying to learn the finer points of plumbing from a YouTube video. "You could've bought it yourself. Then you'd have the joy of hanging new wallpaper and dealing with the clogged pipes all to yourself."

"Oh, no," she said, rapping one ringed knuckle against the clawfoot tub and readjusting a dull maroon scarf that had come loose around her throat. "The house chose you, dear, not me."

When I raised Selena's creep factor with my mom, she sprang to the defense of her new bestie, quoting Mark: "Love thy neighbor as thyself—there is no commandment greater than this."

"We should all be grateful to have a new friend like her," Mom said. "You need to stop seeing the worst in people, and look for the good."

What*ever*. I knew weird when I saw it, and Selena Stone seriously weirded me out. But people with ulterior motives always show themselves sooner or later—I just hoped it happened before the woman made herself an official part of the family.

After the initial sting of the move had worn off, Remi and I turned the constant problems in the house into a sort of game. We made half-hearted guesses about how many cracked panes of glass we'd have to replace, bet pieces of candy on how many times the first-floor toilet would overflow. When that grew old, we over-compensated for the gloom in his bedroom by using charcoal to draw silly scenes and write messages to one another on the walls. We sealed these documents under brightly colored paint, chosen by our mother and Selena as if we could rewrite the history of the house. The distractions worked, and for a while, we could ignore the presence looming behind every corner, inside every shadow.

Then we started to find things in the house. Hidden things that didn't want to be found.

Behind closet shelves, we found doorways, locked from the inside. At first, we thought panels had come loose, but if you pressed on one side, they'd budge the tiniest little bit, old hinges on the other side holding them fast.

Three weeks in, Remi started to hear voices.

"There's someone in the walls," he said. "Someone behind those doors. I can hear them."

"Those doors are just old shortcuts for servants that got sealed up when the house was remodeled," I told him. "Just like the sealed-off door to the attic. If we open them it'll just be walls behind them. I promise."

Regardless, Remi started slipping into my bedroom at night, his stuffed elephant tucked under one arm. I have to admit, his fretting got me to lay awake and listen for the voices. I never heard anything.

But I felt something. I couldn't put my finger on it, but whatever *it* was, it was nothing any of Mom's most ambitious remodel projects could fix. There was something else, something *here*. I saw it when a shadow moved at the edge of my sight. It waited in the corners, behind the doorways. I got the feeling the house had a mind of its own, and it watched our family with even more interest than Selena.

Without telling anyone, not even Remi, I sent out résumés to anything and everything within a one-hundred-mile radius. Not just to jobs online or in the classifieds—any business I thought might put my fancy-pants art degree to use. I figured I could parlay even a halfway decent paycheck into a chance to escape with Remi.

No job offers came. A clandestine call placed from the corner of East Street and Loree to my alma mater's career counselor got me nowhere. So it just pissed me off all the more whenever Selena asked how I planned to spend my time once Remi started back up at Vinton Elementary in the fall—her saccharine tone always hinting at a world of opportunity, with an undertone of doom and gloom. "Oh, wouldn't it be a delight if you could send him to Emmanuel Academy," she'd say, referring to Vinton's Christian private school. I appreciated that Selena didn't speak in colloquialisms like *y'all*, despite that drawling accent. "I'm sure you'll find something, dear," she said, "to keep yourself busy," but trailed off in that way that suggested she wasn't sure at all.

By the end of the first month in Vinton, the voices bugging Remi had grown so severe, he stopped going upstairs altogether. With the fervor only a ten-year-old could muster, he demanded I stay downstairs with him, and I caved to the constant pleading and sea-green eyes like a sheet of paper in a hurricane. We blamed it on the lack of central air conditioning—low on Mom's list of projects since her room had a window unit. Our second story felt like a tropical wasteland crawling with malaria. Mom and Ray protested at first, but neither argued nor offered to help when we took our bedding and built a fort in the den.

We spent more and more time at the local library, from which I launched a ceaseless parade of job applications and scoured the ancient microfiche collection to find anything that would back up the stories Selena told us about the house. Judging by the way she spoke of the place, I half expected to find a shrine dedicated to it. Instead, I found nothing, all the way back to the very first edition of the *Southwest Star Vinton News*.

Like the house didn't exist. Or, if it did, nobody wanted to know about it.

One particularly balmy afternoon, I'd had enough of Selena's endless interrogations. I sat on an old chair my mother had grabbed at the Bargain World in Lake Charles, the kind she called a "chase lawn" chair. Dressed mostly in black with huge boots that could tear through the red and yellow polyester webbing, I looked as out of place on the lawn as I felt in the whole of West Louisiana. Elbows on the aluminum armrests, I kept moving my book to block my view of Selena as she prattled on about an old maid with a broken heart whose father abused her—but the woman hadn't taken the hint.

Fair was fair. If she insisted on talking, I could at least drive the conversation. I stole a look across the yard at Remi sketching on the lawn with Rothko, who, I noticed, needed another round of surgery to repair a ripped limb. In jean shorts and spaghetti straps, Mom knelt on the Spanish tiles beside a bucket of grout, trowel and knife close at hand. The driveway represented such a personal quest for perfection, she took this one task on all alone, allowing me to spend some time reading in the sun. She'd sent Ray to the hardware store over an hour ago, and the fact he hadn't come back said he'd found his new favorite dive bar. His current attempt at sobriety had lasted a total of two weeks. As often as Mom brought up *Gone with the Wind*—a book she'd never read—maybe she had less in common with Scarlett than with Mrs. O'Hara. Scarlett's mother had lost her first love to tragedy, and while the man she married got her out of a bad situation, no one found Mr. O'Hara to be worthy of her.

At least he could afford to send their kids to private school.

"Did you know the previous owners?" I asked, stabbing into Selena's monolog about this crazed spinster running up and down our staircase.

She stammered the punchline, about the old woman hanging herself, surprise evident in the sudden roundness of those crystal blue eyes. Normally she got nothing out of me but a series of grunts and eyerolls.

"But no, in fact, I didn't," Selena said. "This house has been empty for a very long time. But my parents knew the Cobbs quite well."

"What were they like?"

Selena's eyes flattened as she considered me like she could sniff out whatever mischief lurked behind my sudden interest. When I didn't look away, she tried to cover her suspicion with a laugh. She was out of practice. "Well, they weren't good Christian people like you folks," she said.

Without pausing in her work, my mother nodded as if this meant something.

It didn't, at least not to me, and I met Selena's eyes with the slackest, most unimpressed expression I could muster. "I asked if you *knew* the people," I droned in a voice as bored as Philip Seymour Hoffman in *The Talented Mr. Ripley*, "not if you'd passed moral judgment on them. People can be a lot of things and still call themselves good Christians."

Mom clicked her tongue and reminded me manners don't cost a thing, but with the gentle movement of one jeweled hand, Selena motioned her quiet.

"Old Man Cobb," she said without breaking eye contact, "he was a bit of a nasty man, or so said Father. Decent enough before his wife's accident, afterward Cobb's hateful spirit brought on quite a lot of negative energy, and old houses like this, well, they don't need any more than what they already have. I'm sure you know something about negative energy, Britta, dear."

"What was that?" my mother asked, while I shot Selena a look hot enough to singe the tips of her white hair.

"Oh, Joan," Selena chuckled again as she strolled over to the driveway. "Nothing a little prayer can't handle." She patted my mother's arm. "The bayou is a sinful place with a lot of history from darker times, and the house just needs a good cleanse—"

"What kind of accident?" I interrupted.

Selena flashed one of those sugary smiles I'd come to detest. "Pardon?"

I let out a heavy breath and set the book face down on my lap, hitching the aluminum armrests to bring me into a more upright position. "You said Cobb's wife had an accident. I've been going through old newspapers. I've read two dozen articles on Mystle Boudreaux's award-winning bees, and three separate reports of someone called Tinker racing a riding lawn mower down West Street. I've gone all the way through the most brittle scraps of microfiche in that library, and I've never seen a single mention of anything you've told us about this house. Which is odd, don't you think? Because if Mrs. Cobb broke her neck throwing herself off the balcony, or devil monkeys came out of our tree to bust religious icons, you'd think a local crack reporter would love a break from honeybees and riding mowers."

"Didn't you come from a small town, young lady?" Selena leaned in so close I could see ice crystals sparkling in her pale blue eyes. Her lilting voice dropped to a conspiratorial whisper that made my skin crawl. "Personal matters don't always require a public airing." She arched her brow and straightened the collar of her red and white dress, fixed her scarf. "Not to mention this happened way back, many years ago." She glanced up to the top windows of our house, then back to me. "Mrs. Cobb had a child, younger than Remi, in fact. A worrisome, sickly little boy. Never quite right, this child, he liked to play on his own. Well, to just sit, really, on his own ..."

The doe eyes she cast at my mother made my ears hot. Remi still sat drawing across the lawn, focused on the house itself, spared from listening to a word of this.

"Anyway, Mrs. Cobb—her name, if memory serves, was Alcée—worried a great deal about the boy," Selena said. "Took him to her pastor, to the doctor, but they couldn't tell her anything. Finally, Alcée became convinced the child was bedeviled." My mother had set her tools down, her rapt attention on her guest. "Afflicted by some energy that had clung to this house since the first slaves practiced their spirit religions in the crawlspaces. Frustrated with her conventional spiritual advisor, Alcée took her concerns to some old voodoo witch, who gave her a charm to keep the spirits at bay—to protect the boy."

My mother's eyes were wide as Selena took a seat on the grass, looking very pleased with her story. With one bedazzled hand, she spread out her gingham skirt so her legs disappeared, like some garden painting by Manet—minus any sensuality whatsoever.

"But no matter how much you dress it up," Selena said, "the master of darkness doesn't spare the innocent, especially those led willingly into his arms."

Mom clutched at the cross on her neck. "'The thief comes only to kill and destroy.'"

Selena nodded and waved one ringed finger in the air, not ready to be interrupted. "Like the serpent who tricked Eve, the old witch gave Alcée a charm, all right, but it wasn't to keep evil away. That unholy talisman invited it *in*." Mom shot a worried look across the lawn at Remi, and Selena lowered her voice, having gotten a bit worked up.

"The little Cobb child," she said, blue eyes darting between me and my mother, "disappeared from his bedroom that very night. The whole town scoured the marshes and the woods, but the next day Mr. Cobb found the boy up in the attic." Selena stared at the top of our house. Something struck me odd when she crossed herself, but I couldn't put my finger on it. "Poor child had been so ill he must've crawled up there like a cat gone to die. Not long after, Alcée Cobb went outside on her balcony—the one I told you to leave closed off." She spoke quietly to my mother, ignoring me. "And she threw herself right off. Two women have met their death off that railing."

My mother's jaw plunked down on those Spanish tiles at the very same second I started laughing.

"Hey, Mom," I said. "The town historian here says your vision house is haunted. Must have missed that in the listing information."

"'Haunted'?" Selena repeated, blue eyes wide with false innocence. She spread her hands, palms up, out before her. "There's no such thing as ghosts, Britta, dear. Anything impure is the devil's own business. Anyway, old Cobb sealed up the attic and the balcony." She pointed toward the center of town. "And dragged in the pastor from right down at First Baptist to cast the evil out." She clasped her hands almost in prayer. "Cobb should've sought salvation for himself, though. He became a pariah in the town, friendless and cruel. The house has been empty since that man went to his own early grave … but now you've come to return His glory to what the devil tried to destroy."

I jerked on the arms of the chase lawn chair to lurch forward without getting up, while my poor mom pinched her eyes closed and whispered into her fist, squeezing the little necklace.

"Ghosts, demons, angels, and *Him*!" I said. "All the same thing. Fairy tales for people with inferiority complexes to make other people behave."

"Cindy never told me any of that," Mom whispered, too scared to engage with my blasphemy. She squeezed her eyes shut and her face went pale, knuckles white around the cross in her fist—she'd actually snapped the chain and pulled it from her neck.

"The Lord had reason to lead me to a place that has seen such evil ..."

"Good bargain?" To her credit, she still ignored me. I smirked and cast another glance to make sure Remi hadn't come closer. Selena had told us some fucked up tales, but this took the cake. Worrying about your home being haunted was one thing. Hearing some crackpot story about a little boy and his parents being knocked off by the "master of darkness" was something else entirely.

"I don't know, Mom, this gossip tastes stale to me," I said, opening the book back up. "A disappearing boy and a balcony-jumping mom would've made the paper—definitely better above-the-fold material than someone's bees." To be fair, that space usually filled with updates about high school sports teams or Governor Foster's bold stance against the satanic cabal of the ACLU. "Though"—I turned to Selena as I drummed a sharp paradiddle on the open page before me—"small-town decorum or otherwise, I couldn't find a single line of copy about this place in over fifty years. Not one thing that you have told us is documented, Selena." My poor mother made a noise between a cluck and a *tsk*, but our guest had my full attention. "Growing old in this boring old town made you desperate for an urban legend but you ain't creative enough to think of nothing better than the old dark house cliché, are you, *dear*?"

I probably went too far with the mock-swamp accent near the end. And the pet name.

Selena reached out and gripped my mother's hand, her face a textbook diagram of *earnest* as she doubled down on her story. "There is no greater victory for the Lord," she said in a hush, "than to see one of his flock rebuke Satan back into the bowels of Hell where he belongs."

There was my excuse—the devil stole my manners. My twenty-fourth birthday was days away, but maturity accounted for little when the devil got involved.

"You've seen this house in your visions, restored and brought back to glory by your own hand," Selena went on. "That's not just a vision, Joan. It's a prophecy! You will bring this house back to God, and in the doing of that good work, you shall deliver everyone who walks in it." Now she took both hands. "He chose you."

"Oh, a haunted house *and* a chosen one," I said. Selena's blue eyes swung to me, heavy with malice. "Do you see my mom as more of a Buffy, or a Neo, or an Anakin …?"

"Are you talking about *Star Wars*?"

I whipped my head around to where Remi stood grinning. He looked about as carefree as I could remember seeing him, the crease in his forehead all but gone. Mom yanked her hands away from Selena's bejeweled grip and clamped them on his arms, pulling him in. He bumped my shoulder, dropping the sketchbook.

"That's right, honey," Mom said. "Your sister was just telling us a story."

"Guard your flock, Joan," Selena advised, a cruel twist of her lips. Mother nodded blankly in agreement and picked up my brother's sketchbook. "Watch your babies—"

"My goodness." Mom never interrupted Selena, like, *ever*, but it seemed a good time to start. "Look at this, will you?" She beamed as she wrapped one arm over Remi's shoulders and held the drawing for us to see. He'd drawn a pointed box with smaller boxes lined up across the face of it. Our chimney was the only part of the house he'd rendered in any detail.

"It glows with the light of the Lord," Mom said, hugging Remi tighter, and pointing to the top of the drawing. Lines radiated from the roof like Remi meant to show the sun sinking behind it. But rendered in heavy charcoal, the lines of alternating depths seemed to give off something other than light.

CHAPTER FIFTEEN

By the time I left the library, the sun hung low to the west, and I remembered never to question the passage of the time I spent with Mam Byrdie—but I was famished. I wanted to go straight to the house, to the broken scrying mirror, and to Remi, to get this over with, but my hunger had grown way too strong to face any challenge greater than untying my Docs. I had to eat—soon—or it'd be hard to control my shifting. I also hadn't taken a shower, and while personal hygiene requires little effort in a body embalmed with magic, cleaning releases endorphins in canids, and even in the privacy of my motel I had no interest in lying around licking and chewing at myself.

Whether or not I still had a soul, a nice, hot bubble bath would soothe something. A decent night's sleep wouldn't hurt, either. I felt a little too much like the big, bad wolf in *Little Red Riding Hood*—hungry, grouchy, sick of playing nice, and ready to gobble up the next innocent thing that crossed my path. The mood I was used to, but I needed my senses on point. Whatever Selena had done, whoever had killed her, I couldn't fail Remi.

Not again.

I retraced my steps to the Prius—why the hell did the rental company give me a hybrid in rural Louisiana?—tossed the bag on the passenger seat, and slipped behind the steering wheel. I pressed the start button, heard the electric engine engage, but cranking the air conditioning to full blast made the gas motor come to life.

I pulled Mam Byrdie's potion from my pocket and studied

it. Just looking at the cloudy green fluid turned my stomach. I looked through the windshield to make sure no one had taken an interest. I'd gone to the old mambo for advice. Insight. Hell, I would've settled for simple encouragement and a conversation with someone who didn't want to use me for their own gain. What I hadn't asked for was magic. Light, dark, somewhere in between, I did not want to find out what it'd cost.

Considering Mam Byrdie's hang-up with those of the *loup garou* persuasion, whatever concoction was in this little bottle may cause me to spontaneously combust.

I stuffed it into my bag and noticed my cellphone vibrating. I'd been in demand while out of reach. Labaye and Alec had each sent several messages, the two of them texting enough to litter my entire screen with notifications. I thumbed my phone unlocked and scrolled through, wrinkling my nose at the half-hearted apologies.

It's Aaron Labaye. I'm sorry for not meeting you halfway. I shouldn't have been so tight-lipped. This is your case too. Can we talk? Please? I'll meet you at the house?

And ...

Together we can put an end to your quandary and return your brother's spirit to peace. I am at your beck and call should you accept my proposal.

All their messages read like guilt trips, which I had no time for. I powered my phone off and shoved it back in with the vial, then hopped out of the car and made a beeline for the meat counter at the Market Basket.

Less than half an hour later, I peeled off the plastic bag and tossed it in a trash bin on my way out of the grocery store. Liquid seeped through the folds of the brown paper wrap. The tighter I squeezed, the more blood. How long before someone noticed the girl who'd let her whole family get massacred, leaving a trail through the middle of town? Just because I didn't recognize the people I scurried past didn't mean they wouldn't remember me and what I'd done, what I was.

I ducked into a weedy alley between two closed storefronts, thinking it'd get me to my car with less attention. Pressing my back against a cool brick wall in the shadows, I stopped to smell the meat, and my legs twitched with the urge to eat it right there, to mash the flesh between my dull human teeth and let the flavor wash away the poisoned stench still lingering from that goddamned house.

But the thin red juice spattered my black jeans and pulled me back. I'd kept a low profile despite my face off with Labaye that morning. I didn't need Mabel Landry to find me scarfing down raw steak behind the Merchants and Farmers Bank.

I angled the rental car back to the motel on I-10. With my takeout dinner in hand, I ignored the way the counter clerk gawked at my out-of-towner getup and my brown paper bundle of raw meat. If I didn't have the energy to hunt for my dinner, I damn sure didn't have time for his lingering eyes or racing pulse. Nothing suspicious if the poor high school kid at the meat counter hadn't wrapped the package well enough to keep a little blood from seeping through.

I twisted the old-school room key in the lock and slammed the heavy door shut behind me. Everything I'd held inside broke in the privacy and silence of my motel room. Forget bathing in that vinyl bathtub, or sleeping on the paper-thin queen mattress. Forget eating, too.

My last bit of strength vaporized, and I crumbled into the fetal position on the cheap carpet—which smelled none too subtly of foot fungus—my bag, and my dinner splayed out beside me. The emotions I'd held back pushed through the levies behind my eyes, sending a tropical storm surge of tears crashing down my cheeks. I sobbed, my body racking in painful waves, so furious it felt like my wolf meant to claw her way out of the skin prison of this human form, ripping me open in bursts of grief and regret.

I'd run for ten years, away from this nightmare. I'd counted the days since I let my brother die, yet it felt like not a day had passed. I was simultaneously the same naïve girl I'd been back in the day and the walking corpse who shambled away from Vinton. Counting the days, I'd comforted myself with the fact that if I still suffered, if I had to be alone, at least my family's pain had ended fast, with them together. But no. I'd failed Remi worse than I ever imagined, and he'd been locked in that horrible house with nothing but older haints to keep him company.

I had no idea how to save anyone, fix the damage I'd done. It was unbearable. And it was all for nothing. The whole time I'd been tallying up the days, it had really been counting down.

To this. To whatever fresh hell Selena had planned for me.

I rolled and screamed into the carpet, muffling the misery in cheap, filthy fibers. But it wasn't enough.

I lost it, there on that coarse carpet. Fur burst from flesh in a shudder so violent I sprang to my feet—to my hands and feet, to paws. My grief turned into a howl of pain, and I didn't give a damn who heard it through the thin paneled walls.

For a moment, I couldn't separate the woman from the wolf. We cried together, in our shared and consuming misery.

I came to the motel, in human form again, naked and sore. The butcher's paper lay in shreds, nothing left of the pound of flesh I'd purchased.

But I didn't feel sated, not really. Now I could go a long time before eating, but as soon as my eyes opened my legs itched to move. I didn't want another night of running the Moors, though; the buzzing in my thighs didn't feel like that kind of restlessness.

I pulled on a long sleeve black tee, wishing I had my leather jacket, and hopped in the rental. The Prius silently crept out of the parking lot, engine kicking in on the freeway. I almost took the exit that would lead straight to the house, our old house, but decided against it. The engine went silent again as I turned down onto West.

The library sat fat and dark, and I tucked the rental in the shadowed corner of the parking lot. A beat-up old Dodge pickup sat closer to the building, and I bet it'd still be there come morning. The faint signal my phone picked up wouldn't let me download the next part of the podcast, so I listened to some wannabe preacher complain about how the Republicans had settled for a Mormon to try to take out Obama. Hardly a car passed by, so I powered the rental's engine off and hopped out without locking the door, dropping the key into my back pocket.

Wondering if the Coffee Stain stayed open late, I headed down the one well-lit block in town. I couldn't very well walk through Vinton at night in sunglasses, not if the goal were to avoid notice, but it put a new twitch in my thighs to feel this exposed. Maybe my wolf had sensed something.

"Britta Orchid?"

I'd kept my eyes on the sidewalk, so I noticed the fluffy little terrier mix more than the man himself.

The dog pulled on the leash, sniffing eagerly at my legs, as Paul Beaulieu met my eyes. "Wow!" he said. "Sorry about Clarence, he's normally not this friendly."

I stepped back and pretended to keep looking at the dog when really I just wanted to hide my face. I drove my hands in my pants pockets past the wrists. Paul jerked back on the leash, laughed, and apologized again.

"It's all right," I said. "Dogs just normally don't like me is all."

"Wow," he said. "Britta Orchid." He knelt to reel the dog in.

I forced a hard laugh, trying to cover the name. "Yeah, yeah, you said that."

"You really haven't aged a day," he said, and I laughed a little more genuinely.

"There's some gray up there," I said. *But you're right*, I thought, *but only because I am dead, whereas the faint lines around the corners of your smile and the way your skin hangs show the life you've gotten to live, the vital, actual human life pounding in your veins …*

Between all the work on the house and how much Remi hated to be inside it, we spent a lot of that summer out in the sun. Paul lived with his parents two doors down, and couldn't miss the fact a not-totally-repulsive young lady had moved in, so he'd finally said hello.

Paul stood with the little terrier in his arms. "Are you here visiting? I mean, do you have any other family here?"

If he felt obliged to talk to me, I'd have to compliment his mother on his manners, because he sounded genuinely interested, and skilled in dodging the obvious issues around mentioning family to the girl who'd let hers be brutally murdered.

"No family, no," I said. "Just here very briefly."

Paul had been the one person I'd known in Vinton who had nothing to do with the tragedy. Which had to be why I had no memory of him until the moment he stopped me. I never saw him after the night of the murders, never tried to contact him, and over the next ten years, as I relived every awful moment that led to that night, he only slipped further into the past.

"My folks still live on Central," he said. "But I'm just around the corner here."

"Just out walking Clarence," I added.

"Yeah, right." And he didn't seem to be in any kind of hurry. "Hey, I heard the cops had been poking around your house. Mom said there were cruisers all around it."

"Oh. Do you know what that was?"

He didn't and we spoke for a couple of minutes there on the sidewalk, until he gestured behind him and asked where I'd been heading. I told him nowhere in particular, so he gestured in the direction he was going and asked me to walk with him. Clarence stuck close to my ankles.

"Still wearing Doc Martens, huh?"

"Yeah," I said. "Shoes, not boots." I pinched my pant leg at the thigh but couldn't pull it up any.

I hadn't had a normal conversation with a human outside of Corinne, my fellow dispatcher at the juice company, in years, and apparently, Corinne hadn't really kept me in practice. It took him mentioning his parents three times before I had the manners to ask about them, and of course, they were fine, though they sometimes drove him a little crazy.

"Is there someplace we can get a drink?" I asked.

He named a place that didn't ring a bell, either from back in the day or tooling around in my little electric car. We only had to double back and go half a block past the spot we'd met.

He gestured to the door and looped Clarence's leash around the base of a parking sign. My hand hovered inches from the door handle. Not a bar. He'd led me to a Mexican restaurant. It'd certainly have drinks, particularly those of the tequila-infused variety, but bright light filled every corner. I couldn't make out any familiar faces, but anyone who'd lived here ten years ago would look a decade older, and I'd never given them the time of day anyway. Paul remembered me literally as the girl next door, but who inside would remember my face, without even knowing the name of the girl who stood there while her family met their gruesome ends?

"Britta?" he said behind me.

The way my hand had hovered over the door, his hovered near me, and without thinking, without even recognizing the gesture, I reached out and let my fingertips touch his. He laughed, almost a giggle.

"I don't think I'm in the mood for that," I said.

"For what?"

"Mexican." I said the word almost like I asked a question as our fingers touched. I had to look down at Clarence tugging at his twisted leash when I said, "I guess you live pretty close."

I never slept with Paul in 2002. I only cared about Remi, back then. About getting him away from Vinton, from the religious zeal of Joan and Ray Hall, and away from Selena's constant attention.

Paul's building didn't have a lobby so much as an extra-wide hallway, with mirrors on either side, interrupted by a column of mailboxes. The facing mirrors created an infinite reflection in which we got smaller and smaller, further and further away. If I were a vampire I wouldn't reflect at all.

Paul's breath was hot against my skin when I pulled him atop me on the skinny mattress of his bachelor's bed. His fingers brushed across the angles of my face, the swells of my breasts, my hips. But when his lips parted as if to speak, I pressed my body against his and the fire in his eyes burned through the unspoken question. My hands tore at the thin material of clothing between us, pulling away and discarding layers of T-shirts and denim like old skin. Flesh met flesh and I clung to him, my fingers digging bruises into the loose muscles of Paul's arms and shoulders while his hands fumbled against the hidden places of body—insistent, urgent, unfamiliar.

He pushed away from me and I saw the reflection of my hunger—my own *need*—in the gleam of his eyes, the sheen of sweat glistening on his chest in the sweltering heat of the bedroom. The distance was a vacuum, sucking me back to him, and my back arched from the mattress, my limbs wrapping around his body, tightening, pulling him down. His mouth found mine and I sucked his tongue, bit into his kiss as he pushed inside of me.

"Britta," Paul moaned, and I ate the sound of my name off his lips as our skin bonded together in hungry mouths and hungrier hands.

Even with his body against mine, the scent of Clarence the terrier slipped in beside the smell of sex with an undercurrent of prey. My wolf stirred, eager, and a growl of pleasure loosed from my throat. I hooked one leg inside Paul's, pushing him onto his back so I could swing my body over his. Beneath me, a brief flicker of hesitation—surprise—flashed through Paul's eyes, followed by desire. His fingers traced circles on my nipples, my stomach, before his hands found my hips, anchoring my body to his as I rocked above him, forcing him deeper into me.

I fed on him one thrust at a time, need and pleasure swinging like a pendulum in the rhythm of our bodies until all was spent.

The growl didn't wake me, but I only knew I'd woken up because of the sound, quiet and intermittent at the back of my neck. Straight lines came into focus, revealing the edges of a room. I lifted my head and found pale street light coming through gauzy curtains.

Paul Beaulieu lay beside me snoring, his arm warm on my back, one foot between my own where we'd pushed the sheets to the end of the bed.

I floated there, on his bed, weightless, every bit of my body finally at rest. With this other aspect of my appetite sated, I could get some real sleep, not like the tortured nap of that afternoon.

I eased onto my back, careful not to wake him. A tiny scar marred his shoulder. A mole marked the spot where his collarbone disappeared into the muscle. Freckles ran down the biceps, faint enough that another woman might not see them, even with the lights on.

Would his skin have been any smoother at twenty-four?

Someday he would grow lined and loose, muscle pulling away from bone, but hadn't every painter or sculptor who'd ever lived found beauty in the mature human form, or at least found nobility there? In the dark, at night, it would take effort to spot the differences between Paul now and the Paul of ten years ago. From here on in he'd grow both stiffer and softer, but he'd seen his prime, and so now his form would shift. Alec's human form hadn't matured one bit in decades, probably centuries, frozen in a false youth. He'd go from wolf to man and back, but never actually mature.

The same as me.

This man's eyelids danced, maybe dreaming of me. I wanted to kiss the slightly parted lips, but it was time to go. If nothing else, my wolf could move silently. From the corner of the room, a short whine like a leaking balloon reminded me that Clarence slept in his dog bed. He lifted his head to watch me, and I nodded. I dressed in the dark, and slipped out, shoes and socks in hand as I went down the carpeted stairs.

When you sit close to the mirror and look straight at your reflection, it isn't multiplied. Your actual body blocks the image in the glass behind you. I didn't want anyone to catch me pulling on my shoes there in the entryway, but as I met my own green eyes in the reflection, I felt very little shame.

Just as I'd guessed, that beat-up pickup still sat in the library parking lot. I got into the motel room before three a.m., collapsed on the bed without pulling back the sheets, and popped in my earphones. The podcast jumped from Maine to eighteenth-century Europe, and if this story connected to the death on the yacht, I missed it. An Italian occultist named Cagliostro had commissioned a portrait from a German artist, around the time of the American Revolution. The painter died at the hands of thieves raiding his studio. The podcaster explained that we remember Cagliostro as a charlatan, an imposter wizard, but she cited only Wikipedia, to leave the listener open to the possibilities. Why not?

As legend has it, the artist finished the portrait, but Cagliostro never took possession of it. The death of the painter combined with the subject matter birthed the legend of a curse. Maybe Cagliostro had cursed his portraitist, maybe the act of painting the notorious villain damned the painter, but the canvas traveled through the late eighteenth-century European underworld, and my friend and humble podcaster detailed every death associated with the painting. The last documented sighting of it was in London in 1803. No reproduction of the painting was ever made, so no one in the last two hundred years could've really told you what it looked like.

If my esteemed podcaster explained how this painting tied into the death of the yachtsman, the guilt of the niece, and the sleuthing aunt, I fell asleep hard before she got to it.

Just over a hundred years ago, an old spinster named Lisbeth Kelleher owned the house. A spinster is a woman who never married, so I guess you could call me a spinster too, Britta, dear. Some say this woman loved a young man who went off and died in the War of Northern Aggression, but I believe all this happened closer to the turn of the century.

Lisbeth lived her whole life just taking care of her father, an invalid who never once rose from his bed after his daughter dropped out of school to tend to him. Mr. Kelleher, he had a bad heart, see, among other failings, and just lay fading away in the front bedroom with the paneled walls. He complained that his daughter nearly scared the life out of him every time she opened his door, so she started knocking on the banister as she'd walk up the stairs, one tap for every stair, all nineteen of them. Mr. Kelleher would listen and count to know just when she'd open the door.

When the old man finally passed away, Lisbeth kept right on pacing those steps, tapping that rail, until she went mad from loneliness. Sometimes, you can still hear, click, click, click, her knuckles rapping on the banister, up and down the stairs. That poor old maid, she hung herself from the balcony, her father's balcony, and she wasn't the last to do it, neither. I've told your mother she ought to leave it closed off because you can never be too careful.

CHAPTER SIXTEEN

A fat moon hung in the sky as I stepped through the back door of my old house. I'd slept away most of the daylight, listened to just enough of the podcast to solve the mystery of how the portrait connected to the death at sea and made another trip to the Market Basket meat counter to gird myself against what came next. I'd hit rock bottom at the fourth stage of grief and was not proud of what I'd done with it, but I'd climbed back up to angry now, with no intention of making another trip through the loop.

If the bitch turned me into a wolf, the time had come for me to act like it.

Now I stood in the threshold of the back door of my family's former home, listening hard to the rooms before me. For too long, I'd let grief color these spaces. Grief, and fear—I hadn't let myself remember anything else about the place. But this decaying collection of bricks, wood, and nails had seen death before our family, and there'd been life, too. From the mudroom, memories flooded in. I saw myself kneeling on the old countertops, wiping down cabinets. Cooking dinner on the stove for me and my brother. From that entrance I could see the carpet in the den, where Remi sat and drew, Rothko flopped beside him. After four years of college, these walls had seen me reconnect with my baby brother.

But how much damage one little suggestion had done. With only a few words, Selena had lit the flame that put it all to an end. Her plan, carefully set out, had spread like wildfire. Now, so long after it had all burned down, here I stood among the ashes.

I moved through the lower level, and something made me pause outside the parlor. The acrid smell of bleach wafted through the gap in the wide French doors, still tied off with police tape. Beneath the bitter chemical stench pulsed a coppery tang. The crime-scene photos had shown a *lot* of red—but should Selena's blood still be so potent? I hadn't planned on going into the parlor, but a sudden urge overtook me. I raised a hand and called to my wolf. Fingernails lengthened to claws, and I used one to slice through the evidence ribbon, then pulled my fingers back into shape.

I shoved one door open wide enough to see inside the room. It was spotless except for a large, faint stain on Mom's imported Spanish tile. The police had done a good enough job cleaning that it would take luminol to reveal the truth of the crime scene now, but to me, the smear showed a clear shape—a woman, arms splayed, and feet spread.

The witch had died alone and in agony. *Good.* I'd hate to think she'd had any comfort when she drew her last breath. The thought of her suffering made me smile. I'd prefer if Remi didn't have a hand in her fate, but he deserved his vengeance, too.

A second, more faint stain caught my attention.

A footprint—scrubbed away, but the shape still distinct between the blue and white of the tile. Too large for a woman, with a sharper impression on the ball than the heel, as if someone had squatted down. The killer? Too big a footprint for Remi.

I knelt beside the mark when a bang from the floor above startled me. Someone was in the house—I should've scented them as soon as I'd walked through the door if it weren't for the parlor's stench.

The footprint would have to wait.

I shot out of the room to the bottom of the stairs, head cocked to listen. I drew in a breath, but the bleach and the blood from the parlor muddled my senses too much to get a clear scent of anything else.

Another bang and a door opened, upstairs and east. My brother's door. The sound of footsteps. One person, under the assumption they were alone. The footsteps moved past the sealed attic door, neared the top of the stairway. The scent of musky pine and earth drifted down to meet me, now with a bottom note of bitter vanilla.

I moved against the wall, out of the line of sight of the stairs, growing angrier with each footfall as Aaron Labaye made his descent.

Exactly *what* in the name of fuck all was Officer Shiny Badge doing here?

I fought to keep my wolf inside as Labaye's feet passed the landing. He still wore the plainclothes from that morning, with a light windbreaker thrown over. Chalk dust covered his wrinkled jeans, and the five o'clock shadow he'd sported at breakfast had sprouted into full-blown stubble. Even in the dim stairwell, I could see his agitation, his normally sweet smell made pungent.

His left hand held my leather jacket. Remi's trunkless stuffed elephant hung from his right. Now only one dull black eye remained in Rothko's face.

"What are you doing here, Labaye?" I asked in a low growl as I stepped forward. He froze a few stairs from the bottom, eyes wide and mouth agape. His heartbeat slammed in his chest, and his skin went clammy. The man smelled like prey. "And what are you doing with my things?" My pulse raced, neither from fear nor from an empty stomach, neither fight nor flight. That scent of his …

"B-Britta," Labaye sputtered. His stare locked on me, unblinking. He made a valiant effort to play off his shock, but he couldn't trick a wolf. "Your eyes …"

I'd never replaced my contacts after the crying jag on my motel floor. I'd be damned if I'd listen to him go off about fireflies again. What would Alec do in this situation—short of eating the man?

"What are you doing here?" Labaye asked. His Adam's apple shot to the top of his throat before easing back down.

"This is my house," I spoke with care, and stepped back, making room for him to descend the last couple of stairs.

"It's not," he said. "Not for a long time, Britta. It's a crime scene." He pressed himself against the doors as I advanced on him, closing the distance with a growl. The hand that held Rothko brushed the glass doorknob.

I thought of Alec. "I'm listening to this podcast my friend Corinne recommended," I said, and made a slow circle around the foyer. "The crime scene's off the coast of Maine. Corinne thought I'd like it because it's local, and I'm kind of spooky, I guess." I smiled at Labaye and tried to slow my breathing. "See, a guy dies. And someone figures out that people have died in that same spot … many, many times."

Even as his pulse reached a crescendo, a fierceness beat within him—the same as it had when we'd first met in the police station.

"Three hundred years ago, this New England pirate—" I played off Labaye's confused expression. "What?" I said, spreading my fingers across my chest like some scandalized southern belle. "We had them up there, too. Anyway, this pirate used a trick called a Judas lantern." I raised a hand—careful not to move too fast—and extended the middle finger, pointed the thumb and other fingers down, and walked my shadow-puppet horse in front of Labaye's face. "The pirate would saddle a horse with this big torch, and walk it along the shore at night. Sailors would mistake it for another boat, and they'd crash on the rocks." I rolled my hand to imitate the boat but realized it just looked like I'd killed the horse.

"Then our pirate friend would steal their, you know, their booty, and kill the crew." I'd taken my eyes off Labaye in my pacing, as though he held no interest. "This one ship sank straight to the bottom. In fact, the pirate died trying to recover the treasure, which, according to lore, included a painting of this famous sorcerer—"

"Britta," Labaye muttered. "What are you talking about?"

I snatched the jacket and stuffed animal from his hands. "What are you playing at, Labaye?" I barked in his face. "What were you planning to do with these?"

One of his hands reached toward me as the other fumbled for the doorknob behind his back. Something tumbled out of the pocket of his windbreaker in a flash and broke into two black, shimmering pieces on the hardwood floor. Stunned into stillness, I stared at the shards of the scrying mirror.

"Britta," he pleaded, anticipating my reaction. "Please, I'm trying to help you." He started to bend down.

"Bullshit," I barked, and Labaye shot to his feet, hands up like a perp.

The stuffie and the jacket could be called evidence. Souvenirs, even, or, for a killer, trophies. A broken scrying mirror wasn't fit for the recycling bin, pure garbage unless you had a plan to make it work again.

Why try to salvage a tool for summoning the dead unless you meant to use it?

"I swear," he said. "Please, trust me." Labaye's voice was so earnest, I avoided looking too deeply into those big brown eyes, so wide with fright.

This same man, just two days ago, had reached across the interrogation table to comfort me when he'd told me about Selena's death. He'd said I had fireflies in my eyes, this man I'd saved. I almost felt bad for scaring him.

Almost.

The deadbolt wailed as it slid from the lock. Labaye peeled one of the doors open behind him, but I slammed my palm against it, shoving it closed with a loud bang, echoes screaming through my empty house.

"Not so fast, Officer."

Being almost a foot taller than me did not make the man seem any less small as I pressed him against the doors. My fangs lengthened against the back of my lips. Claws dug at the wood of the door under my hand.

Labaye had seen me in my wolf form, but that wasn't nearly as terrifying as the view mid-shift—the one that horror movies liked to portray as our true form, back in the days of Lon Chaney Jr.

A shudder passed through the cop as he met my eyes, and he pressed his back into the doors. A whiff of vanilla hit me, followed by that strange, indefinable extra note, that even more puzzling part of his scent. Half of me wanted to rip out his throat. The other half wanted to jump his bones. Choices, choices.

"Tell me, Officer," I hissed, and the heel of my Doc Marten crunched black glass by mistake. "Why'd you have that in your pocket?"

Labaye opened his mouth, but something over my shoulder stole his attention. His throat made a gurgling sound, and his skin lightened to the pallid hue of raw milk.

A familiar scent flared behind me. Animal and arrogant, earth and ego. I didn't need to look back over my shoulder to know what had made Labaye's eyes go wide.

I was big when I turned, but my beast had nothing on Alec's.

He stood behind me in his wolf form, shoulders higher than my waist, warmth beating off him—his presence changed the game. My *loup guru* was unpredictable, impulsive.

Despite my fury and suspicion, I didn't want Labaye dead. I let my fingers fall across his shoulder. I dropped my hand from the door as I stepped away. Only two pieces and some splinters was all that remained of the scrying mirror—of what had called my brother back from the other side.

"Get out," I growled.

Labaye pulled open the double doors and slid through without looking back.

CHAPTER SEVENTEEN

I didn't care that Alec was livid—so was I.

"*You!*" I slammed the doors shut. I'd really blow the low profile if any locals caught sight of this faceoff.

The huge wolf didn't so much as flinch when I whirled on him. I threw the leather jacket and sad excuse for a stuffed elephant at my feet, gnashing my teeth.

Alec's heat struck my face across the small entryway. Anger stalled any more words, but when they came, they rang with venom.

"What in the hell are you doing here?" I snapped. I'd meant to cover the pieces of black glass with the jacket, but two long triangles stuck out clearly, glinting in the low evening light.

Even in wolf form, Alec could thread the needle between livid and peevish. He stalked across the dingy floorboards without blinking. When he pushed himself up on his hind legs, his ears nearly brushed the ceiling before they slid down the sides of his head, and his torso shortened to that of a man, shifting like rushing liquid. He stopped within striking distance, having returned to human form, all lean muscle and chiseled cheekbones, boots and leather pants, and black coat with the collar already popped. He'd tried to teach me the trick of staying dressed through the transition, but I could never nail it.

"It would appear as if I arrived just in time." He kept his voice cool and flaunted his trademark showman's smirk, challenging and sinister. You could never mistake what Alec was. Even in human form, everything about him screamed *predator*.

I squeezed my fists at my sides and fumed. "I had everything under control, and you cost me answers," I snapped. "And just so we're absolutely clear, *Alec*, I have not agreed to fucking anything. If you're here to seal that deal, you can fuck right off."

"Now that's hostile, Britta. Even for you." Alec's tone had gone from cool to cold, eyes hardening to amber. "I thought we were on friendlier terms." He looked at my oxblood shoes and leaned forward. I flinched. Could he smell Ray's blood, in decade-old stains invisible even to me? Not over the smell of the police crew's cleanup …

Alec straightened and nodded, and I realized he'd been checking out the two black triangles of broken mirrors.

Of course, Alec would waltz in when I needed him least. And in full wolfcoat—why pass up an opportunity for a dramatic entrance? He'd probably expected me to be happy to see him, but his surprise visit said a lot about how much he thought I was capable of.

A fat lot of *nothing*.

His wolf stared out at me from behind his yellow gaze, tickling the little hairs on my arms, phantom paws racing along my skin. Alec hadn't come here to play nice. He was challenging me. Daring me to shift. To assert dominance, see if I was strong enough—literally—to fight off his advances.

My wolf paced within, but I pressed my thick rubber heels into the floorboards and glared up at Alec, resolvedly human. No metaphysical flexing or whatever passed for courtship with wolves.

"Don't challenge me, Alec. I don't have time for it," I hissed. "I asked you to help me free my brother. And you passed. Get lost."

Alec heaved through flared nostrils—would he shift back?—but he only snorted and managed to find his way to a passably contrite expression. His wolf settled within him, and the tension in the air thinned.

"You are not an easy wolf to woo, Britta." With a dismissive sort of grunt, Alec flicked a piece of imaginary lint off the breast of the peacoat. "But I'd be remiss if I didn't seize an opportunity to move things in my favor. You'd make an excellent Luna."

It was all about as romantic as Rhett's proposal to Scarlett at her second husband's funeral, but I'd missed something between the lines on that Skype call—either that or he'd buried the lede. Alec hadn't just asked me to be his mate; he'd asked me to be his *Luna*. A Luna is mate to an alpha. Our reigning alpha, Malakh, might take issue with Alec's ambitions to rise in the pack hierarchy, but I had more pressing trouble.

"It was a dick move, Alec." I refused to look surprised or flattered, and glanced down at my side, fixating on the exact spot where I'd first met Selena. The same spot where Ray had later been reduced to ash. "I don't care how fancy you try to make it sound."

He spread his hands before him. "You have my apologies."

"Yeah, well, your apologies aren't worth much, and you're still an asshole." I wanted to pick up the things I'd grabbed from Labaye, but I'd lose a lot of authority facing off with Alec with a plush elephant in my hand.

"I have been called much worse." He smiled, which only sharpened the angles of his face, and shrugged it off.

I glared back, holding my mouth in a tight scowl. "No, Alec, not yet." Slipping around him, I turned my back to the darkness of the stairwell. One upside to immortality—you could hold a grudge for a really long time. Yet as much as his sudden arrival aggravated me, it might not hurt to have another nose around—one that had more experience with witches.

Assuming I could trust him.

Alec moved closer, cocking his head in a way that looked coy and contemptuous at the same time. "I am sorry, Britta. I do not expect forgiveness, but I'm here to help whether you wish it or not." He pivoted smoothly around me and slid toward the stairs, lifting his nose while I glowered at his back. "This house reeks of old blood and black magic." He turned and wrinkled his nose in disgust. "Under all the chlorine and peroxide. Now, tell me, what did I walk in on? I can only assume our scared little mouse was the policeman you saved." He shot a look at the jacket and stuffed animal by the door. "And why was he in possession of your coat?"

"He was about to tell me before you scared him off." Figured I'd let him enjoy that. "But there's more." I pulled the vial Mam Byrdie had given me from my jeans pocket. I couldn't make out a scent from the liquid, but it didn't mean Alec couldn't get something from it. "An old friend gave me this. I found Remi's spirit trapped in a witch's circle upstairs. She'd used a scrying mirror to communicate with him, but it broke." I shook the vial at him. "The mambo told me to pour this onto a piece of mirror so I can talk to my brother."

Alec raised a skeptical eyebrow, but sighed and swept his arm toward the stairwell in a gesture that said, *Let's get on with it, then.*

I knelt to slip the vial into the jacket pocket, and swept the pieces of mirror under the leather and Rothko, in a neat pile out of the way of the door. Then I stepped around Alec, past the stairs to the spot where the smell of bleach burned the strongest. The copper scent had faded.

"This is where she was killed," I said. I'd left the one parlor door open, the police tape hanging where I'd torn it. I stood next to the gap so Alec could look past me. "Actually, both my mother and Selena died in this room. Selena's body left a stain on the tiles, and I found part of a footprint, but I'm not getting anything else. The cops did a thorough job, bleaching the place clean."

Alec peered past me into the parlor. "You mentioned a body. Have you not seen it for yourself?"

I shook my head and looked away. "The police aren't sharing."

"Then next time don't ask." He sneered, eyes scanning the room behind me. "If they wish us involved, they will give us the information we require, or we will simply take it for ourselves."

I shrugged and turned to head up the stairwell. I guess humans weren't the only ones who could play good cop, bad cop—or, in our case, good wolf, bad wolf.

His leather pants creaked as he followed me. The last time I'd climbed these nineteen steps, a cloud of panic had hung over me, and sweat had beaded out of every pore. The rookie's presence had done a little to dampen my anxiety, but with an elder wolf at my back, knowing what we might find in Remi's room, I felt almost nothing. Was I ready to see the house as just a house? Alec had always urged me to detach from my past.

I had never been here.

I had never died here.

We reached the landing and walked past the painted-shut attic door to Remi's bedroom. This time his door swung open easily, but as I stepped over the threshold, something had changed. It's what you feel when you first set foot in a new motel room, the indefinable pulse of something *different*. I'd felt it before, walking into Alec's apartment to find the stereo on, flies buzzing over a neglected cut of beef.

My brother's room looked just as I'd left it, but it *felt* different, with an altered smell. A hole hung in the heavy atmosphere of the room. No hint of bitter vanilla remained. Just stale, unclean air, the creep of chemical cleaner from below, and the stink of rotting wood.

Alec noticed it, too, pushing past me into the room. He ran his finger over the decade-old glue smear where Remi had peeled the Ninja Turtle sticker from his window. He opened the door to the bathroom my brother and I had shared, then closed it quietly.

"There's an emptiness … something was here but has gone." He paced around the room, an actor measuring his stage. "If someone practiced magic here, it would have left a longer …" he studied the ceiling fan, "aftertaste." He met my eyes where I stood in the doorway. "Someone has cleansed this place, and with more than chemicals."

Labaye had come up to fetch my jacket and Rothko, but I hadn't left them in the bedroom.

I dropped to my hands and knees, feeling for the crack along the inside of the fireplace. My fingers slipped in, and I shoved the small door open, then shimmied through as fast as I could, not caring as my hair caught on the rough brick edges, or when ash caked the thighs of my jeans. *Please be here, please be here.*

The brick-lined chamber was dark, but not black-magic dark—I could see enough. A bundle of wood was stacked in a dim corner, bits of a wood frame and an easel, and longer sticks that had once formed a rocking chair. A small broom lay atop the kindling. Faint chalk marks remained on the floor. The only sign that glass had shattered here was the sparkle of glitter between the boards. The space had been swept, corners cleared even of cobwebs.

Not just cleared. Hollowed.

"You'd never know a witch had called the ghost of a little boy here," I said. That she'd trapped his spirit. No trace of the scrying mirror, no magical circle.

And no Remi. Or any signs his spirit had ever lingered in this place.

I checked the old worn floorboards under my Docs because it felt like they'd been pulled out from beneath me. My heart pounded in my throat. "You've got to be kidding me," I muttered. "Where is everything? It's gone!" I screamed at no one in particular.

Alec's enormous head poked out of the crawlspace, a safe distance from me in his wolfish form. Under normal circumstances, I would've teased him for shifting just to squeeze through without getting his clothes dirty.

He ran his snout across the rough wood floor, tracing the circle from the few marks that remained. I shimmied out of my jeans and shifted, pushing my transformation as fast as I could, leaning forward to land on my paws. The pinprick sting of nettles climbed up my forelegs with the impact. We wound around each other in opposite directions, tracing for scent in the corners of the small chamber, winding in tighter circles to the room's center. I scratched at the boards where the floor met brick wall, like some pup begging to be let out.

Nothing.

Alec snarled and slid around me, back into the narrow passage to the bedroom. I pulled back into human form.

Nettles before, the abrupt change now felt like a million razor blades on my skin. Beyond the pain, a powerful punch of vertigo kept me on hands and knees when I had those again, as I struggled to regain my breath. The early warning tendrils of a migraine stabbed at the edges of my brain. I dressed, to find I'd also torn my shirt, though nowhere too revealing. Perhaps I was getting better at not ruining every item of clothing I owned.

I crawled back through the fireplace to find Alec standing over me, leather pants and black coat as crisp as ever. He growled, "Your human friend betrayed you."

What had Labaye been doing when I found him? "Someone else could've done this before he got here," I said, and Alec just rolled his eyes. Labaye had been scared. Clammy. And not of Big Bad Britta. Whatever brought him here had him spooked, and I didn't think it was police duty.

"I didn't get a chance to ask what he was up to," I said, hesitant to give Alec more ammunition against the man he'd already like to see dead.

"It is enough that he interfered," Alec growled as he walked out of the room. I shot out after him, eager to cover up with the leather jacket I'd left downstairs. "The police have no right to any of this—"

"Alec, Labaye is the police," I said. "They're not just gonna hand over evidence from a murder investigation."

"I'm not concerned with jackets and teddy bears, Britta," he said without looking back. "We need the witch's corpse."

I froze at the top of the stairwell, and Alec paused without turning toward me. "What is it?" he said.

"I didn't tell you everything." I thought of Lisbeth Kelleher as I tapped the banister, her fingernails clicking endlessly as she retraced the walk to her death. Now Alec looked at me, his scowl more contemptuous than ever. "They didn't recover the whole body," I said. "Like, not even close."

"What did they recover?"

I wanted to drive my hands into my pockets and disappear, but the black jeans offered little concealment. The leather jacket would be too warm for the muggy twilight air, but I couldn't wait to get into it. I stalked down the stairs past Alec.

"They only got her heart, one eye, some teeth," I said, flinching so as not to bump his shoulder. "Maybe all the teeth, not sure."

I stopped dead at the bottom of the stairs. The floor where I'd left my jacket, the pieces of mirror, and the stuffed animal was empty, picked clean like the brick-lined chamber above. Only a few tiny shards of glass remained, not much more than dust, the front door wide open.

Labaye's telltale scent of musky pine hung in the air.

Alec didn't reach the first floor on two legs. His wolf shot past me through the doorway into the night, locked on Labaye's scent before I could say anything to stop him. I grasped out at nothing but air and took the rest of the steps in a single jump.

With a groan, I called my wolf to wriggle back into that coat. I dropped to the hardwood floor but landed hard on my knees. Again, I pulled my pants off as fast as I could, and my torso expanded, adding a rib before I could free my shirt over my head—but I couldn't snap back and forth the way Alec could, a consequence of still being a pup.

Then my legs stretched, fibula and tibia creaking audibly as they pulled taut muscle. Claws scraped across the floorboards as metatarsals doubled in length, and I shot out into the night.

I'd need to run faster than Alec. Unlikely. If I couldn't, if I finished in second place, would I find a chewed-up cop?

A dog barked from his leash or pen in some dark yard, then

another, scenting two strange canids running free through the streets, and I thought of Atlanta overrun by strays after the Civil War.

All I needed was a piece of the scrying mirror, maybe my brother's elephant and my jacket. Labaye and Alec could bleed out together for all I cared.

I'd cleared two blocks, sticking to the shadows, before full feeling had flushed through my extremities. Grateful for how few of the streetlights appeared to work, I ignored the backlit windows of the library, Mam Byrdie probably inside at her humfo. I cleared the flimsy chain-link fence in a low jump and cut around the playground through the park.

Blood pounded through my limbs, filled my heart, and it felt so good. I grit my fangs and ran faster, my muscles opening up. This—this feeling, this *freedom*—is why humans do drugs.

I wanted to call out to Alec to stop, to think about what he was doing, but a lot of growling and howling would defeat the purpose of staying in the shadows.

Most of the lights in the Calcasieu Parish Police Department were off. Men's voices, loud and sharp with anger, pierced through my frustration—Alec's voice, his human voice. I caught my breath, hiding by the side of a pickup truck with the driver's door open, heat rising from the hood. Labaye's personal vehicle?

I tried to shift.

Nothing.

And if it worked, I'd be racing into the PD buck naked.

Their voices grew louder as I padded up the steps, the words too mumbled to make out. The tone left little to the imagination.

There'd be blood. I just didn't want them to break the last of the scrying mirror. If I couldn't get my paws on that, I couldn't get to Remi.

So much for low profile.

I slammed through the front doors and went in wolfy.

CHAPTER EIGHTEEN

A aron was having a hard time catching his breath.

He hadn't wanted to go back to the Hall Murder House. As many times as he'd been in the place, it always set his skin on edge, more so since Britta arrived in town. A lot of things had changed since she'd walked into the station, none of which Aaron entirely understood. He had a hard time keeping his priorities straight when she was around, and he'd allowed himself to get too close. He had a job to do that required focus. This was harder than he'd expected, but he didn't have time to think about it now.

That male wolf must've been twice the size of Britta when she turned. Labaye had burst out the front doors. He'd parked—his Chevy S10, not the cruiser—two doors down. When nothing followed to the pickup, he'd gathered every bit of courage he could to go back. Hiding in the weeds and police tape below a window, he'd heard boots ascend the stairs. Britta's Docs didn't make a lot of sound—the other werewolf had probably shifted, dressed, and she'd followed him up. She hadn't stopped to latch the deadbolt, so when he heard the echo of boots on the upstairs floorboards, Aaron poked his head in to see the *evidence* just inside the door. He sliced his hand on a piece of the mirror, which clattered across the other. Voices continued upstairs—the werewolves hadn't heard him. He used Remi's mostly *un*stuffed elephant like a potholder to pick up both pieces of glass, then scrambled to his pickup with as little noise as he could.

As he drove, he wrestled himself out of the windbreaker and

rolled up the shirtsleeve away from the bleeding hand.

He'd got halfway back to the station before noticing the enormous silver wolf in his rearview mirror.

"You okay, Labaye?"

Once inside the precinct, Aaron set the leather jacket and the elephant containing the mirror pieces on his desk and tried to catch his breath long enough to answer McKelvie, the patrolman on duty. McKelvie closed the notepad he'd been scribbling in and stepped away from the front desk.

When the man in the leather pants, black coat, and silver hair slammed through the doors of the precinct, Aaron did not wonder for one split second what he was.

McKelvie wheeled on the man in the long black coat—the wolfman—and shouted. Aaron tried to warn him. He dropped the roll of gauze he'd started to wind around his injured hand—but the wolfman tossed McKelvie aside, the cop's head making a sharp sound on the edge of a bench.

Then the attacker turned flashing eyes on Labaye, who stepped away from the desk where he'd set the jacket and the glass-stuffed bear.

Funny, those eyes didn't look to Aaron one bit like fireflies.

When Britta had shoved him out her front door she'd saved him for a second time. She wasn't around now for a third.

But the silver-haired wolfman did not attack. Aaron drew on him, the gauze red and dancing off his hand, and shouted, "Freeze!"

"Do we really need to do this, *Officer*?" The wolfman spread his arms wide to provide the best target that he could, and he hung his head.

He lurched forward, too fast for Aaron to see, before the cop felt himself rocketed back across the linoleum floor, the gun knocked out of his bloody hand and sent skittering across the floor. His spine slammed into a desk, and when he looked up the leather-clad legs stood so close Aaron might have slid between them.

An iron grip closed around his hand and lifted him to his feet. The cut hadn't hurt so bad before, but now it stabbed up Labaye's arm and through his shoulder. He squeezed his eyes shut against the pain as his boots shuffled, looking for solid ground.

Hot breath in his ear brought Aaron back around. "The witch's remains," the voice said.

"We never found …" he began, but the grip on his hand released, and Aaron crashed to his knees.

"I know all that," the wolf growled, pulling the gauze off his own hand and balling it up. "I shall take whatever you've managed to put together."

Aaron's collar choked him as the wolfman dragged him, legs still scrambling, across the tiles. He couldn't speak—he popped his top button to ease the pressure on his larynx—if he could just catch his breath.

But he flew off the floor again, landing against the wall. Aaron struggled to his knees, his hand bleeding freely now so that blood pooled. The rolled-up sleeve had come loose and dripped red in a splatter on the hard concrete floor. He fumbled for his gun before remembering he'd dropped it. The room echoed with two sharp *Kerrang*s before a dusty metallic scent hit him. Aaron raised his bleary eyes just in time to see the intruder reach for him again and drag him through the smashed open door marked in black and gold decal letters, *Prop Room*.

If he could just catch his breath.

When he managed to grab the man's wrist, he had half a second to marvel—*How could so thin an arm toss me around like this?*—before the world spun again, all straight lines and shelving and white cardboard boxes. Aaron made a lap around the painted concrete floor, albeit backward and on his ass, then he stopped hard.

His back smashed into a cool surface. A door. The wolfman knelt and fumbled with Labaye's keyring.

"The fridge," Aaron said, chasing stars from his eyes. "You found it." He slapped the paw away with his good hand, unhooking the ring from his belt, singling out the refrigeration key. He didn't feel like a coward, just helping along the inevitable.

Staggering to his feet, Aaron wiped the blood from his palm on his thigh and faced his attacker, who opened the five-inch-thick steel door.

Cold air snapped the cop the rest of the way alert. When the wolfman pulled Aaron into the cooler, he did so more gently now, maybe a reward for complicity. Aaron could face him for the first time, sketching every detail of the man's appearance into memory, his sharp cheeks, the thick silver hair. Still, even as a man, Aaron recognized the wolf that he had seen in Britta's house.

"Labaye." The intruder spit his name as he scanned the shelves.

Aaron studied his wounded hand. The bleeding had slowed but would need medical attention. He looked at his attacker and said, "I don't believe I've had the pleasure."

"I am Alec." The wolfman smirked. "You will want to remember that. Now, where is the witch."

Aaron's fingers brushed across shelf after shelf. He ignored the burn in his back as eyes the color of molten gold tracked his movement.

Labaye curled his fists into balls, turning his knuckles white, refreshing the cut on the bad hand. He glared at the shelves.

"Not here," he said. He held his hands apart as if gripping a basketball. "A little red and white cooler." He stepped back, seeming to forget the wolfman at his side. "Where the fuck ..."

A shelf collapsed onto him, and Aaron dove toward the cooler's open steel door. Alec pulled down more shelves, knocked glass containers shattering to the concrete floor. He tore a cardboard box to shreds, tin containers clanging around his boots.

Aaron saw his chance. Diving through the entrance, he grabbed the cold edge of the massive door to propel himself out. He didn't pause to look at the new figure who'd appeared in the doorway of the outer evidence room but spun back around, throwing the steel door shut with all his might.

Alec reached out, just missing Aaron's bad hand. The huge door slammed against the wolfman's forearm and bounced open. As Alec fell to the painted concrete floor, he punched at Aaron's leg, sending him crashing against the wall.

The wolf barked and leaped from the evidence room doorway over Alec to place herself between him and the cop. Aaron climbed to his feet, but fell against a shelf, knocking a loose stack of papers to the floor. Aaron recognized the wolf in front of him before Alec said her name, his arm hanging limp at his side. *Britta.*

"Whoa!" Devereaux shouted, appearing in the doorway behind Alec, service revolver leveled at the wolfman's center mass, cowboy boots planted more than shoulder-width apart. "Everyone!" the cop yelled. "Hold still!"

Britta barked, and Aaron called, "Devereaux, get out!"

Alec spun, his limp arm waving at his side as the other arm shot straight for Devereaux's throat. But not as fast as before.

The pistol barrel flashed. Alec staggered back, almost falling over the she-wolf, but his broken arm found the shelving, and he steadied himself. A second shot slammed him against the shelves, but he didn't go down.

When he raised his head, Alec's eyes burned golden fire. His shoulders twitched, and his chest swelled up, with air or something else, and for a moment he appeared to be a wolf on hind legs. Devereaux stumbled back against the wall, and Aaron thought, *He saw it, too.* Britta sprung away from the wolfman and her tail whacked Aaron's thigh.

Alec threw himself forward to grab Devereaux's wrist just as the gun's muzzle flashed again, the bullet punching a hole through a wooden crate on an upper shelf.

Britta launched herself with such force Aaron fell on his ass. She knocked Alec off Devereaux, then sprang over him, out of the room.

Alec didn't even turn to look at the two cops.

"Jesus H. fucking Christ!" Devereaux shouted. He looked at the ceiling, touching the back of his head to the wall as he pressed his fingers against his jowls to check for wounds. Then he looked at Labaye. "C'mon!"

Aaron followed out through the main room, the older cop's boots clacking across the linoleum, but it felt like they moved through molasses. The leather jacket and the one-eyed, trunkless elephant lay on Aaron's desk where he'd left them. McKelvie also lay where he'd fallen, and Aaron hoped like hell the man hadn't died. McKelvie had a small kid at home, a wife, and Labaye didn't want someone with that kind of life caught up in this.

He stopped just behind Devereaux on the front steps. The older man crouched, hands braced on his knees, breathing heavily. Across the parking lot, one wolf limped into the shadows, and Aaron knew it was Alec, Britta already long gone.

Aaron tried to catch his breath, rested his good hand on his chest as though it could slow his pulse. He closed his eyes, and when he opened them, Devereaux stood looking at him. "Do you know who that was?" the older cop asked, then turned back to look across the parking lot.

Who, not *what*.

"Said his name was Alec," Aaron said. "No last name." He wondered for a moment if Devereaux meant Britta, but he had no interest going there. "Never saw him before he busted in here." Technically, even that was true.

Aaron took a deep breath and let it out, releasing all the tension from his shoulders. His chin fell to his chest. He'd never retrieved his gun from the freezer. Instead of going back in, he dropped to the concrete steps, peeled the sticky mass of shirt away from his body, and set his injured hand in his lap. The loss of blood had turned the arm white.

Aaron Labaye stared out across Vinton at night, where now probably two werewolves prowled, and thought, *Neither one got what they came for.*

CHAPTER NINETEEN

Within two blocks of the police station, it felt like someone had pumped a gallon of water into my skull. My head pounded, and the usual surge of pleasure brought on by running could not overcome the migraine as I raced away from the all-out freakshow in the evidence locker. Normally I could never in a million years outrun Alec, but even for a senior werewolf, a couple of gunshots and a fractured ulna weren't nothing. But I couldn't stop. I ran, paws pounding against the pavement. He *better* be chasing me still, or Labaye and Devereaux would have way more than they could handle.

I didn't want to think about them. Devereaux almost certainly had *not* seen Alec change—Alec could do it so fast, he must have done it out of sight of the cops. Hopefully, the crusty old detective was back at his desk, putting in a frantic call to Animal Control about a pair of rabid wolves that would never be found. It's amazing what humans will accept, rather than believe in things like me. Just ask Dana Scully.

I raced and caught a whisper of padded footfalls behind my own. Coming closer. Uneven. Limping. If I slowed to look, the monster behind me would catch up.

Of course, I was a monster, too.

I smelled her before I saw her. Vanilla and rose. Magic and power. As soon as I recognized Mam Byrdie's scent, the woman's figure slid out of the shadow of a tall hedge. She stood as a silent sentinel in the street, eyes flashing amber and round in the darkness, draped in a frown and silks from her turban to her caftan, the gold and green scarf loose around her neck. She clutched a flickering brass chamberstick in one hand, casting light on the long, bony index finger of her damaged hand, crooked in a beckoning gesture.

Come to me, Wolf, she demanded, and though her lips did not move, the rich sound of her voice echoed within my head, pulsing inside her candlelight.

I skidded to a stop at Mam Byrdie's feet, the steady gleam of power in her eyes undeniable. They shot past me, and she waved the candlestick. I thought she meant to usher me into the shadow of the hedge, but the shadow came to me. The night sounds around us grew softer, and the pain in my head lightened. Her voice cut through the veil, quiet but clear.

"Hush, Wolf." She stroked the hair at the back of my neck.

Alec limped past, not ten feet from us. His snout swept the street. He neither scented nor saw us, but he paused just after he trotted by. Mam Byrdie withdrew her hand from my ruff and waved her fingers down the road, the direction I'd been heading. Alec snapped his head up, sniffed, and shot forward on his unsteady legs, following the scent Byrdie had cast down the road. A good enough witch can fool any of the five senses, no matter how keen. She grinned at me, spared him another glance to make sure he kept on his way, then turned and led me around an old one-level ranch. A television played behind a blue-lit pane, but even if the residents had stuck their heads out the window they couldn't have seen us.

I followed her through the neighborhood and the park, toward the library. I ground my teeth together to push back the pain that returned, hammering in my skull. Time was slipping away. Remi was slipping away. I didn't know what, but *something* was coming. Shadows nipped at my heels as the night closed in.

"Inside," she whispered in a raspy voice as we crossed the parking lot.

She said something under her breath in a language I didn't recognize and blew out her candle, pressing her scarf against her throat so the silk didn't get too near the flame. I stopped to look back past my tail as she climbed the steps into the library.

"Now." She rapped a knuckle on the handrail, the paint stripped down to metal glinting under the moon.

I followed.

Still murmuring, Mam Byrdie locked the door behind us, then pulled a small canister of salt from the sleeve of her caftan. With practiced movements, she poured a thin line of white just inside the door. Satisfied, she leaned forward to peek through the blinds across the top half of the door, and she snapped her tongue at whatever she saw. Sprinkling more salt in her hand, still murmuring under her breath, she flicked the granules with her fingertips so they stuck to the glass.

I caught the last. "Kenbe iwen." *Keep away.*

The old mambo turned to me with a look of exasperation not unlike a disapproving parent frowning at a misbehaving child. The ache in my head had made me whine and I hadn't even noticed.

It may have been the only time I ever saw her blink.

She paused at the front desk to put on her black cat eyeglasses. "You are stuck, aren't you, Wolf?" she stated matter-of-factly and shook her head, moving toward her office behind the rows of bookshelves. She let me pass into the room, and shut the door behind us, pouring a fresh line of salt at the edge of the closed door. She'd set two safety nets now. I hoped we didn't need them.

The room looked bigger than before. You could not guess this space existed in the back office of the tiny library. The minutiae of library business had been tucked away and Mam Byrdie's humfo filled the room. This decorated seat of her power had pushed past the physical bounds of the half-century-old brick-and-mortar building.

Covered in a swath of black silk and beset with dozens of

candles, the altar seemed alive—as I scanned the rest of the room, the altar moved at the edge of my vision, but when I looked back nothing had changed. It drew breath in the beat of the candle flames, exhaled incense in sweet vanilla, and rose, patchouli, and cedar.

Other items lay scattered about on the humfo, things that made my head throb all the harder. A skull with one eye socket caved in. Pots of melted wax. The disassembled claw of an animal not belonging to the natural world, further removed than me. Dead flowers and effigies of dark-skinned saints whose names I did not know. A small pile of eggshell white stones.

I spun around too fast and my head swam. Mam Byrdie crouched, face level with mine, gaze hard and penetrating. The spark I'd seen in her eyes had roared into a blazing fire. Startled, I tried to back away, but my legs hit the humfo, trapping me between the mambo and her altar. My wolf's senses engaged, but when I tried to leap past Mam Byrdie my body refused, forced into stillness. A growl welled in the back of my throat then flattened into silence. The amber fire in Mam Byrdie's eyes held me in place as the power I had felt before washed over me with a familiar scent.

In a voice I would have thought too deep and guttural to be hers, Mam Byrdie spoke a rhyme that held no meaning but sounded more terrifying than any noise I'd ever heard. Her eyes rolled back into her skull, and her fist unfurled, missing that ring finger. In a gust of breath, she blew powder from her palm into my eyes. Numbness stole the last of my senses, and I gasped for air—felt like I could get none, felt at once like I was falling, and being held up. The world went dark in a whiff of medicinal vanilla and rose—of magic—and I collapsed in a tangle of fur to the hardwood floor.

TEN YEARS EARLIER

Her bad hand gripping the safety-yellow handrail, our town librarian eased down onto the second stair at the edge of the parking lot. She straightened her brightly colored skirt over her knees, then unrolled the top of a small brown paper bag and pulled out a sandwich wrapped in wax paper. Ham and cheddar today. Setting the bag on the concrete step—something heavy in the bottom made it stand up—she peeled the paper away from the top of the sandwich. It tore just a little.

"If anything comes flying out of the trees," I said. "They're not, I don't know, little magnolia monkeys or something ... They'd be ghosts, right?" Mam Byrdie met my eye, and I lowered my voice even more. "I mean, I can wrap my head around spirits, but there's no *monsters*, are there?"

I tugged at my bangs, which I'd cut too short. Mam Byrdie saw sunglasses as a sign of disrespect, maybe dishonesty, but I wanted something between me and the hot Texas sun—pardon me, West Louisiana sun. Same thing. The heat had melted the cheese in her sandwich, the light stabbing at her desk through the library's tall east-facing windows. My dad told me he'd set sandwiches on his dashboard, and by lunch he'd have grilled cheese. I counted twice to be sure this'd be my thirteenth birthday without him. Twenty-four was just a few sleeps away.

"What are you asking me, *sha*?" The wax paper came away from the side of Mam Byrdie's sandwich with a thin orange glob. She scraped at the half-melted cheese with a long unpainted nail and popped it in her mouth without breaking eye contact. A pair of toddlers screeched from the fenced-in playground as their grandmother talked on her phone. Maybe she was calling in backup.

I scraped the thick soles of my boots across the concrete, liking the sound, and the pebbles that shot from underfoot. A lady in a wide, flowered hat walked up the steps, saying hello to the mambo dining on her *croque monsieur*, ignoring my black-clad ass. I pretended not to notice, and picked some imaginary speck from the top laces of my ten-hole Docs, barely having to bend for it. People in Vinton didn't even know the word *goth*. *It's fuckin' 2002, people, yer southern belles don't ring no more*, I thought, and scraped more gravel.

The front door to the library eased shut behind Missus Sun-hat, and I scanned the parking lot, spotted no more arrivals.

"I'm just trying to sort out some of the crap this old lady is telling me," I said, returning to the thread of our conversation without the worry of thirsty ears nearby. "Me and my brother." I dropped onto the top step with a grunt, leaving room for patrons to pass. Whatever was in the house affected Remi way more than it did me, which only made me worry twice as hard.

Edmée Byrdie studied me, chewing her sandwich. I tried to dead-eye her, but of course, I blinked first. Maybe she needed me to put it in the form of a question, but I felt I'd said enough, and before long she gave in.

"Shakespeare has a useful quote on the subject," she said, "but I butcher it whenever I try to apply it. Maybe I'll check when I go inside." She spoke with care as she peeled the last of the wax paper. "No, *sha*, the shadows hold more than the spirits of the dead." She scanned the edges of the parking lot, but not for patrons.

She placed the sandwich on her thigh, pinched diagonal corners of the wax paper. "I cannot speak for your home," Mam Byrdie said, "or that magnolia tree. But if you open yourself to the real world, which hides all around you … or if you cannot resist its pull, you will meet strange things. Little and large, hairy and scaled. Not quite the things of storybooks, no." She pulled the corners of the wax paper and folded it into a sharp crease.

Without looking at me, she nodded in time to some private lullaby, folding the paper again, until the thickness made it too hard to bend. "They can be far worse," she said, "and far, far more mysterious than the works of Mr. Stoker or Messrs. Grimm."

She forced her features into a kind expression and met my eye. "So keep your sweet boy away from that tree," she said and leaned across the stairs to pat my knee. "Just in case your mama's friend tells it true."

"You think whatever's up there is dangerous?"

"Oh, child." Her smile froze in place and she bobbed her chin, looking at the wax paper triangle in the palm of her hand. "If there is something, please consider it a threat."

"In a kind of, *better safe than sorry* way, though, right?" I wasn't thinking about myself. At that moment Remi probably sat in our yard drawing. Probably in the shade beneath the magnolia tree.

Mam Byrdie dropped the waxed triangle into her bag, pulled out a peach, then stood and paced. Wind pushed the bag off the stair, and I dropped a thick rubber heel on it.

"Think of it like this," she said, keeping her voice soft and hushed. "Forget that they are monsters. That they are not human." She took a bite and chose her words with care as she chewed. "Consider only that they think, that they may *feel*." She pressed the tip of a finger to the corner of her mouth to get a drip of juice without ruining her lipstick. "And that they live their entire lives— which might stretch on for many, many years, much longer than old Mam Byrdie's life—in shadows. Up in twisted old branches. Avoiding the eyes of man."

The library door opened, and a woman walked out, a tote bag bumping heavily against her knee. Mam Byrdie nodded and smiled around a bite of peach. Nicotine filled the creases in the woman's skin like grout and I held my breath as she passed. The smoker got in her faded Volvo before Mam Byrdie had swallowed.

"Seeking shelter, feeding, maybe raising young … or else isolated even from their own kind. On fear of death, they hide, and all the while, man pushes farther into the shadow, into the bayou, the mountain." She slurped some juice off the glistening flesh of the fruit, then smiled. "How do you imagine they feel about you?"

The summer heat sent a chill down my spine. I decided right then to give in and set up a bedroom in the downstairs den, get Remi away from the windows under the magnolia branches. "You … you said little or large. So, there are bigger ones—bigger monsters."

She bit the last of the peach from the pit and sat next to me in the center of the stairs. "There is all manner of things that make their home in these parts," she said, our eyes locked. "Do you know the term *loup garou?* You might know the word *werewolf,* but here in the bayou, we call them *loup garou*—man-wolf. Not monsters, but beasts nonetheless. A great pack once prowled this land." She hung her head, lost in thought for a moment. Without looking up, she went on. "The woman who trained your Mam Byrdie said, 'A wolf be a powerful familiar if turned by black magic.' But," she punched the air with her bad hand, the pointer finger straight up, "it is only the most powerful of mambo who can tame those silver-haired beasts."

Byrdie met my eye, and I smiled, but she pulled an exaggerated frown and shook her head. She sucked the pit and dropped it into the brown paper bag.

"Man calls dog best friend." She waved a hand at the cars in the parking lot, as if addressing a crowd. "All these bulldogs and rottweilers and poodles, they would sooner die than see you hurt."

She smiled, but then turned on me as grim as I'd ever seen her.

"But whether it is witch or wolf, when magic turns a soul …" She grasped the yellow railing and climbed back to her feet, holding her bad hand out to me. "Some evil, *sha,* wants to live forever."

My eyes snapped open. I pushed myself into a sitting position, and pain shot through my head again. Couldn't I at least have slept the migraine off? I rubbed at my eyes to force them to adjust to the darkness.

I stared at the fingers before my face, turning my palms over in the dim light—a woman again, not a wolf. I wore a long, soft dress that covered my knees. Not my own clothes, but comfortable—and it was black. At least Mam Byrdie hadn't dressed me in a virginal white sacrificial gown. A small mercy.

Despite the skulls and various gris-gris, the glittering air made the humfo look more like Seurat or Signac than Goya. I sat up in a makeshift nest of blankets and pillows. Mam Byrdie stood with her back to me. The scarf wound 'round her neck and the ash-colored braids covered the marks I'd seen there the day before. She hummed softly as she lit fresh candles on the little altar and arranged the incense on a tray beside a tiny teacup filled with pale green milk.

Hearing me stir, Mam Byrdie turned, her expression softer than it had been before, more familiar and human. "Good," she said, bending to lay the platter on the floor in front of me. Pillar candles stood on either side of us, flames flickering inside the tall tubes of glass.

I tucked my feet up into the end of the dress, desperate for cover. "What did you do to me?" I didn't mean to snap. Happy to be plain old Britta again, I hadn't forgotten how she'd blasted me in the face with magic. She could've bypassed the theatrics and just said, *Hold still*, and I would have. Probably.

Mam Byrdie *tsk*ed. I dropped my head into my hands as she adjusted the incense in a thin layer on the tray.

The collective accouterments of magic made my stomach churn. My skull throbbed. I hated the stuff, and now it was my idea to practice it? But if I'd go on a blind date with the devil himself to speak to my little brother again, to give him one second's peace, then one little spell couldn't hurt much … or could it?

"I didn't get the mirror," I said, then tried to remember where I'd left the vial. I jerked away as she lit incense, remembering the powder puffed into my eyes.

Mam Byrdie didn't react when I flinched. "We don't need the witch's mirror," she said. "I have something better."

In a rush of silks, Mam Byrdie dropped to the floor, cross-legged in front of me. She bent her neck as she spun down, and the flowing petals of her scarf drooped so I saw the scars in her dark skin. When she lifted her head, the spark flashed again in those golden eyes. Right before she'd helped me get away from Alec, her eyes had flashed like that. Bright and inhuman.

Fireflies.

"I know what you are," I said.

Mam Byrdie hated wolves. I never would have guessed she was one.

My heart pounded, waiting for her to speak. "I am the same as you." Even she—big bad Vaudon mambo—would not say the word. She pulled a tiny vial from the folds of her skirt and handed it to me. "For your head," she said and mimed rubbing her temples.

"A wolf," I said it for her, anointing each pointer finger with oil, then putting the cap back on. "You hate it every bit as much as I do. Cursed. Undead."

This time she laughed, but it was kind. "No, *sha.* You know, some who dabble with the tarot cannot distinguish *Death* from *change,* but I feel very much alive, thank you." She reached in the blankets beside me and dug around while I rubbed the sides of my forehead, like applying moisturizer.

"You see a reflection of yourself distorted by grief and pain." She set the tray down and pulled a sheet of paper from the blanket. "You say you are cursed. Broken. And those things may be true, but you are *here*—"The edge on this last was so sharp it nearly cut the air between us. "You are a survivor, Britta Orchid. We both are. If you insist on calling yourself a monster, then stand and be the beast." She handed the paper to me.

A drawing of the library, as it looked ten years ago, half of the bricks rendered in charcoal. "Remi's drawing," I said. No trace of the migraine remained. "You saved this?" I thought of the other one, his new drawing, folded in the front pocket of my pants back at the house.

The old mambo smiled sadly, looking at the paper in my lap.

"He didn't finish …" Tears turned the metallic tang of blood in my mouth salty, and I swallowed. The mambo pushed the incense and teacup to the corners of the tray and placed the drawing in the middle.

"Guilt can be a terrible burden, Britta Orchid." She met my eyes and smiled. I wanted to say something, to say I deserved whatever pain I felt, but she spoke first.

"Not a day passes," she said, "that I do not think of your brother."

"Mam Byrdie, you didn't know, you—"

She shushed me, waved my words away, then tapped a crooked finger on the edge of the serving platter. "Now, pour the cup over the drawing, *sha*. You must cast the spell. Ask your brother what the witch intended, and free him at last."

I reached for the cup, then froze. I met her eye again. "Mam Byrdie, Selena's … the remains." The look on her face betrayed nothing as she waited for me to say it. "Did you steal them from the police station?"

The old woman's stoic face broke with laughter. "Oh no, Britta, my sweet," she said. "You fret about being cursed … Loa punishes with restraint." She shook. "But if I start playing with bodies I'll come back as a diab and my misery will know no bounds." She pointed at the teacup and glared from under arched brows. "We do good magic here, *sha*."

I grimaced and plucked the teacup from the tray, trying not to gag. The vial she'd given me before hadn't smelled, but this packed a punch, abhorrent, potent. Bacon grease left to swelter in the bayou sun. I held my breath and dumped the fluid on Remi's beautiful drawing.

The charcoal lines bled, seemed to move. Light danced over, or perhaps through, the simple piece of typing paper, and for a moment I thought I sat outside in daylight looking up at the building, the glint of sunlight in the corners of my eyes. Glimpses of faces passed in rapid succession, their features blurring together so that none were distinct but all seemed familiar.

"Speak his name," Mam Byrdie instructed. "Tell the mirror who you wish to see."

It took three tries to get it out. "Remi," I said, my voice finally emerging in a whisper when I got to my feet. I cleared my throat while more faces flickered across the glass. A woman's face that might have been my mother's brushed by, and the breath caught in my throat. The last time I'd seen her, blood had covered a face twisted in fear. Had I almost been able to forget that? More faces passed, and memories crowded in, so many faces who I could beg for forgiveness. But I didn't need these reminders of the people I'd failed.

"Remi Orchid," I called again, this time clearer. Firmer. More definite. I didn't even hear myself get the surname wrong.

My chin fell to my chest and I stared into black grains of ash swirling in a pale green pool at my feet. The charcoal dust of Remi's drawing swirled off the paper across the surface of the tray. How much of that potion had the teacup held?

I hadn't been aware of the rushing sound until it stopped. The air around us fell still. The mambo's eyes closed, her lips moving, maybe in prayer. Then a breeze blew, soft at first and then faster, a wraithlike wind in a quiet room. Mam Byrdie cupped her hands over one of the candles to protect the flame, the pinkie and middle finger on her bad hand crossing to cover the gap, her lips moving faster, silently encouraging the light to persist.

A whisper brushed past my ear and the tall candle Byrdie couldn't reach went out. A shadow rose from the emptiness before me, up from the pale green pool. Black and solid at first, the form took shape from the absence of light, softening as limbs faded from blurry shadow slowly into focus.

A small boy stood before me, ten years old, features indistinct, shifting, but recognizable. A curl of hair hung to the shadow's neck, over the rounded curve of tiny shoulders. My brother swelled up from the darkness.

"Keep calling him, *sha*," Mam Byrdie whispered, her hands still wrapped around the candlelight. "Direct the magic. Bring him back."

I said it with confidence this time. "Remi Hall. I call my brother, Remi Hall."

Come back to me, Rem.

The shadow vibrated, details becoming clear like someone emerging from under water. Spectral and colored in soft blue and green, the spirit of my brother stood before me with a shivery quality, an image formed of white noise on a bad television station. Not like I had seen him in the circle—calmer, more himself than before.

I didn't see worry in that line across his forehead.

My brother and I stared at each other.

He didn't move, but continued to waver, a reflection on a rippling pool.

I raised a hand, wanting to touch him but terrified that I could. Terrified that I couldn't, that one brush of fingers would ruin the mirage. I either had to wrap my arms around him or run screaming from the library. The spirit smiled, the curve of its lips crackling as if they'd suddenly flip into a scowl, or be swallowed into the darkness.

Mam Byrdie's creole lilt broke into my thoughts. "The spell will not hold. Be quick, Britta."

I blinked. Opened my mouth to speak. No sound.

"Hi, Britta." My little brother's voice echoed unnaturally, but the pitch, the timbre, that little bit of southeast Texas twang was the same as the last time I'd heard him that day in the library. Before he'd left with his father, before I'd run after him through the house ... and I'd heard it in a thousand dreams since.

"Remi." I grimaced, tears stabbing the backs of my eyes with each quick syllable of his name. *Let them fall*, I thought. *Just let me grab him and squeeze this ghost into something solid.* But I took a deep breath, straightened my back, and clenched my fists as if to hold the air around me. "Tell me how to help you."

The image flickered, darkening. Remi's smile cracked, his lips moved, the sound delayed. "She wants you, Britta."

"*Sha*, hurry," Mam Byrdie urged. The candle flame flared and sent up a nimbus of smoke, and Mam Byrdie winced but didn't withdraw her hands. I looked at the platter by my feet, the clear green liquid soaking the last of the incense there, all the charcoal having floated into the air. Time was running out.

Again, I thought, but pushed that away.

"Remi, tell me how to help." I hadn't used the big sister voice in years. "What do I do? How do I fix this?"

"No, Britta. She is ... waiting," he said, the last word only reaching me as an echo. "*Please*." Phantom tears bubbled in ghost eyes. The line across his forehead twisted with concern. My nails bit crescent moons into my palms, and my knuckles went white and hard like bone in the faltering light.

"Remi, Selena Stone is dead." My voice cracked. "She *will* let you go." I tried to sound firm. "Tell me what to do." Only a little green potion remained in the tray now. All the incense had burned to white ash.

Remi shook his head. He started to speak, but his eyes snapped to the side as if he saw something move—maybe a spirit whose name I hadn't meant to call. Like smoke struck by a sharp wind, my brother vanished, then came back less stable, face contorted in fear.

"No, Britta, don't worry about me—you have to run." His voice rose into panic, his face twisted in terror as a new sour smell filled the room. His mouth moved but I just heard the wind hard against my ear.

Mam Byrdie spoke ancient words in the low, guttural tone of the beast inside her—I tried to block her out to hear my brother. Something was coming. She held it off, buying me time. But she'd lowered her hands and the candle blew out.

"What do I do?" I screamed at the shadow of my brother. Blood poured down my fingers, dripped onto my wrists. Onto the floor.

Remi faded in and out. I'd lose him all over again.

"Selena wants you," he said. "But it's not just her!" His mouth moved, nothing came out, then, "You have to run, Britta!"

The terror in his voice compelled me. "He pretends to care," Remi said, but rushing air swept up the rest. I flung myself forward, to grab him, to wrestle his spirit through the veil, safely into my arms.

I fell through him, and when I turned around, I saw nothing.

"Who?" I screamed. "Who, Remi?"

The room had gone quiet.

Mam Byrdie touched the tall candlestick she'd let go out. She had warned me that guilt could be an awful burden. The blank look in her eyes as she studied the smoking wick said the burden lived in her bones, too.

She bent to pick up the bone-dry platter I'd stepped over, and a fine ash drifted off it, weightless, onto her shoes.

Remi was gone.

CHAPTER TWENTY

TEN YEARS EARLIER

My brother called my name in a heavy whisper, the two syllables tangled up as he tried to control his voice. I pictured him speaking through hands cupped at the sides of his mouth. He thought he could sound farther away than he was. Cute.

"Britta, come and find me," he said, struggling to contain a laugh.

"Okay, kid. Ready or not!" Turning away from the corner, I dropped my hands from my face and blinked down the hall toward the crowded sunroom. Light poured in through the wall of windows, but no amount of sunshine could unshadow the strange feeling in this part of the house. My Docs stood on a box at the threshold of the room where I'd put them after my first round of hiding. The thick heavy soles didn't make a lot of noise, but you couldn't exactly sneak around. One boot had tipped over and lay on its side, and the shadow of the other stretched the length of the hall.

Without a sound, I crept along in my socks. I stopped at Remi's door, and listened for a moment, then went past the permanently sealed attic door, toward our parents' room, which was off-limits.

Being upstairs made my skin crawl. It had been days since we'd ventured to the second story, but with the hallway in front of the parlor stacked with boxed tile, we decided we could risk it up here during the day. Mom didn't want my help retiling the parlor

with her horrendous blue and white patterned tile. Dutch Delft.
I had to admit it complemented the stuff in the driveway, but the
whole bottom floor smelled like mortar, and the air hung thick
with tile dust—which should throw a nice damper on their prayer
circle that evening. Remi and I had been flushed out of our den-
turned-bedroom, and going outside was not an option until the
temperature dropped below a thousand degrees.

It still took a good amount of coaxing to get Remi up the
steps past the landing, but I'd had enough M&Ms in my pocket to
do the trick. Luring the sweet little thing up with candy made me
feel like the witch in *Hansel and Gretel*, but I had to be a big, bad
sister once or twice.

"You won't find me this time," Remi squealed from the room
at the top of the stairs.

I'd gotten the kid *in* the sunroom, but that was as far as
he'd go. Five rounds into hide and seek and we'd run out of things
to hide behind. Mom's unpacking had thus far been limited to
the downstairs, leaving the sunroom a maze of stacked boxes and
furniture.

A lump in the corner shifted under a tattered down comforter that probably used to be blue. I smiled and stepped between
boxes, but ran into a headboard and had to double back. The pile
under the blanket filled the old armchair the way a young man
often might. Remi had never been the best at hide and seek. He
had way too much fun getting caught. And I liked to hear Remi
having fun.

Over the past two weeks, my brother had gone from som-
ber to morose. He'd managed to turn pale during a blazing hot
summer. His hair had dried out to the consistency of old straw.
He'd stopped sleeping and developed big purple bruises under his
green eyes, and whatever was ailing him hadn't improved since
we'd moved in together downstairs. I'd tried everything—day trips
to the art supply store, ice cream, hiding out in the library, movie

binges—but I never got more than a reluctant smile out of the kid. On my end, I hadn't heard anything but crickets on the résumés I'd sent, and my checking account was getting dangerously low.

My first summer out of college was a total bust.

"Have you found me yet?" the gray, boy-shaped blanket tittered from the corner of the sunroom.

"Oh, I will *always* find you," I teased.

But I figured I'd let him have a few extra seconds under wraps. Let him think he had me fooled. If we could get through this summer in good enough spirits, maybe I could go to grad school, support Remi and myself in some cheap apartment on a stipend. I'd been teaching Remi how to work with charcoal over the summer. Maybe I could get a certificate and teach other kids, too—anything to get us the hell away from Vinton. If I waited much longer, Remi would end up a shriveled cornhusk. I stopped talking to Mom about Remi's crippling depression when she kept promising to pray about it.

Super helpful. The prayers, and the holy water Selena gave her to rub on all the doorjambs.

I tiptoed to the armchair, reached out to claim my victory. The threadbare fabric trembled, and the down seemed all gone from the paper-thin blanket. I could almost make out the features of my brother underneath, his nose pointed right at me, and I wondered if he could see me through the fabric. My fingers curled around the corner of the comforter as a voice called out behind me.

"Boo, Britta!" my brother yelled from the doorway. I spun around, a gasp lodged in my throat. I stared, open-mouthed, at the little boy tucked behind the sunroom doorway. Having won, Remi beamed, the best he'd looked in weeks. "Gotcha!" he grinned. The circles under his eyes made him look like a happy little raccoon. I'd enjoy the moment if my heart weren't pounding so hard. "Now you hide," Remi said.

I'd let go of the comforter when Remi surprised me. Whatever sat beneath it looked less like a person now. A cold, prickling sensation crawled up my legs, iced over my tongue.

I did not touch the blanket again. No way. I waited to see if it would move, then swallowed down the lump in my throat and stepped away without looking back.

Why in the hell had I lured Remi upstairs? He had reason to hate it, reasons we both hated being up here.

My voice shook. "Hey, how about we go downstairs, kid?"

"No way, Britta." Remi leaned into the door so it shoved a stack of cardboard boxes. "You know the rules. I don't score a complete victory 'til I find you next round."

I'd crossed the room to my brother, but whatever had hidden under the blanket still watched me—maybe not from that chair, but its eyes bored into the back of my skull as I stood facing Remi. The blanket no longer held the shape of a boy now, but more animal, more *inhuman*. I thought of the things hiding in the magnolia tree out front, and the hairs on my arm stood on end. I brushed my fingertips over to see how rigid the stippled skin was.

There are no such things as ghosts, I told myself, but I'd stopped believing that not too long after crossing the Texas/Louisiana border.

"I forfeit, dude. You win. Completely." I took one more step and felt measurably better once I had my brother's hand in mine. "Maybe Mom's done tiling."

"Just one more time, Britta … please?" Remi whined and pulled a face. "Selena is down there."

"No, I don't think she is."

"She is," he said. "Can't you tell?" I wish I'd thought to ask what he meant by that. "Mom said they're gonna do a prayer circle."

I'd tried not to contaminate the kid with my dislike of Mom's friend—last thing I wanted was to make him worry more—but the way he wrinkled his nose said Selena had done a good job of alienating him on her own. The last time he'd walked in on a prayer circle he'd gotten recruited. Apparently, having a nightmare or two was evidence of demon-haunting, so they had to douse him. I watched, leaning on the mantel, arms crossed, wanting to break the whole show up with the fireplace poker. First, Mom had prayed over him, then Ray mumbled something incoherent, and finally, Selena took a turn.

He'd never said a word about it until now—wouldn't talk about it. Selena just pissed me off, but the woman scared my brother. Almost as scared as he was of the second floor, in fact.

I sighed. Here I was, breaking up the game just because I'd spooked myself. I shook away the shivers and braved a glance back into the sunroom. Whatever I'd seen before, golden light hit a blanket covering a couple of boxes, the kind of innocent arrangement some instructor might set up before class—still life with drapery, nothing more. Silly to think I would've seen anything else. Besides, if Remi could handle being up here, then I could, too.

"One more time, okay?" I said. "Then we go do something else?"

A genuine smile spread across Remi's face, and this time my knees turned to pudding—in a good way. The little gap between his front teeth, the sparkle in my brother's eye, the way his chin tipped up as if the smile would pull him off the ground. I could handle any big, scary blanket, face down whatever monsters the bayou could throw at me, if it earned me one of those smiles.

"Deal," he agreed, pressing his face to the doorjamb to count me out.

"Don't peek," I said, scanning the stacked boxes.

"I won't," he promised, pulling his fingers tightly together. "Ten ..."

I had ten seconds. Less if he skipped a couple of numbers, which was likely. A quick survey of the room revealed no good options. And my eyes kept going to the chair. Nine seconds. Eight seconds. I tiptoed past him into the hallway and considered the stairwell.

Seven seconds. If I went belly down on the stairs he might walk by without spotting me.

A subtle movement down the hall caught my eye. Behind me, Remi's counting sounded far away, underwater. My vision narrowed into a tunnel.

Just before my brother's bedroom, the door to the attic hung open. Wide open. *Impossible.* The doorway was sealed—caulked and painted over. Before we ever got here. I'd tried to open it several times, in vain attempts to convince Remi nothing lurked upstairs to whisper to him.

How in the hell could it come open? My tunnel vision stretched out before me.

The shifty little boy blanket figure got upgraded from a figment of my imagination back to Terror Threat Level Red, whereas my body temperature dropped to zero.

Remi must have finished his count at some point because he stood beside me. His hand slid inside of mine. On a second tug, I tried to look at him without taking my eye off the attic door but only saw that Remi had not walked out to find me. I'd backed all the way into the sunroom and bumped into him. Had I interrupted the poor kid's count just to suck him into crisis mode?

He started to ask what I was doing, then he saw what I saw. "Britta," he whispered. "We have to go." A tremor had crept into his voice, wiping out any hint of the laughter that had been there so briefly. *Goddammit.*

He yanked on my hand again, and I managed to peel my eyes from the door to look at him. He was even paler than usual, lips thin with fear. One of us would have to take the first step, but Remi wrapped himself around my body, clinging to a tree in a storm. "We shouldn't be up here," he whispered. Tears marbled his grass-green eyes.

To get to the stairs, we'd need to move toward the open attic door.

I started to speak, but the door banged shut as if someone had jerked it from inside.

I shoved Remi forward, my grip tight on his shoulder. "Go," I shouted, and we shot into the stairwell. The same sensation prickled up my legs again and I almost fell over Remi on the top step. Eyes crawled across my back. I didn't look up at the landing, didn't stop until our feet touched the hardwood floor of the entryway.

If I'd imagined the shape under the comforter, I had not imagined the sealed door opening and slamming shut on its own.

We crashed into Selena, who must have let herself in through the back door. A cloth bag fell from her shoulder and a couple of candles stuck out, the black wicks showing they'd been used already. She wore a flowing white dress and a pale, mottled mauve scarf—never the colorful, beautiful scarves Mam Byrdie always wore. She looked as if she meant to make herself comfortable for a long visit. As usual.

Ray had anchored himself on the sofa in the living room and didn't raise his head. He'd fallen asleep, pretending to read. He'd been drinking again and trying to hide it. No one else seemed to smell it on his breath. The man hadn't even opened the classifieds since we'd moved in. I guess Vinton wasn't hiring washed-up bodybuilders.

Selena picked up the bag, running her ringed fingers around the bottom of it to check for breaks. "Hello, children," she greeted us, her voice bright and cool. Even with my heart already thundering, a word from her could kick it up a notch. Tomorrow, I'd be twenty-four, a college graduate. Not a child. But Selena wasn't really talking to me anyway. Her eyes were only for Remi.

"Did a door slam?" she asked, peering around me at the stairwell as she picked up her bag.

I couldn't give her the benefit of seeing that all her goddamned stories hadn't just made Remi a nervous wreck, but me as well. I might have a BA in Art History, but I'd mastered in Apathetic. "Wind knocked something shut." I shrugged. "It's drafty."

"Not really," she muttered. Her icy blue eyes had given Remi a mean case of hypothermia. He stared back, feet frozen to the wood floor. I squeezed his shoulder to draw him against me, then joined the staring contest and glared at Selena. Which she'd notice just as soon as she took her eyes off my little brother.

Something had changed about her. Her white hair had deepened to the kind of cornfed blond you can't get with dye, and her skin seemed smoother, a richer olive than before. This new beauty regimen irked me. My brother had dried out, but this bitch had blossomed.

"What do you want, Selena?" I said. "We're busy."

A snore scraped the back of Ray's throat and his book tumbled to the floor.

Thanks for the backup, guy.

Selena's lips curled, a Cheshire cat smiling poison at my brother. "Something bothering you upstairs, Remi, dear?" she cooed.

My brother's body stiffened under my fingers. Her forced sweetness curdled my insides. Forget luring us into an oven with candy-coated bait, this witchy woman would definitely stuff us into an oven if I gave her half a chance.

Remi just gurgled, and Selena's eyes sparkled with satisfaction. "You're looking a little rough around the edges, dear," she said, hitching the cloth bag on her shoulder and crouching so their eyes were level. "Your mother and I, we'll get you feeling better this evening. You aren't getting a lick of sleep—" She nodded toward the den. "Spread out on the floor like that, are you, Remi, dear?"

"C'mon, Rem." I pulled him out of her reach and angled myself between them. I didn't know what Selena was playing at, but she could pick on somebody her own size.

She straightened, taller than me, not by much but enough to look down at me. It did not achieve the desired effect. The threat in her eyes only chased away any pretense of sweetness.

We didn't like each other, plain and simple, and frankly, my dear, I did not give a damn.

I glared at Selena and nudged Remi back toward the front doors. "Come on, kid," I said without breaking eye contact. "Let's go for a walk."

"And what about you, Britta, dear?" Selena's voice stabbed at me. "The house, how has it been treating you?"

Her rigid smile lacked any humor or warmth, but I'd swear the slow way she spoke, and that stiff posture held back laughter roaring behind her ice-blue eyes, ready to rush out.

"It's just a house," I said, matching her cadence.

"It is a *home*," she said, wagging a ringed finger, then the whole jangly hand as if to take in the rooms around us.

The threat in her eyes vanished the second the parlor doors opened behind her.

Mom dropped a cardboard box on top of the stack in the hall. Inside, tiles clattered loud enough that even Ray stirred. One thin arm flopped across his chest, but he didn't wake up. Benefits of a booze-filled snooze.

Selena raised both hands in greeting, bracelets rattling and warmed up that fake smile. "Joan," she cooed, gathering my mother in an embrace. "Does this mean you finished?" They hugged like long-lost sisters, Mom's hands covered with dust the same white as her guest's dress. Then, Selena slid the cloth bag down her arm to show my mom the items inside. A small tin of blue paint, several little stoppered jars of water, some half-melted candles. A length of rope. Some strand of string or thread—or hair—wrapped with a thin white ribbon. A book that could only be a Bible.

"What's all that?" I asked.

Mom didn't look up from the bag, but I could see her face, slack, showing no emotion.

Selena, on the other hand, looked triumphant. "Cleaning supplies," she said.

Maybe the jars were for cleaning, but I didn't see any Windex or paper towels, and I'd bet Mam Byrdie could've ID'd that hairball.

But it was Remi who asked, "What are you cleaning?" his voice small beside me. I wound my loose arm around his trembling shoulders.

"Well, you could say we're cleaning out the house, dear." Selena's smile exposed too many teeth, then she dropped to one knee in front of him. "I intend to do everything in my power to make it easier for you to sleep."

The words would've sounded kind coming out of any other mouth, but her voice hitched on *power* in a way that made my neck itch.

"What is that supposed to mean?" I snapped, looking from one woman to the other. "Mom?"

Mom's bland, self-righteous grin slid back into place, any hesitation gone under Selena's watchful gaze. "Selena's right, Britta. I can feel it, too." She nodded, meeting my eye as if she could cow me into assent. "This is our house," she said. "The Lord's house." She lowered her voice and leaned toward me, but we all stood close enough to hear. She didn't want to wake Ray.

"I have heard the devil knocking at our door," she said, "since we got here. Selena will help us rid the house of his infestation." She straightened her spine and clenched dusty fists, looking at her son, eyes blind with love that had been twisted into something else. "And whatever has latched on to my son."

Piper Laurie throwing Sissy Spacek into the closet under the stairs. Ernest Borgnine yelling about a stench in the nostrils of God. That priest in the *Poltergeist* sequel, way scarier than anything in the first one. Flashbacks to every bad horror movie with religious overtones blinked past as I stared at the candles poking out of Selena's bag. A bubble spun around somewhere in my belly. Best case scenario I could hope for was Father Karras slapping the crap out of Linda Blair. Only fucking problem, my brother was not possessed.

Never mind what had just happened upstairs. The voices that Remi heard. All the knocking and tapping. The eyes watching us. Fine, Selena, I'd give you haunted, fine. Some weird stuff went on in this old house way beyond a little neglect and age. So bust out a Ouija board and I'll play along. But keep your fucking hands off my brother.

"Oh my God, Mom." I mustered up every ounce of authority you get with a college degree and four years in Texas's most populous city, but just sounded like a petulant teen yowling at her mom. "Don't tell me you're going to have an exorcism."

"Britta, dear," Selena clucked. "Please, don't be so dramatic. It's just a little blessing through the power of prayer."

"You're talking about exorcising a demon out of my little brother, and *I'm* being dramatic?" The sick feeling in the pit of my stomach threatened to spill up my throat. "No way. You stay away from him."

My mother's voice called after me, but Remi and I were already running toward the safety of the library, heat radiating off the asphalt like a mirage.

Mr. and Mrs. Marcorelle bought the house from the original owners, the Lemieuxs. Mr. Marcorelle built that carriage house and owned shops in Lake Charles. He spent much of the week there, so after the children grew and moved on, he often left his wife here with only the servants.

A pair of Black girls ran the house for Mrs. Marcorelle, two sisters who'd fled Saint-Dominique by way of New Orleans. She treated them kindly for the most part, but without warmth. It was not uncommon in those days for a family to barely lay eyes on their servants, with the help of a fine-tuned schedule and the sort of passageways you and that little brother of yours have found between the various rooms.

Mrs. Marcorelle only had the women of her church to socialize with, so she confided in them about the sounds she heard through the walls, late at night. It was from them that she first learned about voodoo, and when she heard muttering in a strange language, those women said she was smart to worry.

Her husband disagreed. He derided her, insulted her. She tried and failed to catch the girls in their deviltry. When she and her friends took their concerns to the parish priest, the good pastor did just as you would expect. He spoke to Mr. Marcorelle, who chastised his wife all the more harshly.

Determined to catch the girls in the act, Mrs. Marcorelle pretended to go to sleep, but in her stockinged feet and dressed all in black, she went through that attic door, the one now sealed, next to Remi's bedroom. Mrs. Marcorelle heard voices and saw the glow of candlelight down the passageway. Rather than springing out of bed and banging doors, this time she just had to tiptoe 'round a corner to find her own husband and one of the servant girls, their chests bared, drawing strange symbols on each other in hot red wax.

Mrs. Marcorelle ran barefoot from the house and spent the night with one of her church friends before traveling all the way to New England to be with a cousin. Vinton never heard from her again.

Word got around about what she saw, but Mr. Marcorelle, he laughed it off, said his wife had gone to help an ailing relative. As long as people kept asking he said, "Oh, she'll be back soon." You see, Mr. Marcorelle was an ardent supporter of the Southern Cause, a personal friend of Thomas Moore, and no one much cared what a group of church women had to say about him. However, he left Louisiana before the war. Some say he headed to Atlanta to work more closely with the Confederacy, but others say he went a good deal farther south, with those two sisters.

CHAPTER TWENTY-ONE

I found Alec in my motel room licking his wounds. Figuratively speaking, anyway.

"You and Labaye decide who's the bigger bad?" I tossed the room key on the laminate-finished desk next to him. I didn't make eye contact.

The soft gray glow of dawn lit the horizon outside. I didn't ask how Alec got in, didn't even wonder. Tired, exhausted in a way sleep would never cure, I wasn't happy to see my pack mate for too many reasons to list. I wanted to rest, maybe take a shower. Eat something I didn't have to kill. Check for any clean clothes in my carry-on. Figure out which one of these two guys was out to get me, what to do about it, and how to help Remi—and avoid dying for real in the process.

The door fell shut behind me, sucking itself closed. I dropped the armload of clothes I'd recovered from behind Remi's fireplace, threw myself on the bed, and busied myself undoing the laces of my oxblood Docs, which I'd slipped on sans the socks. I'd left the room pretty late yesterday, so housekeeping hadn't ventured into the monster's lair. The butcher's paper from my Market Basket takeout had started to stink.

Alec reclined shirtless in the desk chair and glared over at me. He'd tucked a bloodstained pillow between his waist and the flimsy armrest.

"I'm not mad at you," he said, "for picking the wrong side back there. It was impulsive of me, going in like that." He poked around in his ribcage with something and used it to flick a small piece of metal out. The crunched remains of soft steel rolled down the pillow and disappeared into the pattern of the carpet. I thought of the foot-fungus smell of the motel floor and figured he was smart to keep his boots on. "Killing a pair of cops in their own precinct," he said, "might have come back to haunt me."

If he hadn't been plucking bullets out of his torso, he could've passed for Canova's *Endymion*, the black leather pants contrasting against his pale skin. He reached into the ice bucket on the desk, pulled out a dripping pink hand towel, and wiped the blood from his hip. The glare he'd greeted me with had softened, and Alec looked more or less as he always did, as though the evening's activities had been a pleasant stroll in the park instead of an all-out brawl in a police evidence locker. He tended to his injuries with the interest a dog would show as it groomed itself. But one arm moved with care and effort, and I guessed the bones Labaye had snapped with the locker door had only begun to knit back together. The tattered shreds of Alec's shirt hung over the back of the chair, but the peacoat seemed to have made it through the ordeal unharmed, hanging loosely from a hook by the door. Labaye had made a mark on old Alec, though, that's for sure.

Good for him. Though I still wasn't sure which of these two idiots to root for.

"You surprised me, going after him on two legs," I said. "Then I thought, Alec doesn't want to risk turning my cop buddy." I managed to wrestle both shoes off and toss them thudding across the floor.

"What?" he barked. "I wouldn't have turned your 'buddy.'" The facecloth wiped away the red to show bullet holes already scarred over. "I would have killed him."

"You don't want to spread the curse to any likely competition." Splaying my toes, I leaned against the headboard. Without socks, the Doc Martens had wrought havoc on my little piggies, but it was so much easier to breathe when I didn't have to stand.

"Britta, we are not cursed, we are not undead," Alec sputtered. He raised his fist, showing off the complimentary motel pen he'd been jabbing between his ribs. "Does dead flesh heal, Britta?" He slapped his chest. "What kind of curse makes its victim indestructible?" Even when Alec got angry he managed to look a little regal, but only I could get him so exasperated.

He sighed. We'd both had a long night. "Instead of provoking me," he said, "you should be wondering about your witch's missing remains."

"I had an idea, but it didn't pan out." I exhaled and sunk lower into the mattress.

"Is that where you went?" Alec asked, poking a finger at the spot on his stomach, smooth and perfect again. A shot like that would have had me down for days, but Alec was old, and the older the wolf, the faster they healed. "I tried to find you," he said, "but lost your scent."

"Are you my mother now, Alec?" The words lacked the sting I'd hoped for.

He leveled a disapproving look in my direction, and he could not have known how well it matched the one my actual mother would have shot my way. He set the bloody pen on the stained cloth and rose to his feet with liquid grace. Stalking toward me, predatory and sensual, he spread bare arms wide open like he was coming in for a hug.

The glimpse I'd had of my mother's face in the library flashed again, momentarily obscuring Alec's advance. Something inside me snapped. It had been so much easier to stay mad at her. To blame her, to hate her for bringing Selena into our lives. But poor, poor Joan Hall had only ever acted out of love, even if it was misguided.

"I'm your friend, your true friend," Alec said, right over me, his voice calm, softer than I ever remembered hearing him.

He pulled me off the bed and to my feet, into his arms, and I let him. His fingers curled around the knob of one shoulder, and his other hand lifted my chin to look at his face. I let him do that, too—it wasn't worth the energy to struggle. I'd thought seeing Remi would energize me, but it just left me more hollow than ever. Maybe I didn't have the strength to do this after all. Maybe even from the grave Selena could defeat me.

Alec's hand squeezed my shoulder, his thumb massaging a little circle on my collarbone. It felt good to have strong hands on me, stronger than Paul Beaulieu's the other night. Alec's fingers pressed my shoulder like hitting a release button. How many times had I told myself I'd never let him touch me like this? And what had Remi said—*He pretends to care.* Maybe he meant Alec, it was hard to imagine him sincerely caring about anyone, but he'd never hurt me.

Though with Alec it was never black and white—hurt me or not hurt me. Other than his infallible black peacoat and his silver wolfcoat, he existed entirely in the gray.

I snapped my eyes open and lost myself in the burning gold of Alec's attention. It was too hot to be sympathy, too fierce for affection, all sharp around the edges. A fire passed between us. Passion is never placid, not quiet or shy—maybe a little mutual contempt helps mask the fear you could lose yourself in someone else. Perhaps Alec and I just ran down the razor's edge of good old-fashioned wolf lust and rage, the line between the two often blurry and sometimes bloody. I'd never been interested in Alec, not *that* way, but sometimes my wolf felt differently. She responded to power and passion—we all respond to what we have in short supply. Her heat rushed through me, but it wasn't just my wolf whose hunger Alec stoked. Not this time.

"I'm your friend." Alec breathed the words, voice soft as my hand touched his cheek. He pulled me up against his unnatural heartbeat. His lips brushed mine, and the heat under my skin nearly boiled over. "But I would be your mate if you'd have me," he said. "Be my Luna, so we can free your brother together."

I blinked. My hand on his face froze so solid I could scrape out his eyes. And just like that, Alec's salt-fire words brought the world back into focus.

I backed out of his grasp, cooling off in every sense of the word. I wished the dress Mam Byrdie had put me in went down to my ankles, wished it was sackcloth instead of cotton.

My breath rushed out in a frustrated heave. "I gave you my answer, Alec." I spit each word at him. "It's still no."

"Why not?" His amber eyes sparkled, he grinned. Alec inched closer, nothing sensual in his approach, just a fiery challenge, voice cool behind the trademark smirk he'd greeted me with at the house. "You desire me," he said. "Your wolf approves. We're a perfect match, Britta." The smirk vanished and he tilted his chin down. "At my side, you would be stronger than you could ever dream of being on your own."

The wall pressed against my back. If he came any closer, this time I'd fight.

His smile returned, smug as hell. He liked having a woman cornered.

There. That was the Alec I knew.

I swept my eyes slowly down his torso, the black pants and boots, everything Alec had to offer. I still had the body of an art student, but eventually life undead would render me in Neoclassical marble, the way it had Alec. Physically, he was flawless. Unfortunately, the long list of his defects covered every other area.

"I don't owe you an explanation," I growled. "Take *no* like a good boy and back off."

The flame in his eyes turned to coal, his face slack. "You've made a mistake tonight, Britta," he deadpanned. He didn't step away. "Almost."

Alec sneered, and, after a long glare, stomped back to the

desk. He rolled his shoulders and suddenly seemed an inch taller—seemed to make up his mind about something. The air shifted, and I stood in the room with a stranger.

"When I am alpha, you will regret this decision," he said and scratched a spot of crusted blood from his hip.

I'd almost forgotten Alec's plans. "You've got a long climb ahead if you plan to reach the top," I said, trying to recall a time when he might have come up with this idea of wolf domination. Probably he'd been planning since before I'd known him—maybe he only brought me to Malakh in the first place to someday unseat him. Very proactive, Alec.

The hairs on the back of my neck stood on end, and my wolf bared her teeth in an entirely new way.

"I wouldn't bite off more than I can chew," I said. "Distemper isn't a good trait in a leader."

Alec just smirked. "I have quite an appetite, Britta. I will happily show you how big it is."

I reconsidered my former assumption that Alec wouldn't hurt me. He might not kill me, but he might just hurt me to prove he could. And, judging by the way the grin widened to show teeth, he might enjoy it, too.

When scared, act defiant, right?

I rolled my eyes. "If the fight's between you and Malakh, you've already lost. Once he hears you want to depose him ..." I dragged a finger across my throat and stuck my tongue out the side of my mouth.

He advanced. I backed up despite myself. Reflexes. Damn. The heat rolled off Alec.

"You would have been such a good Luna," he said with that rare full smile. I could see he forced it. "Strong, but malleable." His eyes passed across the V-neck of my dress. "Full of anger. Eager to redirect your guilt," he spat, and our eyes locked hard together. "Oh, Britta, you could be so much if ... if you didn't use that strength to hold yourself back." He straightened his arms down his sides. He clenched both fists, but the hand that had been slammed in the cooler door didn't close all the way. He laughed. "I thought I could shift your perspective, so to speak. But you're too stubborn for your own good, and—" He shrugged. "Emotionally, too weak."

He exhaled for effect, face twisting into a mask of sadness. "It's a shame it must be this way, Britta. On the other hand, you may actually be more useful as a martyr." Alec loves a reaction. I didn't give him one. "I kill you," he went on, "and Malakh will have no choice but to confront me for my crime. You see, if you and I attacked Malakh unprovoked, others might dissent when I rose to alpha. But no one will really care if I kill you. Malakh will be obliged to face me, the law of the pack and all." He laughed. "Malakh challenges me, I kill him. A cleaner line of succession."

Okay, so maybe he *would* kill me.

Alec's teeth lengthened into fangs and his fingers stretched into claws. Blood pounded through his limbs. I could almost see the heat rise off him.

I looked at my Docs across the carpet and wished I'd kept them on, wish I'd recovered the leather jacket.

If Alec changed in this room, he'd tear me to pieces and just run back to Maine.

"I talked to my brother tonight," I said, voice as flat and unafraid as I could make it. Alec paused mid-shift. "Summoned his spirit with help from a friend—a powerful friend. He warned me about you, Alec."

My wolf paced along the inside of her skin prison.

A cruel smile carved itself across his face, a wolf's smile, long and full of fangs. "You let your brother die, Britta. Soon you'll be with him." He lisped a little—if he changed any more, at least he wouldn't be able to taunt me. "*That* is your curse."

He growled and slammed a hand on either side of my head, his claws stabbing into the sheetrock above my shoulders.

But Alec went easy on the arm that Labaye had broken, and that was my chance. My body was a kiln, it sucked up Alec's heat. My wolf snarled, grinding her paws into my veins. I swung a fist with all my might, tight across my chest, and punched Alec's forearm. Felt the bone give under my knuckles.

He whirled and sat hard on the bed. I lunged for the door, got it open just an inch before he slammed me into the cheap composite head first, shutting the door so hard it rattled the whole room. The bad arm hung tight to his ribcage, but the other forearm clotheslined me into the door and held me there.

Rage rushed through me. I dropped the veil I kept between my wolf and me, called her, and she came running. Her fur ruffled against my skin, and I grabbed both hands around Alec's throat and held tight. The magic I'd tried for a decade to control rushed through my body, freed by his betrayal.

If you insist on calling yourself a monster, then stand and be the beast, Mam Byrdie had said just hours ago.

Alec sensed my turn, and with a quick jerk, made for my throat. I slammed my knee into his still-human groin and sent him to the floor. One boot flailed out and sent the chair slamming against the wall. I fell on top of him on the carpet, stabbed my claws into his bad forearm, and his crotch.

"If you're going to pin someone," I barked with my still-human mouth, flexing my hands, enjoying his grimace, "hold them by the meat, see?"

Alec struggled beneath me, but he couldn't move. When he looked at me again fear had overtaken the surprise in his yellow eyes.

"Shut the fuck up in there!" A voice came from next door. A second voice said something and the two went back and forth, then pounded the wall.

"Prey … for us …" Alec hissed and winked. "Come on, Britta," he whispered and inhaled deeply, his snout an inch from mine. "Are you going to allow these rednecks to speak to you like that?"

"All I care about is Remi."

My voice faltered as I said it, and Alec rolled out from under me. "I apologize, Britta," he said, as I lay on my side on the stinking carpet. He straightened, then bent the bad arm, testing the elbow and wincing. "But I've given you my answer. I can't help you."

"You asshole," I said. I hugged myself, running my hands over my bare arms. The wolfcoat had receded.

Alec got to his feet before me. Even with the broken arm, he was the better wolf.

He ran his hands over the desk. "I'm sorry we couldn't work something out, Britta." I had his blood in my fingernails but hadn't left a mark on him. When he crouched beside me, I scrabbled back away from the door, my back hitting the bed. Alec laughed.

He took his peacoat from the hook and shrugged into it, still babying the bad arm. He put a hand to his ear, raised an eyebrow in a caricature of listening. One of my neighbors snored, inaudible to anyone but the two of us.

Alec opened the door, and said, "Please, get into bed, Britta. You might catch something lying on that carpet." After the door shut, I listened to his boots tapping down the carpeted hallway.

CHAPTER TWENTY-TWO

Devereaux drove his old Lincoln to the ER in Sulphur without sirens or lights, but made it in fifteen minutes flat on the state highway, faster than the interstate at that time of night, all while polishing off two Marlboros. At the hospital, he and Labaye deferred to the other late-night clientele, despite a kind offer from the registrar to get the injured rookie roomed right away.

An older woman rolled her wheelchair back and forth in front of the window. She asked to be seen by a certain person, and would not let up no matter how many times the registrar explained that the doctor she requested—demanded—worked the neonatal ward. Devereaux rolled his eyes at the younger policeman, whose laugh broke into a cough he tried to cover up.

Aaron pressed the bad fist to his lips. Devereaux had cleaned the cut, then wrapped the hand up like a boxer's, while two paramedics loaded Officer McKelvie out of the precinct and into the ambulance. With one jumbo bandage and a yard of gauze from the first-aid locker, Devereaux had done a reasonable job on Aaron's hand, but it'd need stitches, and half a dozen other aches and pains warranted attention. Labaye's fingers stuck out crooked from the gauze. He just hoped none were broken.

Devereaux walked back into the ER from his second smoke break, a fresh one tucked behind his ear. He said something, but the sound bounced off Aaron's ears, faded in a rush, and he had to ask the man to repeat it.

"You ever come to the old hospital?" Devereaux said. He'd

taken his jacket and tie off, folded them on the chair beside him. Four purple lines bruised Devereaux right under the twitchy jowls. Alec's grip had left a softer blue blur of a mark around the wrist when he'd disarmed the detective. The bruises looked sickly in the fluorescent light at two a.m., and Labaye knew the effect must look far worse on him.

"What? Yeah, of course." Aaron forced a smile. His face was about the only thing that didn't hurt. "You know, you can probably get out of here, Devereaux. Doesn't look like he got you too bad. Someone can pick me up later."

"This is where we took Britta and her family that night." Devereaux let his words hang in the air a minute. "Before they built the new place," he said, sweeping his eyes around the ER. Aaron had been to the old hospital at least once as a teenager, but couldn't remember what it looked like then. He didn't figure Devereaux was thinking much about the architecture.

"We knew that the kid, the little boy," Devereaux went on, "he was dead as soon as we got there. The parents, jeez, never mind." He leaned back with a huge sigh, kicked his boots out, and threw his arms across the backs of the beige padded chairs. Aaron shifted forward on reflex, and pain stabbed down his back. Devereaux drew his arm away and wiped his mustache.

An ambulance pulled up outside the dark glass doors. It stopped with its beacons on, but no siren and no one got out. The automatic doors stood open for a few minutes, and the room warmed up just enough to notice. Aaron liked the blue popping into the shadows around him, flashing across the other man's eyes.

Devereaux pulled on his mustache again and shifted his weight in the seat to face Aaron.

"Look, Labaye," he said, and the men locked eyes. Rather than fade over the course of the day, Devereaux's coffee breath stank worse than ever this time of night. "You know what's going on with that girl, right?"

Aaron cocked his head to one side and waited. He didn't want to grin but needed to look curious.

"What I'm saying is," Devereaux whispered, "*I* know."

Aaron drew a serious face. "You're still talking about Britta Orchid?"

Devereaux faced front again and gripped his knees. The automatic doors closed, and the air started to chill again. He flicked his eyes at the younger cop. "I know she's a victim in all this. I get that." He checked Aaron's eyes for a reaction, and when he got none, he grunted and tugged on the mustache. "You gotta steer clear of this whole frigging thing, kid," Devereaux said.

"Wait," Aaron said. "Do you think Miss Orchid has something to do with the death of Selena Stone after all?"

Devereaux studied Aaron's face. He scratched the side of his head and had to replace the cigarette behind the ear. After a couple of false starts, he said, "I saw it one time before." He heaved a sigh. "You can look right into the ... into the face of weird shit," he stressed the words as though they held a particular meaning, "and tell yourself it's something else." Devereaux waited, and when Aaron didn't speak, he added, "It's better to call it what it is, and—" He pounded his thigh to punctuate the last few words. "Just act smart."

In the corner of his eye, Aaron saw the ambulance pull away, and the blue light vanished from Devereaux's face, leaving only the bruise on his neck.

Alec's grip had been so powerful, the wrist so thin. Aaron flashed back to his first meeting with Britta in the interview room. He hadn't known then how well she could've backed up all that bluster, but he figured he had a pretty good idea now.

Through a long silence, neither man looked away.

Labaye's name rang out from the overhead speaker. He dropped the serious look and allowed a smirk. He raised his good hand and floated a fist in front of Deveraux, who looked at it for a moment as if he didn't know what it was, then lifted his fist in slow motion and bumped it against Labaye's.

"Call it a night," Aaron said. "They'll want to really check me out, I think. But seriously, Ernie, thank you. You had my back back there."

Officer Labaye limped across the lobby toward a door held open by a young woman with jet black hair and dark chocolate eyes, a sheet of paper in her free hand. He nursed the charley horse the werewolf had given him as a parting shot and didn't look back to see if the detective was watching him go.

Britta stepped aside and waved an arm to usher Aaron in through the motel door. She surprised him by not grabbing the leather jacket out of his good hand. He waved at her with his other hand so she'd see the bandage immediately, but she'd already turned away.

The dress, although black, didn't seem quite her style.

Outside, the overcast sunrise had resolved into a bright early morning. He couldn't tell if she'd slept. In Britta's small room, a few unpleasant stenches competed for his attention, a shredded shirt lay over the back of a chair, and an ice bucket and a bloody face cloth sat on the cheap Formica desk.

"We busted a meth head down the hall," he said, "my second week."

"Bet you say that to all the girls." Britta collapsed on the bed.

He hung her jacket on a hook by the door.

She was quiet for a moment, and Aaron gave her time to gather her thoughts before she blinked and shifted her gaze back to him. He'd never known a woman to speak so much through her eyes. Now she studied his splinted hand, the ring finger propped straight out, and she seemed to tally up his visible bruises. Besides the hand and wrist, his back hurt the worst, but if he didn't move she couldn't tell.

Her eyes looked animal and fierce, but not like when she'd confronted him in the house. She may still be angry, but the Britta he'd faced earlier wouldn't have let him in the room, certainly wouldn't turn her back on him to lie down. To make sure she wouldn't think he tried hiding it, he flashed his windbreaker open so she could see the shoulder holster, though he'd be reluctant to use it with his hand the way it was.

"What are you doing here, Labaye?" she grunted into the pillow. "You're low on the list of people I want to see right now."

Despite her tone, a smile tugged at the corner of her lips, though he could have imagined it. She sat up, crossed her arms, and leaned against the wall.

When she didn't ask him to go, Aaron made another scan of the scene. What seemed to be fresh punctures, maybe from claws, marked the sheetrock. A pillow stained bright red had been tossed in a corner.

He waved his injured hand at the chair and she nodded, so he limped over and sat down, gently, so as to not rattle his aching back. Warm satisfaction melted away some of the aches in his shoulders when he spotted a little knot of lead on the desk, wet and red. Alec had been here.

"You look like hell by the way," Britta said and crossed her arms high and defiant over her chest.

His ribs hurt when he laughed, the chortle turned into a cough again. He pulled his hand into his lap, wincing at the sharp stab of pain that fired up his arm. "You ought to see the other guy."

"That guy was my one friend the last ten years. Pretty sure I just sent him running home with his tail between his legs."

"So to speak," he added.

Britta sniffed the air, then wiped at her nose without uncrossing her arms. "Hiding anything else under your windbreaker?" She closed her eyes and shook her head. "Injury-wise, I mean."

His weak smile took too much effort. "Just the usual."

She unwound her arms. She seemed a different person altogether in that black dress, bare feet stretched across the mattress. Softer, somehow, perhaps more like the girl she might have been before the … incident. He didn't figure her one to succumb to flattery but couldn't resist.

"You, on the other hand, are a sight for sore eyes," he said.

Just like that, her arms were back over her breasts. Her chin went up and she stared at him through narrowed eyes, her tone sharper than the pain in his broken finger. "Why were you in my house earlier?"

He cleared his throat. "After we found Selena's remains, we searched the house top to bottom without finding the space behind the fireplace. You were good enough to take me there, so I had to process it …" He shot her as best a reassuring look as he could manage. "And I had to do it alone if I wanted to leave out certain aspects of my experience there. I was on my way out when I bumped into you and your … friend."

Britta scoffed. "Alec is no longer my friend."

Aaron raised an eyebrow but kept his mouth shut. He jerked the thumb on his good hand toward the leather jacket hanging by the door. "Got you that. Nice dress, by the way."

She shot him a scowl worthy of a petulant toddler and reached out her hand toward the jacket. He got to his feet with effort, grabbed the jacket, and tossed it on the bed.

She slid into it, pulling the zipper halfway up. She exhaled long and slow and sank into the mattress.

"So," she said, "speaking of the witch. Was that all an act, telling Alec you lost her remains?"

"Excuse me?" he said. "No, I was going to ask you about that. If you didn't take them, and he didn't, any thoughts on who did?"

"No." She didn't look at him when she answered, but Aaron decided not to push his luck. If she didn't want to share her secrets, now wasn't the time to push.

"Actually I was hiding something else, I guess," he added, dipping his good hand into his jacket pocket.

Britta looked at him, eyes fully flame on, as he produced the small vial of cloudy green fluid. Aaron noted her hand move to where her jeans pocket would be.

"Where'd you get that?" she asked.

He approached with caution, holding it out to her. "With the jacket. Any idea what it is?"

She surprised him with the truth. "If we had any of the scrying mirror left, we could use it to summon Remi." Her face fell as she said it.

Aaron reached inside his windbreaker and pulled out a fuzzy gray chunk of cloth not much bigger than his hand. It clinked when he set it on the bed, and Britta jerked her feet away. When she gasped, he knew she recognized the fabric. He unfolded it to reveal two fragile slices of black glass, each the size of a playing card torn diagonally. "Will this work?"

Britta's lips moved a few times before any words came out. "The fuck, Labaye. This is how you process a crime scene?"

"Sorry about Roscoe."

"Rothko." She dropped the vial on the bed. "Like the painter. Art grad, remember?" she added when he quirked an eyebrow.

Britta plucked one piece of the mirror up with care, turning it to catch her own reflection, or maybe looking for something else. "It's shattered. Obviously. I just don't know how much of it I need for the magic to work."

He held out his hand and she gave the glass to him, then collapsed onto her pillow. He laid one piece of mirror on top of the other and folded the scrap of Remi's stuffed elephant around them. He picked up the little bundle in his good hand, the vial of green potion in the other, and set them both on the laminate desk next to the ice bucket.

When he turned around, Britta's eyes were closed.

Grateful to have a moment just to look at her, Aaron pulled his jacket off with care and dropped it over the back of the chair. He knew he shouldn't let himself get too attached, but the unfamiliar sensation moved in his stomach again, pulling so deeply from within it might have been his soul that stirred. It wasn't just desire he felt when he looked at her, but something else. Something stronger. He didn't have a word for it any more than he had a way to deny its existence.

Britta didn't open her eyes again until he sat down, and even then, she averted her gaze. The weight of things unsaid made the air in the room thick, but not unpleasant.

"So, what now?" he asked.

"I need a nap. You could, too."

She was right. Aaron sank into the chair, as far as you can sink in the kind of bargain basement office chair found in a highway motel. "Nap," he instructed. "I'm a little sore, but not tired. I'll keep watch."

"I don't need you to protect me, Labaye," Britta said, but for once her words had no bite. The pounding of nearby eighteen-wheelers barreling along the interstate punctuated the quiet of the room. "I can take care of myself."

"Got any music?" he asked, and she surprised him by patting the mattress beside her.

Moving over to make as much room as possible, Britta fiddled with her phone on the bedside table. Labaye limped around the far side of the bed, kicked off his tactical boots so they banged against the decades-old baseboard heater, and lay on top of the covers beside her. The tension in his back eased slowly and his heart thrummed in his ears.

Taking a nap, Aaron told himself, trying not to feel Britta's warmth at his side.

His heartbeat was in his neck as Britta rolled over and looked at him. A woman's soft voice spoke from her phone. Aaron had only ever touched Britta in her wolf form, and now she lay next to him, flesh and heat in her leather jacket and the early morning light coming through gaps in the thick, dark curtains drawn across the long window, and he had never wanted anything more than to touch this woman. He rested his bandaged hand on his hip, so he didn't need to leave too much space between them.

Britta Orchid looked at him, her face soft, serene, and she took a deep breath, then crinkled her nose.

Aaron had a terrible thought.

"Do I smell bad?" he asked. He'd gone a whole day, not to mention fought a goddamned werewolf, since his last shower.

She closed her eyes and let out a soft laugh. She rolled away from him, but to his complete surprise, she scooted back, curling spoon-like into the curve of his body.

"No," she said, "you don't." The soothing tones of the podcast sounded like a lullaby.

His heart opened. His midsection felt hollowed out. And he realized he might not be able to let her go.

He braced for impact and put his arm around her. Britta stiffened at the touch, then relaxed, and within minutes her breath had fallen into the rhythm of sleep.

CHAPTER TWENTY-THREE

It was a beautiful morning, sunny but not too hot, bright but not glaring, and the warm breeze that rustled the trees along Rice Street sent silver highlights dancing at the edge of my vision. I pushed my loose hair back and sipped from the to-go cup. We'd had to ask for the cardboard cozies, which probably cost extra since they had *The Coffee Stain* printed on them.

"The main character's this older woman, right?" Labaye said. He kept his bad hand in the pocket of his windbreaker as we walked around the playground by the library. I wondered if Mam Byrdie watched me from inside.

He hadn't slept a wink, so I'd asked him to bring me up to date on the podcast I'd snored through. "Yeah," I said. "She wants to prove her niece didn't kill her fiancé."

"The niece's fiancé?" he said. "Not the aunt's?"

"Jesus, Labaye, did you listen or not?"

He almost spit coffee. "Well, you didn't mention any of these characters the other night."

I leaned back into the playground fence, more comfortable now in black jeans, long sleeve black T, Docs, and thank God that leather jacket. "I tried to draw you in with the crime scene."

"Sure, appeal to my professionalism." Labaye kicked at the dirt path. "A sunken ship, with a haunted portrait of some wizard." I nodded, holding in a laugh. "Okay," he said and shook his head, serious again. "So, the aunt knew this curse wasn't the most promising way to clear her niece's name. Especially after they recovered

217

a bloody hammer covered with the niece's fingerprints."

"Oh." I raised my eyebrows.

I didn't know if our morning walk was more to neutralize the heat we'd generated, curled up on my bed, or to delay the inevitable trip back to the house. We still had to stop by the Market Basket to see if they had what we needed—the nearest hardware store was half an hour out of town.

I thought of Scarlett O'Hara's visit to the mill to distract Ashley while his wife prepped for his birthday bash. When Ashley's sister caught him and Scarlett in an innocent hug, rumor of an affair raged across Atlanta. As Labaye explained how the podcast ended, I scanned the park, the streets around it, less worried about sparking romantic gossip than having someone recognize the girl who'd let her baby brother die. I pictured the villagers gathering their torches and their pitchforks. Of course, if they knew what I really was, perhaps it would be silver bullets instead.

"The police took apart his boat and found the hammer inside the hull. So that was kind of it for the niece. By then the aunt was obsessed with the painting, though. She got this professional diver to look for the old sunken ship. Problem is, the aunt insisted on going down with him. He swears she didn't pay him extra, but why did he do it? See, he's on the podcast, talks about the moment they found the canvas. But three hundred years of saltwater can wreak havoc on an oil painting. The aunt was so upset, she tangled her lines or something, and drowned—right there over the canvas. So ... cursed? Of course, there's no telling if the blank canvas they found was *that* portrait, the wizard guy. Maybe it used to be a bowl of fruit. Now the aunt's dead, who knows if there ever was a haunted painting, and the best part—the podcaster interviewed the diver in prison. Thirteen months for involuntary manslaughter. He had no business taking the aunt that deep. The niece's lawyers denied requests for an interview, as her trial drags on and on." Labaye shook his head.

"Good morning, Britta."

I had dropped my vigilance on the good townsfolk of Vinton.

There, alongside the fence, stood Paul Beaulieu, and his little dog, too.

"Oh, uh, hello, Paul," I said. I kept my eyes on the dog, Clarence, and made awkward gestures between the two men. "This is Officer Labaye."

"Aaron," my accomplice said, extending his good hand to Paul while looking at me. "Nice to meet you."

Manners don't cost a thing.

"Paul lived next door." If I could have been more concise I think I would have.

They shook hands and smiled. Paul said, "You never said goodbye."

I drummed a sharp paradiddle on the fence post and my mouth made the tightest, flattest line it could. I have no lips and I must scream.

"I'm sorry about that," I said. "I'm just glad that I got to see you." A lock of hair, silver-gray as moonlight, blew in front of my eyes. I did nothing to remove it.

Paul asked, in a small-talk sort of way, if Labaye had hurt the hand chasing bad guys, and Labaye technically did not lie but answered in a way you'd think involved a broken window. Paul didn't ask about the bruises, if he noticed them, and said his uncle had been a cop in Lake Charles—but stopped midsentence when I hazarded a glance his way. He locked eyes on me, confused.

I'd left my contacts in the motel lavatory.

Labaye set his to-go cup on the grass and knelt down to pet Clarence. Smart move, wish I'd thought of that.

"Paul, it was so nice to meet you," Labaye said, as he scratched hard at the back of Clarence's neck. There's really nothing that feels quite like that. "Miss Orchid and I have a little police business to conclude," he said without looking up. "So, if you and this fine young man will excuse us …"

We said our goodbyes, and in my head, I silently thanked Paul for keeping it polite.

Labaye followed me across the library parking lot toward his Chevy parked at the corner. My heart started to pump again, and immediately my temperature soared. I wanted to run, not to get away so much as to feel the blood hammer through my legs, my four long, lethal legs. I passed a trashcan set inside a concrete container and whipped my cup at the plastic dome lid.

But the empty cup bounced off the swing door, which did not swing one bit. The cup rolled across the hot top, and behind me, Labaye burst out laughing. I turned to glare at him, and he just shook his head, leaned over to pick up the cup with his bad hand, the injured ring finger poking out straight. With seemingly no effort at all, and with a damaged wing at that, he landed both our cups in the bin and let the lid pendulum back and forth as he limped past me, rattling the keyring on his belt.

CHAPTER TWENTY-FOUR

Bleach weighed down the air in the Hall Murder House, so I couldn't break apart the individual scents under its sharp odor. There should have been other smells—rotting carpet, mildew, Labaye, the chalk in our shopping bag, even traces of Alec's presence last night—but all I got was chemicals. Bleach permeated everything. More, it seemed, than the day before.

If anything nasty lurked upstairs or in the crawlspaces, I'd never smell it coming. My best preternatural defense mechanism had been rendered useless by Clorox.

I took little sniffs so my lungs didn't catch fire. The acrid air made an odd juxtaposition to the vibe in the house, soft and gray and sterile as a tomb. Daylight filtered in through the dirty windowpanes, filling the house with a kind of spectral fog. And while the sun climbed higher outside, it stayed colder than it should be in here. The chill in the air suggested the house knew what was coming.

I looked up into the stairwell. Labaye threw the deadbolt behind me and rattled each of the glass doorknobs. Black splinters of the scrying mirror made a shiny bruise on the dusty floorboards at his feet.

Those first few solid hours of sleep I'd gotten since coming to Louisiana, with Labaye curled up at my back, had lulled me into a false sense of security. I looked back at him, at the grocery bag tucked in his good arm, full of the things I needed to summon Remi. I patted my jacket pocket just hard enough to hear glass click together.

I'd walked through those front doors less nervous than any of the times I'd come in this week. No memories, no reticence. It seemed impossible that I had ever lived here, much less died in some little room behind a fireplace. I stood scanning the first floor of nothing more than a crappy, old, depressing house whose better days ended more than a century ago.

It wasn't just the confidence I'd felt when Alec and I had walked upstairs. I felt power, felt it now as my foot landed on the first step.

Be the beast, Mam Byrdie had instructed me. And I was.

If this place had any bogeyman, it was me.

"We're doing this?" Labaye's voice slid over my shoulder before I could make it to stair two, his breath tickling my neck. He'd clammed up since the park. If we needed to talk about Paul, it would wait. He switched the bag to the other arm, maybe to keep his good hand free.

I resisted the urge to shiver as his palm touched the small of my back. His pulse thumped against my spine, even through the leather jacket, and something stirred low in my stomach. The touch showed no particular affection—he could've been motioning me into a holding cell—but at the moment it felt like more. My wolf thought so, too. She arched her back into the warm spot where his hand made contact.

I pressed her down into the hollow space inside.

"Getting a little touchy there, Officer," I said, "for someone who's barely said two words since the grocery store."

His fingers went stiff before they fell away. "Sorry. I guess I'm just … preoccupied."

"Laconic is my thing, Labaye. You're the chatty one."

"Guess you're rubbing off on me," he shot back, and I hoped he wasn't making a pun about the cuddling.

I pivoted to face him. In our first meeting, he'd proven he could wait out a silence as well as me.

He shifted the bag back to the other arm. "I'm just checking things off in my head," he said. "Making sure we didn't forget anything."

I patted my jacket pocket and jerked my chin at the bag. "Good idea, about the sidewalk chalk. I wouldn't have thought of that. Candles, salt. That better do it," I said. "Not like either of us have done this before."

He shrugged, fingers darting inside his windbreaker, probably to check the holster. Sweat trickled around the pulse in his throat. "That's exactly what I'm worried about."

I made a conscious effort to soften my tone as the scent of his fear mixed with his usual musk. "Why don't you stay down here." I nodded at the gun hiding under his windbreaker. "Stand guard for me."

He sucked up a whiff of bleach like a champ, and his dark eyes bored into mine. "I don't think that's an option."

"This isn't your fight. It's mine."

He shook his head. The man looked grim but stood firm.

I smiled as I turned back up the stairs.

For better or worse, Labaye was with me.

Remi's old bedroom was dark, the walls faded to gray even at high noon.

Labaye pushed the small door at the back of the fireplace open with his boot, but I crawled through first. He handed me a small black Maglite, which I clicked on for his benefit. He pushed the bag ahead of him as he followed, struggling with the stiffness from the night before, and unfolded himself at my side in the brick-lined alcove, brushing a layer of ash from his jeans. I didn't bother worrying about mine, though it stood out more on black.

The cleaning crew had never doused the crawlspace in bleach, so I could better smell his fear. I stood the Maglite up in a corner, casting sharp shadows up the bricks, dimly filling the space above the rafters.

My stomach grumbled.

Not with hunger. Definitely not desire. Or whatever it was about Labaye that usually got to me.

This place. The dread had set in at the top of the stairs, grown heavier as we turned from the sunroom, with every step past Mom's room, creeping toward the sealed attic door. I swallowed the lump in my throat and tried to breathe my racing pulse down to a light trot.

It's just a room. Just a room. *Right.*

I'd sure managed to muse a bunch of stoic bullshit standing two feet inside the fucking front door.

Nothing to see here, just a little brick box sandwiched high in the guts of an old house. With Selena's circle broken, I could even see in the dark, though not into the blackest corners. I took a deep breath, let it rustle the fur of the wolf inside. Dust from a broken mirror—nothing big enough to work with—old chalk dust, and the pieces of easel and the rocking chair told the story of the fight between Labaye and my poor little brother.

It's just a room.

Pushing my hand in my jacket pocket, I thumbed the vial to the side and squeezed poor, deflated, old Rothko. The two pieces of glass inside him scraped together. We had the mirror, we had Mam Byrdie's potion. Selena was dead. I was a wolf. Against my better judgment, I trusted Labaye.

We'd be okay, probably.

I got back to the Maglite standing by the mouth of the crawlspace and realized I'd been pacing.

Stepping into the center of the room, I said, "We have to make a circle." I turned in place, tracing the air with arms out to illustrate. Labaye had already forced himself down into a crouch on the dark boards, knees along one of the chalk marks that remained of the former circle. "Can you make it out from that?" I said.

Without a word, he reached toward me, and I handed him the vial, and the two pieces of mirror wrapped up in Rothko. The vial fell from between our hands but didn't break. It rolled a couple of inches and stopped in the seam between two floorboards.

"Oh," I said and pulled from my jeans pocket the folded-up drawing of the boy and the wolf, of my brother and me. "I learned another trick."

But Labaye had turned to rummage in the bag. He pulled out the piece of yellow sidewalk chalk, which we trusted would read white. It surprised me how Labaye traced a near-perfect circle from what little remained of Selena's. He scooted around me, keeping his knees clear of the line he drew and mumbled under his breath. First I thought he was cursing his sore knees and back, but then I caught the words of a French prayer.

If Labaye's last experience here bothered him, it didn't show. I didn't ask. There was something to be said for shoving bad memories as far down as they could go.

The air in the brick-lined chamber thickened. The restored circle charged the air, potent, pregnant. A subtle whiff of baking surprised me, understated and mildly appetizing, then stronger, like an entire bottle of extract had toppled over. Remi's drawing crinkled as I squeezed my fist. The weight of everything I'd seen the past few days landed on me like I hadn't slept a wink, and my limbs turned to lead, though I didn't feel like I could even sit.

I stood in the middle of Labaye's circle, distracted by the odor of magic, my body suddenly made of cement. I tried to step over the chalk line, but couldn't lift my foot from the dark, rough boards. A headache pierced my temples. Darkness pushed in from either side and the empty room felt suddenly crowded. When Mam Byrdie's power had shown itself to me, it felt like drowning. Now the space around me constricted, though nothing touched me. I stood upright but felt like I was being pressed beneath stone. I tried to lift an arm. Whatever strength I put toward it just squeezed back as though someone else reached inside me. Only the fingers of one hand could move. All on their own. The drawing fell to the floor, next to Mam Byrdie's potion. The tiny vial hopped out of the gap in the floorboards, rolled in a gentle curve, and stopped at the edge of the circle next to the dusty knee of my cuddle buddy, who still muttered some Cajun prayer.

"Labaye." I choked his name out. Blackness overtook my vision, until only Labaye sat at the center of a long tunnel, in a pinpoint of hazy light. "Labaye," I said. "Stop. I have to get out of the circle before—"

With his good hand, he pulled something from his jeans pocket, and pressed it against the chalk line, then raised his voice. "*Fermez*," he said.

I gagged, lungs contracting to squeeze out all the air. I struggled to speak, so it came out a growl. "The hell, Labaye? Let me *out* so we can do this."

We both looked at his hand. Some tangle of thread or hair, a pale knot, poked out where he touched the chalk line. I held my breath waiting for him to break the seal with just a swipe of his fingertips. But he pulled his hand back and, with a flick of his wrist, sent Mam Byrdie's vial skittering across the boards to shatter against the brick wall.

The pale knot of hair sat on the chalk line, gray in the dim light. No, silver.

My hair. My fur. Twisted together like something you'd pull from under a couch. I had no idea when he'd gotten the fur, but he must have cut the hair while I slept.

It was only when he laughed that the floor seemed to fall out from under me. He laughed, and it shook the bricks loose from the mortar. The migraine screamed like a rake across the chalkboard inside my skull.

The noise dropped away, and I knew Labaye had just let out

a little chuckle, but the simple sound had confirmed the horrible feeling that had bloomed in the pit of my stomach.

The man at the edge of the circle transformed as if those long tan fingers merely pulled away a mask I'd mistaken for a real face.

He still had those soulful, dark eyes, the handsome, good cop grin—but the face belonged to a stranger.

He patted his good hand against a thigh. Yellow chalk dust puffed from his long fingers. He looked down at both hands, maybe to hide a smile. "Afraid I can't do that, Britta."

"Like hell." I tried to lunge at him, struggled against my invisible bounds. I ground flat, useless teeth like it made a damn bit of difference.

The harder I pushed, the tighter the vanilla air pressed in. If I drew on the full strength of my wolf I could probably suffocate and end this once and for all.

I'd let myself be charmed by a white trash redneck cop—allowed myself to trust. To be betrayed.

He pretends to care.

They, Remi. Not *he*. I looked at my brother's drawing, near where my boots were rooted to the rough floorboards. They always pretend to care. But you never ever would have grown up to be that type of man.

Labaye reached over with his bad hand and grabbed Rothko, poor Rothko, great and powerful elephant, once worshipped by the Hindus, feared even by the so-called King of the Jungle, now an oven mitt used to pick up shards of glass.

"Miss Orchid," he said, peeling the gray felt away from the pieces of scrying mirror. Couldn't fault him for resorting to surnames, but probably not a good sign. "I really am sorry to have misled you."

Or maybe he was simply afraid of her.

"Selena," I seethed, my words venom, poisoned by all the unhappy truths that had just shown themselves in eight simple words. His willingness to help. His insistence on following my every move. Even the overpowering scent. I'd been stupid enough to think all this said something special. "You've been … working for her this whole time."

Labaye let out a breath. His eyebrows arched and he nodded, and I caught a glimpse of a grin, but it slipped right away. He had the nerve to act impressed.

"I guess that's what you'd call it." He laid one piece of mirror on the chalk line by his knee and folded the scrap of elephant hide back around the other piece, which he set down farther from the circle. His hand disappeared into the bag, pulled out a pair of candles, and the canister of salt with the little girl skipping through the rain.

"For about as long as I can remember, actually." He needed both hands to get himself to his feet, then he made a lap around the circle, sprinkling salt just outside the chalk line—all the better to keep me in.

"Nearly as long as she's been waiting for you," he said.

"Yeah, well, she's dead now."

He laughed. I cringed. I was still figuring this out way too fucking slow.

He flung another heavy spray of the stuff along the edge of the crawlspace back to the bedroom. "She knew you wouldn't be able to resist nosing around her 'death' if you thought it involved Remi."

"There never were any remains," I said. "Body parts. That's why Alec couldn't find them. How the hell did you—?"

"How'd we convince a police department to investigate a murder if there were no remains?" Labaye set the canister of salt back in the grocery bag, and got to his feet again, turning toward the darkest corner of the room. I strained to see through the darkness, to ignore the bitter, medicinal vanilla. The stink of magic. The hungry hurt radiating off the yellow chalk line. His heat made him visible as he knelt in the black space, to pick something up in each hand, objects I could only make out as he approached the circle again.

He set down a red and white cooler no bigger than a basketball. A metal pail hung from the splinted finger of his bad hand, and he knelt. The cooler bore a red, thorny *Biohazard* sticker, and when he flipped it open, a strip of white tape on the lid read *Stone Hom.*

My wolf flexed, and I shot forward. The effort felt like hammer-blows up and down my thighs, and the air above the chalk line shot invisible flames through the hand that I reached toward Labaye.

I recoiled back to the center, expecting to see the flesh shredded off my whole forearm. But something outside the circle distracted me.

Labaye turned toward a pale spot in the air, like a beam of light in a storm. A figure took shape beside him, the head not much higher than the kneeling cop's.

My brother.

Not the angelic image Mam Byrdie had called, but the hollow-eyed wraith Selena had sicced on Labaye the other night in some mock battle for my benefit, a sharp worry line marking his forehead.

"What does she want? What else can she take?" I tried to keep my voice measured, but wanted to scream. Instead, I struck out against the circle, beating at a brick wall that wasn't there, and the pain gave me the excuse to scream.

Something flashed in Labaye's brown eyes, a quick glimpse of uncertainty. "You have to ask her yourself."

Remi's pale figure dimmed, but he smiled, and that smile still melted my heart. I searched the eyes for some light, but Selena had been sucking the light out of my brother from the moment she met him. He'd looked so good when Mam Byrdie called him to the library, but I stared into this real face of death, my beautiful imprisoned Remi, and the pain left me and I knew I would tear

Labaye to pieces before the night was out.

"It'll be okay, Remi," I said, but he didn't seem to hear.

Labaye pulled three Pyrex containers from the cooler, two the size of whiskey glasses and a larger one. Something else passed over Labaye, maybe nausea. Remi's slack face showed no interest, but he watched Labaye closely nonetheless.

"I tried to keep them tied together," Labaye said, "but the lab guys insisted."

He unscrewed the aluminum lids, one by one, and a strong odor cut through the vanilla, something organic and rotting but with an unfamiliar chemical undertone. A smile passed across Remi's face but vanished as soon as I looked.

Labaye carefully set down, just outside the circle, an eyeball, and a purple human heart bisected by a vein so red it looked black. Labaye reached for the optic nerve, which had flopped near the salt line, and tucked it closer to the orb. He tipped the third jar to make a small cairn of human teeth between the two organs.

It took a few tries to form the words, but I managed a pretty coherent whimper. "What's it mean?"

Labaye reached into the bucket and began to pull out items, but I couldn't pay attention to that.

The ghostly form of my little brother crouched over the remains of Selena Stone, of the woman who killed him, and I had the horrible thought that I'd have to watch him eat them.

Labaye dropped a bundle of herbs or incense between Remi's feet, and it burst into a slow purple flame that wavered and bent more than flickered but crackled loud and fast as pine in a campfire. The same purple that had consumed my mother back in the day. The glow cast sickly amber shadows around the chamber and brought out the yellow in the chalk line. Labaye's face took on the pallor of old bruises as he gawked at my brother. The air shimmered between the organs and Remi, and the air melted, shapes running together in a blur between his feet.

"Remi!" I screamed as his face fell out of focus, but my lungs were squeezed into silence.

He stood taller, stretched out his arms toward the rafters. The purple faded into white, until this wraith, this Remi doppelgänger, revealed the witch herself.

"Selena Stone," Labaye said her name once, and a blast of phantom wind knocked me onto my back.

CHAPTER TWENTY-FIVE

TEN YEARS EARLIER

The sky outside the library had begun to turn purple the last time I'd checked on Remi. I hadn't looked down at the magazine for quite a few minutes when my brother burst through the door, causing Mam Byrdie to stand from her computer screen.

"Everything okay?" I asked too loud. Now everyone else turned from what they were doing.

But Remi smiled and smacked a sheet of paper on the open pages of *Art Papers*. The sketchbook slapped beside me on the table and he pulled up a seat.

"Wow, Remi," I said, more softly. "Nice work." He'd copied the lines of the library well enough that I'd have recognized it even if I hadn't known where he'd been sitting.

"Now I just gotta fill it in." He pulled the drawing away and started to render tiny rectangles. His new favorite thing. The charcoal shaded in each brick individually, leaving the mortar white, creating shadow and depth with the patience of a student. I didn't point out that the pediment above the entrance, like the one over our own front doors, had a painted facing, no bricks.

Mam Byrdie still had her eye on us. She smiled, nodded, then went back to her screen.

I caught the odor of stale beer that hovered like a dusty cloud around my stepfather before I saw him.

Blurry-eyed and ruddy-cheeked, the former bodybuilder

looked more out of place among the middle schoolers and retirees than I'd ever seen him. Dude did *not* belong in a library. He navigated between rows of books and small reading nooks with all the grace of a bull in a china shop until he arrived, panting, at our small table in the back of the main room. I had not actually seen Ray drunk in months, but he looked different than I remembered—practically brain dead. Maybe not a far cry from his natural state, but definitely off. Blood supply terminated, all synaptic activity ceased.

"You two need to come on back to the house." His voice slurred too loudly in the quiet space. Just the sound of it jerked Remi so much his charcoal snapped. The librarian's head whipped up, dark eyes harpooning Ray's back from across the room as she removed her glasses. The look gave *me* chills and it wasn't even meant for me.

Ray smiled at his son, the meanest smile I'd ever seen, not one his face had ever contorted into before. "Selena wants to pray over you."

"*You* need to go back to the house," I stage-whispered at him, flipping a page I hadn't read. "You and Mom and Crazy have fun playing church."

I turned back to the article about some Nashville sculptor I couldn't be less interested in, and Ray puffed himself up in my peripheral vision, a bullfrog bracing for a fight. But his face went slack like he was asleep with his eyes open. The more this guy drank, the dumber he got. My brother sat frozen, hands pressed flat to either side of his half-rendered drawing. His skin had turned red around eyes glassy with tears.

"In case you forgot," Ray muttered. "I am the parent here, young lady. Not," he wheezed hard, "you."

I closed the magazine and met Ray Hall's eyes. I couldn't put my finger on it, but just in that moment, if I hadn't known it was Ray, I might not have recognized him.

My heart hammered in my chest. "Yeah, Ray," I sputtered, "I *had* forgotten. 'Cause you sure as shit aren't *my* father." I sneered and grabbed Remi's hand. "And I'm not a child. So, I'm getting him out of here."

Ray dropped a meaty paw on top of mine and Remi's, the worst-ever team huddle, and the poor kid looked like he might crumble. Thick fingers pressed into my wrist, and I couldn't help but wince. My anger boiled up. Ray was big, mean, and dumb, but he'd never been violent. The grip suggested this might change.

"I am taking him home," he said in a measured tone. "There's nothing for you to do but come with us."

It took everything I had not to rocket out of my chair and shove the man away from my brother. I slid out of my chair and straightened to my full height—a good foot or so shorter than the one-time bodybuilder. Not that I thought my stepfather would ever hit me, not that he ever had. But when I looked in those eyes, I wondered if someone else was pulling his strings.

"Pardon me." If anything could've eased that tension, I'd have bet on the lilting rhythm of Mam Byrdie's Creole accent. "Sir," she said, standing at the corner of the table between Ray and me. "Your children are always welcome here. Your son is a little angel." She smiled at Remi, but he didn't look up.

Her gentle intervention did not have the desired effect.

"No, pardon me." Ray used his outdoor voice, which had no place in the library, and got absolutely everyone looking again. "Ma'am," he said, his tone matching the sour twist of his face. "Are you telling me how to parent my kids?"

Every face that had turned to us, the old women and the kids Remi's age, a pair of college students who'd peeked out from behind a spinner rack of softcovers—every single face in the library that afternoon was white. Every face except the woman in a caftan and long gray braids bound in a headscarf, minus a finger, who'd had the gall to insert herself between this man and his children.

A nasty smile curled Ray's lips. He slipped around Mam Byrdie and me and set his paw on Remi's shoulder, pulled the boy from his chair.

My hands balled into fists at my side. "Let him go, Ray."

The Ray-thing ignored me as it angled Remi toward the door. "Your mother wants you *both* home," he said but didn't even glance back.

The expression on Remi's face as he looked over his shoulder would figure into my nightmares as much as anything else I saw that day. His voice trembled when he said my name, barely loud enough to be considered a whisper.

Ray gave him a little push, and Remi stumbled toward the door.

I lurched forward, but now Mam Byrdie put her hand on my arm, three fingernails digging into my skin while she smiled after Remi. "You go on, *sha*," she cooed. "Everything will be okay."

I did not like watching Ray leave with Remi, but the librarian clung to me, blocking my exit. She waited until the little bell rang and the door had closed behind them, then turned to me and dropped her sweet librarian smile. Her Creole lilt deepened to a low octave.

Like Ray, the old woman became someone new.

"You're a strong woman, Britta, *sha*," she said. "That man is weak, and a fool, but he's not wicked enough to hurt you. You get home to your brother, and you stick to him like glue." I heard the unmistakable sound of Mom's truck roar to life. Great, he was drunk *and* driving. "Tomorrow, you do what you've been scheming over, *sha*, and you get that boy away from here once and for all. Let this be your last night in that house."

Frustration and fear burned inside of me, pulsing out of my skin, setting me on fire. Maybe the old woman felt it, too, because her grip loosened on my arm, and I jerked away. I ran to the door, wasting just one last questioning glance on the librarian, who'd picked up the unfinished drawing of the library that Remi had left on the table.

I ran as fast as I could to the house.

By the time I could see Mom's dinged-up old Ford F150 in the driveway, its cab was empty. Remi and I had walked to the library in part because Selena had parked me in, and her car still sat behind my little hatchback. I'd have to tear up the lawn if I needed to make a break for it tonight.

My feet throbbed and my calves burned inside my ten-hole Doc Martens, and my heart threatened to pound out of my chest as I walked the last steps up the porcelain tiles of the driveway. Something very bad was happening, I could feel it in my bones. Something evil. I paused at the back door, wished I'd begged Mam Byrdie to come, that I'd found the words to explain the horrible sense of doom I felt over whatever Selena had been planning since the day we arrived in town.

But the mambo had told me I was strong, so I slammed into the backdoor so hard it bounced off the opposite wall. Something crashed behind it, but I couldn't care less.

I could barely see through the gloom of the mudroom and kitchen, darker than they should have been at that time of day, and the place had a pungent, saccharine scent—a burned, sugary smell. I gagged.

Before my vision had adjusted, I heard a man's scream from the front of the house. Something heavy fell. Terror bolted my feet to the kitchen floor where I stood, but I pulled them free and tried not to make a sound in those giant boots as I made my way through the maze of doors connecting the rooms of the first floor.

Ray struggled on his side, his back against the front doors of the house. He reached up for a glass doorknob, but his fingers slipped off. Whatever had happened in the last few minutes had made him instantly sober, and he seemed smaller than usual. He held his stomach, face twisted in pain. In the dim light of the entryway, he looked sick, his hands coated in some dull sheen.

My stomach lurched when I realized it was blood.

"Britta," he gasped, one hand peeling away from his stomach to reach for me. "Britta, you need to get them and go." The closer I got, the worse he looked. He struggled to his knees, his face growing pinched and gaunt. It had been a while since my stepfather lost the bulk he'd carried as a younger man, but now his flesh shriveled in upon itself until his jeans and T-shirt hung like clothes thrown over a railing.

This couldn't be Ray. It couldn't get to its feet because it had been dead for a long time.

"Where are they?" I hung on the banister, afraid to move closer.

"Parlor," he croaked, voice as dry as dead leaves, then he crumbled to the floor, his skull clacking off the hardwood.

I blinked a few times and squatted beside him, holding back vomit as I touched the skeletal wrist to find no pulse.

My hand recoiled from the skin as cold as glass. It gave way under my touch, sticking to my fingertips and floating off Ray's bones like disturbed ash. What remained of his other hand fell away from his stomach, and my vision blurred from a second wave of nausea. The T-shirt wasn't torn. There was no wound. The blood that coated his hands, the doorknob, it belonged to someone else—either Mom or Remi.

I scrambled to my feet, not caring about the noise my boots made and slid through the door to the study Remi and I had turned into a bedroom. The door between this room and Mom's parlor stood open just enough to show the flickering purple light within. A new smell in the air covered the burned sugar. It smelled like pennies.

It smelled like blood.

Selena's voice called from beyond the door, a smug, singsong quality in the way she said my name that even now, in that moment, deepened my hatred for her.

"*Brrrritta.*"

"Mom?" I yelled back. "Remi?" Closing my eyes, I said a silent prayer one of them would answer. If they could speak, they were not dead. If I could barter their lives, I'd gladly sign a contract with God and baby Jesus, because it was pretty clear all Selena's talk of prayer circles was meant for someone else.

"They're in here, Britta, dear." Selena's voice. "Come and join us." If they couldn't speak …

My arms and legs trembled, my pulse kicked into overdrive as if the sickly-sweet stink could jack up my blood sugar. It didn't feel like adrenaline, it felt electric, like a switch inside me had clicked on.

With a deep breath, I pulled the parlor door wide and stepped through. It took everything I had not to scream.

Mom lay motionless, covered in blood. Her long, graying hair had been clipped. Her arms seemed to reach out, pale legs stretched across the delft tile floor, so she looked like an animal twisted on a spit. Candles burned inches away from her hands and her feet, both bound with thin white rope. Gory black and red holes pierced her palms and the soles of her feet, but I didn't see any hammers or spikes lying around, and the fireplace poker stood by the hearth with the matching tongs, shovel, and broom, each clean and dry. My mother's fresh wounds still hiccupped blood, which pooled on the blue and white tiles, the horrid scene tinted purple by strange flames in the fireplace.

My mother's eyes rolled frantically, she moaned and struggled when she saw me, but something beyond the ropes seemed to keep her arms and legs outstretched, and a gag muffled any words. I recognized the dust-colored cloth in her mouth as a scarf Selena had worn, and my fingers balled into fists so tight my joints ached. She lay across the center of a circle, the outline sparkling—salt?—against the tile, catching the light of the candles and the fireplace. Strange characters had been etched in chalk around the circle's perimeter, a series of sharp angles and curves, some ending in points and others in what might have been a pair of horns. I didn't have to understand them to know that whatever message the symbols represented was evil, unholy.

Selena sat in a high-backed rocking chair across the circle from me. Beside her, a candle burned on a small table, with a fancy knife and some knotted mess of wood or leather.

Remi perched on Selena's lap like a doll, hugging Rothko tight against his chest. The light from the candle flashed in the elephant's glassy black eyes. Selena had one hand on the side of Remi's neck, and in the other, she held a bundle of what must have been my mother's hair, twisted into the shape of a person. Remi had his stuffy, and I didn't need a mambo to tell me that Selena held a voodoo doll of my mother …

Ray wasn't the only one who'd undergone a transformation. Where the life had been sucked out of my stepdad, it had been flushed into Selena. Her smooth skin glowed, wrinkle-free, and her white hair had deepened into golden copper. She even sat straighter, her legs longer, more supple. She looked twenty years younger.

Some evil wants to live forever. Mam Byrdie's words came back to me.

"Let my brother go," I said. "And quit whatever stigmata bullshit you're playing at with my mom."

Something flickered across the witch's face, but it disappeared in a blink. She smiled and coiled her fingers around my brother's throat.

She raised the little bundle of hair as if making a toast. "Stigmata," she cooed to the voodoo doll. "Interesting, but you're a bit off. I have designed a spell with the help of your loving family, Britta, dear, and you're just in time for the finale."

I swallowed and moved around the circle toward the fireplace. I pulled the iron poker from the toolset and brandished it in Selena's direction.

Selena took her hand away from Remi to touch her face, her

hair. "Immortality requires a rather involved recipe, as you might expect, and the ingredients can be frightfully hard to attain, but your family provided a wonderful resource." She pushed Remi to his feet and dragged him around the edge of the circle. The back of the rocking chair knocked against the wall.

I moved opposite them, my mother's body a median between us. The toe of my Doc just touched the circle's white outline, and I almost fell over as my leg snapped back in pain, like the salt had teeth that could bite through an inch of rubber sole.

I forced the sting into words. "What ingredients?"

Selena pinched the doll's head, rubbed her fingertips together so the hairs crackled, and my mother writhed on her tile floor. I stepped toward her, but the circle knocked me back again, and I yelped as needles stabbed up both legs.

"It's easy to harvest a man's strength and vitality when he goes to such lengths to make himself weak," Selena said, running a hand down her restored curves. "Alcohol really is a nasty thing."

I looked at the tips of my fingers, where the ashes of Ray's skin still clung, then gripped the poker in both hands and slipped between the rocking chair and the salt line.

"A mother's love," she went on, and gestured to my mother, twitching on the floor. I thought Selena's hand passed over the salt line, but couldn't be sure. My brother moved along beside her, obedient and dazed. "And what greater love does a mother have than for her children?" Now she leaned all the way into the circle, while Remi hung back. She dipped her index finger in the blood that pooled around Mom's feet, stood back, and rubbed it on Remi's cheek, and then the other, like marking a novice hunter's face the first time he sees a fox killed. Electricity surged inside me, and the fireplace flashed purple in response. Mom moaned, the sound weaker now.

"You scared her!" I lunged around the circle after her. "So she'd let you do what you want to him!"

"Oh," Selena cooed, her mouth spreading into a wide grin.

She shuddered like something had tickled her, and pulled my brother along by the shoulder. "But, Britta, dear, you're important, too."

"What the fuck does that mean?" I tried to control my voice. Tears cooled my cheeks.

"You feel it, don't you?" She moved her hand onto Remi's neck. "The power? My magic, it calls to you." She waved the voo-doo doll of my mother's hair at me.

"Like hell." I lunged again, avoiding the circle of snapping salt. "Let Remi go."

She stopped next to the table by her chair, hugged him. Kissed his cheek. His lips trembled, he squeezed Rothko with his whole body, and Selena let him go, bending down beside my mother's head again. She touched the little tangle of hair to the candle, and the crackling flame spiked up between us.

My mother yowled in pain, and without rising, Selena spun to the table, grabbed the knife, and with both hands drove it into Remi's stomach.

I threw myself over my mother and swung the poker wildly at Selena, ignoring the pain that sliced through my legs, biting and burning to my hips. Remi dropped the stuffed elephant onto the salt line and grasped at his belly, his hands filling with blood. A spasm of fresh pain knocked me to my knees, and I knocked over Selena's table.

She broke into a laugh and shoved Remi toward me. "Such power," she exclaimed.

Remi's body wound around mine as my mother screamed. On my knees, I wrenched Remi away as purple flames engulfed our mother, twisted around her. I dropped the poker and squeezed Remi in my arms, covered his stomach with my hand, forcing his face into the crook of my neck. I hugged him so tight I felt his bones against mine. My thoughts pulsed inside my head, the worst barely forming as they tumbled over each other—*blood, don't die, so much blood, Mom, Remi.*

Selena, on her knees, grabbed the table I'd tipped over. She'd dropped the dagger, and picked up something else—the knotted mess, some gris-gris or monkey's paw.

Mom's body, like Ray's, had smoldered into a mass of blackened ash, and no longer looked like her at all, though it retained a human outline. The smell of vanilla and copper was replaced with the stink of burned hair and my mother's death. Rothko stared up from the edge of the circle with lifeless black eyes. I grabbed the fireplace poker that lay across him, pushing Remi behind me as I climbed to my feet.

Selena stood next to the rocking chair with the monkey's paw in hand, her eyes purple fire, her grin a twisted sneer.

"One more ingredient left," she snarled. "And that's the last thing I need for my spell to be complete. Your sacrifice."

The words barely registered. "Run!" I screamed at my brother Remi and swung wildly at the witch.

"Britta, no—"

My Doc Marten slipped on the tiles, maybe in my brother's blood, or Mom's. Selena spun, but the poker struck her face, knocking her over the chair where she crashed onto the table.

Remi's big, green eyes stared at me, wide and afraid and full of trust, his hands still gripping his belly and turning a darker red. Watching his life drain out of him, I almost lost my nerve. I would have taken his hand and run if I had any hope Selena wouldn't catch us.

"Run!" I screamed. "I'll find you, Rem! Get help!"

He darted out of the parlor, but Selena scrambled after him, the knife in one hand and that gnarly paw in the other. I reached for her, but fell into the circle, pain slicing back and forth through my arms, my legs, up through my chest. I pushed myself off my mother's body and rolled out of the circle but had to reach back in for the poker lying across her ashen arms. I used my left arm so my right would still be strong enough to cave in Selena's head.

I shot out of the room after her, knocking over a stack of boxes, sending the last of Mom's tiles clattering across the hallway. As I rounded a corner, first I saw her, then I heard Remi scream.

Did he recognize his father in that scorched husk, blocking the front door? He stood in place, red-stained hands fluttering at his sides. I yelled for him, and he looked back, saw me, but Selena stood between us. Wasting no time, the kid shot up the stairs, little feet hammering up those nineteen steps.

Please pick a better hiding place than the sunroom. I threw myself at Selena, barreled into her, and we crashed into the front door, scattering Ray's remains, which still had some bone in it. She dropped the knife and the gris-gris, but I didn't drop my poker.

Selena got a handful of my hair. "He can't hide," she said. "He's already mine." She grinned, but her nose was bent and gushing blood, her cheek torn wide open, showing bone. Her eyeball bulged, too much white.

Electricity and rage blasted through me. Whatever power Selena thought she could get out of me, I'd use it to kill her instead.

"Over my dead body."

I pulled away, and the bitch kept the handful of my hair.

Then I stabbed the poker hard into her solar plexus, and it hooked under her ribcage when I tried to jerk it back out.

CHAPTER TWENTY-SIX

When I opened my eyes again, it was not Labaye I found myself looking at.

It was *her*.

"Welcome home, Britta, dear," Selena said. The pattern of the brick wall, rough rectangles like Remi might have drawn, showed through her thin and papery form in the chamber's purple glow. She appeared made of spiderwebs, but still with the same ice blue eyes as back in the day.

"I am so, so glad," she sneered, "to see you again."

I howled as I threw myself forward, but landed inside the circle on hands and knees, my fingers touching the drawing Remi's ghost had left for Labaye to find. I clawed at the chalk line until my fingertips streaked the floorboards red. My wolf roared and we kicked and scratched at the trap I'd led us into.

I pressed against the circle, to get at Selena like I had in that parlor ten years ago.

This circle, rimmed in the same symbols that had trapped my mother, didn't budge. Pain shot through me. My knees gave out and I fell into the fetal position inside the prison Labaye had drawn.

"What did you do to my brother?" The words ripped out of me in a ragged burst. I bit down as my voice devolved into a scream, my arms and gut contracting against the pain.

Selena flickered. She might have been laughing.

"Do you see this, Aaron?" Selena's head turned at an angle only a ghost could manage. For a second I had no idea who she was talking to. I felt a twinge of satisfaction that I'd only ever called him by that name once.

Aaron Labaye could go right ahead and fuck himself.

He'd retreated into the sick ocher shadows at the limit of my sight, kneeling well outside the candle's glow. But I felt his eyes on me. Could smell him—all pine, and musk, and *betrayal*.

"She won't cooperate if you torture her," he said, but his words lacked conviction. He sounded frightened. Maybe he didn't like watching me writhe around on the floor.

"Give me my brother," I grunted.

Selena shook her head. "Britta Orchid is already so tortured—" She returned her gaze to me. "But she still hasn't put together that I never had her poor baby brother's spirit."

I tried to spit words out, but couldn't manage through the agonizing heaves.

Labaye tried to make some point about it being good that Selena never had Remi.

I couldn't take my eyes off her.

I'd come home to identify a body that didn't exist, and I'd stayed to free a brother who wasn't here.

The drawing Labaye had handed me that first day, Remi and the wolf, my brother and me, lay beside me in the circle, just a stick drawing. It showed none of Remi's emerging talent, none of his careful charcoal strokes. The wolf looked more like a horse, with one small circle of yellow highlighter for an eye.

A good enough witch can fool all five senses, no matter how keen.

Selena had become more solid, no longer the flimsy specter dressed up as my baby brother, but a figure dense as flesh, wrapped in Halloween gauze. Her bare feet on the floorboards seemed to support weight now. With the fading purple flames, and Labaye skulking in the amber shadows, the chamber looked like a garish parody of Goya.

I found the strength to snap off another question. "What do you want?"

"Oh, it's simple, dear." Selena smiled, using her sweetest voice. "What I always wanted. You. Forever."

She wiggled her fingers in the air between the rafters. Again the image of cobwebs struck me, but now the air took on a hint of physical substance, which her hands seemed to suck in.

"I spent almost ten years bringing this Plan B to fruition," she said. "When I found Aaron, he wasn't much older than your brother when he ... well, when he passed away."

She stepped up and kneeled so close I'd swear her face crossed the edge of the circle. "He is rather handsome, isn't he?" she whispered. "Have you noticed the way he *smells*? Oh, I'm sure you have."

My stomach clenched again.

"You know," she said softly, "the spell that makes two people fall in love, that one is much harder to cast—" Her eyes shot back to the sallow darkness behind her. "Than the one needed to find a pair already destined to fall in love." She arched her brow, and those icy blue eyes sizzled with sincerity. "If Aaron hadn't had the spark, Britta, he never could have been right for you."

I looked for Labaye in the shadows. I could barely see him, but I could smell him—that musky pine and secret scent. A blaze flared from his corner, and butane and wax filled my sinuses.

"The fact is," Selena cooed, "I've provided you quite a service, although it's finally time that you perform the greater one for me."

Labaye knelt over the bucket and the cooler, holding a large candle. He shifted around, agitated. I recognized the expression that stared back at me. The first time he'd seen the glow in my eyes, the fireflies. This wasn't the man who'd trapped me in the circle, but the man I'd let touch me in my wolf form. The one I'd let lay beside me while I slept.

"So, he has magic in him," I grunted. "He can become a wolf, too."

That earned an approving smile from the witch. "Well done, Britta, dear. You're catching up."

I swiped at her. The circle's outline bit hard. When I pulled my hand back, I was surprised to see all the fingers still in place.

I was too angry to be scared, too scared to be cautious.

The last time I'd tangled with this witchy bitch, in this very space, I'd been the one to walk away. Cursed, undead, alone, but like Mam Byrdie had said—I had *survived*.

I'd do it again. This time Remi's life *wasn't* on the line, and I had nothing left to lose.

I was Big, Bad Britta, and Selena was a ghost. Fuck her.

"Aaron held the same spark that had drawn me to you," she said, running jazz hands through the air. "All the way in Texas, before those mysterious visions lured your mother to this house."

More of Mam Byrdie's words came back. *A wolf be a powerful familiar if turned by black magic.*

Okay. The bitch was right. I *was* catching on.

"But to insure my investment," Selena said, "I filled little Aaron's head with visions of his own, dreams about wolves, noble and strong, dreams that left him predisposed to certain … ideas."

The candle cast shadows up to exaggerate Labaye's scowl. He jammed a thin wooden rod into the bucket, stirring God knows what.

No wonder he was so freaking interested in me.

He *wanted* to be a wolf, to be torn. Maybe he just hadn't expected his soul to be Selena's bargaining chip.

"Oh, but Britta, don't you see—it's not Remi we'll set free tonight." As she spoke, Labaye scooted forward from the shadows, dragging his bucket, the wood rod bumping on the rim. He reached his injured hand toward a light spot on the floor.

"It's you, Britta, dear," Selena said. "You'll finally have real relief from the burden."

Rothko—the last scrap of him—had blended into the rough

floorboards. When we'd first come into the room, all Labaye had to do was put out his hand and I'd given it to him.

"The guilt, the curse," Selena went on. "Your mambo friend, she whipped up that concoction to help you free your brother …" She jerked a thumb to where Mam Byrdie's vial had shattered on the bricks.

Labaye unfolded the piece of felt that used to be Rothko, and removed a piece of the mirror with the same hand he'd cut on it the night before.

"Aaron is putting together a potion to free you, Britta, dear."

The contents of the bucket hissed when he dropped in the black shard, and I could smell it now, boggy and mossy and sulfuric. He scowled and turned his head away from a lavender cloud.

I wanted to ask if he'd bothered to ask any questions before turning to the dark side.

But I just snapped at Selena. "Got it." I rose to my knees and crossed my arms high over my chest. "I tear him, you kill me, then he's your familiar?" Behind her, Labaye's eyes bugged and he mouthed the word *No.*

"What?" Selena's icy eyes flashed at him, and he buried his face in the bucket, missing the sharp shake of her head. Maybe that sulfur stink would poison the son of a bitch.

Despite all her talk about nice smells, Selena looked like she felt the same way about Labaye as I did. "No, Britta, dear," she said, "I need *you.*" Her eyes went from my own, down over my body, the way a guy might ogle my tits in a bar—but it felt like she saw through me. Still, she stressed, "*You.* Forever."

Selena got to her feet, and I climbed to mine, though she had the room to move. "I took what I needed from your mother, from poor drunk Ray, and from your brother." She stepped past Labaye, over the piece of mirror still wrapped in that last piece of Rothko. Candles cast her dancing shadow on the brick walls of the room, up into the rafters.

"And I made you what you are," she said, punching each word in a staccato rhythm as she slowly circled. "But I never got to reap the benefit. So, why would I kill you now?"

In the corner of my eye, Labaye nodded like an idiot without looking up.

Selena made two fists and put them together. "The curse bound the soul to this wolf-enchanted body. But I don't need the soul. I'll free that from the body." She opened one hand to flutter away and pressed the other fist to her heart in a pledge. "And keep your wolf in my thrall. You see, I'm not looking for a *familiar*," she said sarcastically. "I want a pack."

Her eyes went back and forth from my face to Labaye's behind me.

I just thought about Alec.

Again she fluttered one hand below the rafters. "So, I'll release the spirit of that tragic child, of Britta Orchid—"

"Wait," I said. "My spirit? What happens to that?"

Her face twisted up like a kid caught in a lie. "Well, you see, any major spell requires a sacrifice."

My eyes wandered across the murky yellow shadows. Poor Labaye wiped at his sweating brow with the splinted hand, having a hard time getting his mind around the fact that he'd trapped the woman—or, the woman's *body*, anyway—he was destined to spend forever with.

Had he been drawn to me, too? I fought the idea that this enormous lie, this betrayal, hid behind some kind of sincerity.

Fought the idea, but it fought back.

Either way, the dude was about to get a two-for-one deal—a new wolfcoat of his own, and someone to spend his immortality with. Bad news was he'd spend it tethered to Selena. I almost felt bad for him.

Almost.

I met his eyes. He blinked. I didn't.

"I didn't know," he said.

Selena wheeled on him. "You didn't know, you didn't know," she said in a mocking shriek, and he recoiled, almost spilled the steaming bucket. "Aaron, all you ever asked about was the wolf. And you've heard her, Aaron, dear. She calls it a curse!" Selena widened her blue eyes and threw open her arms. "She thinks she's *undead!*" She jabbed a finger into her flat palm. "Each of us is getting what we want."

I looked at my cuddle buddy stirring his potion and wondered when I'd stopped assuming the worst.

I must've laughed because Selena turned on me. "Is something funny, Britta, dear?"

I fixed my mouth in a scowl and said, "Always thought my trust issues ran in the other direction."

She shook it off. "Your wolf, I will keep her. And she'll turn your intended—" She gestured to Labaye without looking at him. "And together they'll raise my litter." Labaye's head whipped in her direction. I saw the look I'd tried to get from him back in the interrogation room.

"My pack will conquer all others," Selena said. "One by one, until I am alpha to all of the wolves of this world."

The room's purple glow hid Labaye's bruises enough that you could forget how bad Alec had beat the shit out of him, but he turned to me with wet eyes, and I wished like hell I had the energy to tell him that the only word for that look was *sheepish.*

CHAPTER TWENTY-SEVEN

TEN YEARS EARLIER

I tightened my grip on the poker, tried to yank it free from Selena's abdomen. She screamed, grabbed the shaft with one hand, and clawed at me with the other, stretching out the hole in the knee of my jeans.

With a deep breath, I closed my eyes and thought about Remi, hiding somewhere upstairs. The weird adrenaline heat rose to a full boil, and I wrapped myself around it. A tingling sensation rippled up my arm.

Selena got a hand around my ankle, and tried to knock me off balance by shoving my foot straight up—but I threw all my weight on it, and brought the thick Doc Marten heel down right next to where the poker entered her midsection. Her eyes bugged and her mouth rounded in a silent cartoon scream. Blood squirted from the broken nose and the tear in her cheek. Slatterpaint.

Staggering back across her knife and the gris-gris, I wound up, took aim at the cut I'd opened on the side of her head, and tried for a field goal. Her face spun and snapped back, and I brought the foot down on her ear, and again, and again.

With Selena out cold it was easier to wiggle the poker out of her solar plexus.

"Remi!" I called.

The witch didn't look so intimidating curled up in the fetal position on the floor beside Ray. No, not Ray. Beside a pile of ash. A pile of ash that used to be Remi's dad. I looked up into the shadows of the stairwell, listened for my brother's voice, but did not call out again.

I prodded at Selena's body and used the poker to roll her onto her stomach. A pool of blood spread dark and quick from beneath her now.

I needed to get Remi and get out the backdoor, didn't have the bandwidth to care about anything else right now. I kicked the knife and the monkey paw away, and held tight to the banister all the way up those nineteen stairs, afraid of slipping with all that blood on my boots.

At the landing, I pressed my back against the wall, hugged the poker to my chest.

"Remi," I called in a stage whisper. I checked the sunroom. Said his name again, and stared at the threadbare down comforter draped over the chair, then listened.

Nothing.

"Remi, where are you?" My voice sounded freaked out, even to me.

Something moved behind me. I spun around just in time to see his shadow slip into the master bedroom, our parents' room. "Damn it, Remi." I followed, bloodying the carpet Mom had just put in.

The figure that stepped out onto Mom's balcony was not my brother, though she wasn't much taller. Her skirts spread out in a wide hoop, not circa Scarlett O'Hara, but southern belle in decline, for sure.

Lisbeth Kelleher paused at the railing that Mom and I had never blocked off, despite Selena's warnings. Miss Kelleher grabbed a rope that had already been tied there, placed a loop around her neck, and she jumped.

The crack made me spin back out into the hall. The painted-over attic door banged open. The floorboards trembled beneath my feet with the impact.

"Remi!" I screamed despite myself.

I raced to the attic door because I only cared about getting Remi out of the house. Seated on the rickety attic stairs in a thick layer of dust, half a dozen dark little creatures stared out, with wild hair and teeth that flashed in the shadows, long limbs with too many joints. One got to its feet and leaped, and I slammed the door shut, pressing the poker against the creature as if to bar it. But as I pulled my head back, I saw the seams of the door still painted shut, like always.

I listened for some sound from those little monsters from the magnolia tree but heard a voice whimpering from my brother's bedroom. I whirled toward his door, the bloodied end of the poker out in front of me. Before I dared go in, I peered over the banister. I could only see halfway down the stairwell, but nothing was coming up the stairs.

As I crept into Remi's bedroom, I called again. The mint-green paint he'd picked out felt acidic on my eyes. When they built the house, the green they would've used had arsenic as an ingredient. It helped keep the bugs away, but the green drapes Scarlett O'Hara had made her fancy dress from probably doused her skin in poison as she supplicated herself to Rhett Butler. The blue splotches around the ceiling line had done nothing to protect Remi from the haints.

"Remi," I said. "Answer me."

"In here." His voice sounded far away, tinny, from the bottom of a well. "The fireplace."

I inched toward a fireplace that had never in our brief residency been lit. The poker I'd brought along from downstairs waved out in front of me, a dowsing rod in a windstorm. I set it down and dropped to all fours to squint up into the flue. A section of bricks at the back of the fireplace had been pulled away—a door on a hinge disguised as a mortar seam, just large enough to crawl through, drag marks tracking through dry grime.

I couldn't see anything through the door. "Rem?"

No answer.

He'd complained of voices from inside the fireplace. Ice replaced the anger that had been keeping me warm.

I snatched the poker, holding it awkwardly as I scrambled through the little opening on my hands and knees, which forced my pounding heart into my throat. The poker head scraped the floorboards ahead of me as I crawled into pitch black.

As my eyes adjusted, I got to my feet, leaned against the wall beside the crawlspace, and followed the bricks up to low rafters just overhead.

The poker clattered to the floor when I spotted my brother across the small space, curled up, back pressed against the wall. A dark pool spread out from his stomach, ending in a straight line where the blood seeped down into a gap between two boards.

I knelt beside him and the blood soaked through one pant leg, warm on my skin. Remi's blood. Even in my arms, Remi seemed very far from me. I took hold of his shoulder, scooped one hand under his neck. I'd seen more blood coming out of Mom downstairs, but Remi was small, so small. And there was so much red.

If I could've spoken, if I could have even cried, I might not have heard the movement as fast as I did.

I whirled around and saw the shadow first. The dim light from Remi's bedroom only made a softer spot in the darkness where it entered this brick-lined chamber, but something blocked the light, cast a shadow as it crawled this way.

The taloned paw of some cadaverous dog entered first, and a glow seemed to follow it. Then, the horrible pale head entered, soaked in blood down one side, masking a broken face, icy blue eyes peering out from under a great white swirl of hair.

I lunged for the poker, but Selena stepped over it, tearing at the back of my shirt with the gris-gris. Cloth and skin raked open.

I crashed to the floor, pain stabbing from head to toe from

the tear in my back, worse than the sting of the circle downstairs. I braced for another blow from Selena, but instead Remi shrieked, and I snapped up to my knees.

"Stop," I screamed. "Stop hurting him!"

Remi's cries cut as deep as anything else I'd felt that day. Selena leaned against the wall, as though she needed it for support. She'd drawn Remi up to his feet, and held him by the throat, shaking him. Blood ran down the front of them both, mixed together on her white dress. Without her scarves, Selena's neck looked too long, spindly, and insect-like.

I shook myself, grabbed my weapon, and closed the short distance, leading with the point of the poker, which found its place back in the hole in her abdomen.

Selena spit blood in my face and dropped my brother. She couldn't fall because I held her up. The tip of the poker ground against the bricks behind her. Her heartbeat came through the shaft, through the palms of my hands. I spun and let her fall off to the center of the floor.

I should have knelt down to Remi, but I wouldn't turn my back on this thing, not like some bimbo from a horror movie, not again. She'd fallen onto the side of the head I'd smashed in downstairs, so I had a clean profile facing me, and went to work. The ear was the first to go, then the back of the head opened up, but I had to be sure.

I kneeled over my brother, wiping my hands on my shirt so I wouldn't get more of the witch's blood on him.

A second ago he'd been crying.

The tears were still wet on his face.

I sat in the grass. Not under the magnolia tree, never there again. I held Remi, my arms around his body, alternating between sobbing and screaming. I ignored the burning place in my back. If the sirens were on, I didn't hear them, but I saw the lights.

A big black shape spoke to us. I thought it was Ray, but it had a mustache, wore a suit and tie. I nuzzled against Remi and wished he'd move, wished his eyes would open, his chest would rise.

Wished he would look at me and smile.

But the color had all run out of his face, his lips already pale blue. I breathed deep, searched for his scent, inhaled nothing but copper. I pressed my cheek against the cold slab of his face, my tears mixing with all our blood.

I love you, I tried to say, but my lips didn't work. The man with the mustache tried to pull my brother from my arms, but I clung to him, to this tiny, broken body that even stiff and lifeless was the most precious thing in the entire world.

"Look at her back."

"Yeah, I'll get it patched up, just get him."

"No, look. Stopped bleeding."

With one last, shuddering breath, I took in as much as I could of the last heat from Remi's body. I let the man with the mustache scoop my brother up in his arms, and only then noticed another pair of hands on my shoulders.

"Weird. Can't be that long ago, the blood around, it's still wet ..."

I turned to face a uniformed man with jet black hair and dusky skin, not much older than me. We watched the other man get to his feet holding my brother, lifting him carefully, a babe tucked in the crook of his arms. Memory flashed through my mind of an infant Remi, gurgling as he stared up at me with curious green eyes. Rosebud lips puckering to form my name.

The long thick hair of the man in the uniform made me think for just a moment that my father had returned, so I let go, and collapsed into his arms.

"No, no," I muttered, remembering. "He's dead, too."

CHAPTER TWENTY-EIGHT

I shuffled back and forth inside the circle while Labaye stirred the concoction that would "free" me from my body so Selena could claim my wolf. No longer frozen in place, I didn't exactly have a lot of room to move around. Just getting the toe of my Doc near the chalk line sent a thousand volts through my leg.

Someone had gotten better at casting circles. And she'd taught Labaye everything she knew.

Each time I blinked, my mind's eye filled with the slack, soulless black eyes I'd stared into only moments ago. I searched those eyes for the light that once burned so bright in my brother, the light of my heart. It was a uniquely hellish form of torture to face the woman who'd worn him like a mask, who waited now to kill me.

Selena was nothing if not creative.

If I could find a way out of this alive—at least with all of my elements still intact—I'd damn sure take it. I wasn't dead yet—there was still time.

Yeah, right. I needed to get rid of that optimism before it got me killed.

Labaye's eyes landed on me from his safe spot on the other side of the room. He knelt with the bucket between his knees, gripping the thin wooden rod with both hands as he stirred his bubbling tin cauldron like some cartoon villain. The sharp mossy stink got in my eyes, and I avoided his with a concentrated effort. I toed the edge of the circle, and it felt like putting my full weight down on broken glass, pain racing up my leg in a million small bites. The thick rubber sole of my Docs had begun to melt, which I definitely didn't remember from ten years ago.

Big, Bad Britta was big, bad stuck in every sense of the word.

Selena herself hung back for the moment, her face vacant in the shadows of the brick-lined chamber. She whispered to herself, too quiet for me to even recognize the language, a hellish prayer or meditation. Maybe she'd retreated into some purgatory to conserve her energy. It couldn't be easy to tear someone's soul from their body, could it? No easier than manifesting as the brother you killed just to fuck with them and destroy their hope.

Nah, that part had probably been a blast for her.

It was too hard to think of Remi. Too distracting, and I had to keep my wits about me.

Labaye scurried out of his corner, bringing the bucket toward the circle. I didn't bother looking over.

"I didn't know everything." His voice shook.

I rolled my eyes and plopped down cross-legged in the center of the circle. The fake drawing blew across the chalk and salt lines. If only it were so easy …

My feet hurt. I glared at Labaye. The purple light rendered his expression of self-loathing like one big bruise on a sad clown's face. He tended to his stinking devil potion as pitiful as a drunk hanging his head over a toilet about to puke, but I had no pity to give.

"Come on, Labaye." I glanced over Selena's way as her bone white hands did some perversion of crossing herself, then I turned back to glare at my suitor. "Don't puss out right before you clear the finish line." I ran my fingertip over the board just inside the lines, and pain shot up my wrist. "And didn't know *what*?" I snapped, pushing myself back up onto my feet.

"I knew she'd get you to turn me. To *tear* me, you call it, right? I knew she wanted us both." Labaye dropped his head even lower so his chin touched his chest. "The other part. I didn't know all that. The moment I met you, I … I felt something for you." His teeth clacked together. "I had no idea that was part of her plan, that she knew we'd fall in love."

In love. I rolled my eyes. "Yeah, well she got that part wrong. If we don't get to choose our mates, it should at least be someone we like. Now, back to your corner."

Labaye finally manned up and met my eyes, extending the fingers of his good hand. I'd swat the goddamned thing away if I had to reach through the circle to do it—but he lowered it, and picked up the pale silver knot of my fur and hair that he'd set on the chalk line.

No wonder he was making his grand apology. It was go time.

"I'm sorry, Britta." He closed his fist around my little hairball. "I don't have any more of a choice than you do."

I lurched against the circle—agony shot through my palms, running up my arms like teeth tearing off muscle and scraping bone. Even my wolf winced, though her power flared inside me. "Bullshit," I said, and pushed through the pain and fury. "There is *always* a choice."

He sighed and smiled so softly I couldn't tell if it was sad or menacing. Everything had a way of looking sinister under purple light.

"You're right," he said.

Labaye opened his fist and dropped the hairball into his hardware-store cauldron. For a moment, the light dimmed and the room went silent. Selena even paused in her mantra. Then, the brick walls lit up in shades of furious violet. The air moved, the candles blazed to life, coloring the shadows around the edges of the room. The chalk and salt ring shimmered awake, and misty white tendrils of flames curled up from the enchanted line. Labaye pushed the smoking bucket right up to the edge of the circle, the smell of black magic heavy in the air.

"Britta, dear, are you ready?" Selena sounded excited, eager. "Time to say goodbye."

Labaye shifted nervously at her side. I stepped toward the

bucket, to the edge of the chalk, avoiding the licking flames of the circle. If it had felt like teeth before, it'd chew clean through me now.

The wind that stirred the thick air shifted, and the boggy steam off the bucket hit me full in the face.

"I'm not drinking that," I said.

"Oh, Britta, dear. The smell, it isn't to your liking?" Selena mocked, clicking her teeth against her tongue. "I'm certain I'll come to value that sensitive snout of yours." She waved a willowy hand out as if she'd pierce the circle and pet my face.

Labaye shuffled beside her as she set her bare toes on the rim of the bucket. "You don't need to drink it," she said. "Just know that soon, if I command it, you will gobble down your own scat."

I chomped down on my temper, but Labaye, he dove at her leg, knocking the bucket away. It skittered across the boards, spewing the potion he'd slaved over, changing the smell of the whole chamber. Selena herself almost went over, but she caught her balance, screaming his name, his first name.

He spun in the other direction, to avoid the muck that pooled away from the circle—but he grabbed something gray off the floor.

Selena turned on him as he peeled pretend elephant hide away from a piece of black glass, got up on one knee, and with his bandaged hand drove the last shard of scrying mirror into her ribs.

She shrieked like a crow as her hands scratched at her side. The glass fell to the floorboards and broke in two. I didn't want to miss my own shot at this witch monster, so I leaped at her, but the barrier of the circle knocked me back, and every bone felt like shattered glass stabbing through muscle and organ.

Facing away from me on all fours, Labaye shot a leg out just as Selena latched a long taloned hand around his throat, and hauled him up.

The heel of his tactical boot wiped a narrow gap across both chalk and salt. The pressure around me lessened but didn't give way.

"I need you," I said to my wolf. She responded instantly.

Bones twisted so my feet came right out of the shoes. I shrugged out of the jacket, claws shredding the lining as I sprung over the salt and chalk lines.

Still, it hurt, it sliced through every inch of me as I left the circle. I'd make her hurt worse. My jaw gaped, spit flew from my fangs, fur poured behind claws sharper than the gris-gris she'd stabbed into me all those years ago.

She rolled, a white blur in the flashing purple light. She hauled Labaye off the ground like he weighed no more than a blanket.

Like Remi's dead body in the cop's arms.

I slammed into Labaye hard, threw him out of my way with clumsy paws, and I bit down on the witch's arm.

She shrieked again and slapped a palm across my forehead. The circle's sting couldn't compare to the jolt from that hand, but I knocked it away with my maw and clamped down with molars that snapped the arm in two.

Then I got her by the throat.

If she'd been a ghost, some ethereal haint, she might have slipped through my teeth. But while her pathetic Officer Renfield had stirred her witch's brew, now spilled all across the floor, she'd been gathering mass. The neck doesn't have a lot of muscle to get through. The rich taste of copper exploded in my mouth. As the trachea popped, and my canines connected on the far side of her cervical vertebrae, that bitch tasted better than any two-day-dead Market Basket side of beef.

It wasn't Britta so much as the wolf Selena had wanted so bad, who planted her claws into the floorboards and whipped around with the full force of her body. The big she-wolf growled at top volume, jaws locked on her prey, which she thrashed back and forth until the head snapped clean off.

She panted over the pale corpse. She licked the gore off her muzzle and barked one time at the headless woman with two broken arms.

The spill moved slowly across the boards, and the wolf sniffed at it but recoiled from the sharp smell of something dead much longer than one would expect. The blood that she cleaned from her paw tasted different than the witch's blood. Not better, per se, because she'd rather not have shed this blood, and she hung her head as she set amber eyes on the man she'd torn through to get at the witch.

CHAPTER TWENTY-NINE

Labaye bled out on the rough boards, his blood mixing with the potion he'd spent so much time on, mixing with the other red flow from Selena's neck.

My hands, just hands again, should have been pale, but Labaye's blood painted them dark red.

I'd ripped his windbreaker, ripped the shirt away. Oh, I'd torn him, all right. Two sets of gashes marked his tan chest, marked him for dead. This idiot had wanted to be a werewolf and got himself killed.

No. When it came down to it, he'd tried to help me, and I'd killed him. No one could say it wasn't my fault this time.

If I lapped the stinking potion off the floor maybe it would free me after all, send me on to Remi and to my mother, and even poor Ray. To Daddy. Or maybe I'd just be another ghost in this goddamned house. Maybe that's all I'd been all along.

"No," I groaned, dropping to my knees beside Labaye. My thoughts were scrambled, conflicted, and contradictory, but one thing was clear. Whether he was chosen to be my mate or not, whether or not he was blameless in all this, I didn't want him to die. "Labaye," I barely shook his shoulder and blood bubbled from the cut closest to his throat. I pulled my hand back, and he groaned in response. "What were you thinking?" I said.

He managed a weak version of his good cop smile, teeth, and lips the same shade of red. "Yer welcome."

I told myself if he could joke, he'd be okay. That optimism, again. His Adam's apple traveled slowly down his throat to swim back up, taking far more effort than it should. Sweat beaded on his skin, and it smelled wrong. Color drained from his face. Almost none of that earthy aroma—no pine, no musk—hung in the air, while the puddle of blood beneath him spread, filling in the seams between the boards. Dull eyes stared into the rafters, and I realized the candles had all burned down, the purple fire had been snuffed out with Selena. Poor Labaye couldn't see a thing.

"Why didn't you just let her do it?" I asked. "Let me die?"

His body shuddered—maybe he'd tried to shrug.

"Stupid." I only half meant it.

"Brave," Labaye managed with another weak smile. He shuddered again, mouth twisting to show a top row of red teeth.

I pushed back onto my heels, pressed the palms of my hands to my temples, and tried to remember anything I'd learned about tearing. Vampire stories made the whole thing pretty complicated, from Anne Rice to the little daggers in *The Hunger* to the "sire bond" from *Vampire Diaries*. How we do it, though, was a blank spot in my training—no doubt a deliberate omission on behalf of my *loup guru*. He had plans of his own. I'd personally been turned a whole different way, Selena's nasty gris-gris deal, so I'd never witnessed the miracle before me now in the shape of a local officer suffering multiple sucking chest wounds.

But if a wolf tore a human—which I'd done, knuckles deep—and they had magic, they could turn.

If they didn't die. And once they turned ... they pretty much would not die.

So, how would I differentiate between a tear that kills and one that turns?

Labaye took a deep, wracking breath that I could see in the blood bubbling on his lips.

"So hot in here," he said, and finally met my eyes. "S'posed to get cold at the end."

I sniffed to hold back tears, but his blood acted like smelling salts on me.

"Hot," he said. "I feel hot."

"You have magic in you." It had smelled too pleasant, too enticing, nothing like the bitter vanilla I'd come to expect—but it was magic nonetheless.

Our eyes locked. He focused right on me.

So he *could* see in the dark now. But if he was turning, the blood should stop, and it still ran down his chest, carrying that scent of his, of pine and musk and the magic I hadn't recognized.

Because it wasn't just any magic, but a special mark. For me.

"Selena picked you for that." My power flared through me. "Just hang on …"

"Not going anywhere, Br—" He winced so hard blood eked through his teeth, through the cut under his collarbone.

I kicked Mom's dead friend just to be sure. I slipped my leather jacket back on, searched through the muck, running my fingers across the floor, and pulled up Rothko. The gray scraps dripped with the sulfur stink of the potion. I found two last bits of mirror, no bigger than silver dollars, and stuffed it all in my pocket.

I lay a hand on Labaye's chest while I slipped the ring of keys from his belt, looking for one with the little squat cross, the Chevrolet logo, at the top. With what looked like a lot of exertion, Labaye's good hand found its way on top of mine, the skin clammy and hot, laundry pulled too early from the drier. He opened his mouth, sucking air like a fish without water. Blood bubbled between his lips, and his skin had gone from tan to blue, now to gray.

I crossed his arms over his chest, sarcophagus-style. Grabbing under his armpits, I dragged him through the crawlspace into Remi's bedroom. At the darkest point in that tunnel, he stopped moaning.

The midday light blinded me. I propped Labaye up against the corner of the fireplace and shot a glance out the window to make sure nothing watched from the magnolia tree.

His chest rose and fell in a shallow and rocky rhythm. I took a deep breath myself, glad to be away from the sulfur swamp stench of the potion, though it still clung to us, and fresh blood seeped from Labaye's wounds.

"Damn it, Aaron," I said. "Don't you leave me, too."

A burst of his unique musk filled the air. His eyelids fluttered open, revealing clouded eyes more gray than brown, and he sat still for a moment. Recognition opened his features as he took in Remi's bedroom. He moved the fingers of his good hand up to the tears in his chest, blinked a few times, and stared at me.

A grin broke across his face, and I felt one move across mine.

"You finally called me by my first name," he whispered as he moved the hand to my cheek. An ice-cold fingertip dotted the space near my eye. "Fireflies," he said.

His hand dropped into his lap, and I reached for it. His eyes blinked open and closed, and I looked for any hint of gold in the dull brown iris.

Labaye gave my hand a faint squeeze. His words were breathy, his deep voice reduced to a whisper.

"Y'know what happens if you save me."

"You'll be a wolf."

"Not that." He sighed, and the breath went on a long time, like something leaving him. "You know she was right."

Labaye's grip went slack and his hand fell from mine. I could barely smell his magic anymore, the scent so faint I had to fill my lungs with air just for a trace of it.

"So, how do I finish it?" I shook him, I wouldn't lose anyone else tonight.

He opened his eyes but let his head rock back and forth. "Left that out of my training. She was strictly need-to-know," he said. "Kind of a control freak."

"Fuck that." I slipped an arm under his shoulder, the other

under his knees. "I'm in control."

He howled in pain when I forced my leg under his back and hoisted him up. Even buried within me, my wolf was strong enough to get him out of Remi's room and past the sealed attic door. We went slow on the stairs, careful not to slip in the blood that still dripped from him, overpowering his fading scent, which had called to me right from the start.

"Aaron, let go," I said when he grabbed the banister and almost made me lose my balance.

That's when I heard footsteps—boots—walking past the parlor.

I froze. Labaye winced and I shushed him.

Of course. Of course, Alec hadn't left, of course, he wouldn't sit by while I turned another wolf.

I saw the pistol first. Then the big man in the mustache and suit rounded the corner at the entryway.

"You hurt?" Devereaux asked. I hadn't recognized the stink of the cigarette burning in his lips.

I had to think for a second, but the bloody heap in my arms had passed out again so I leaned my ass into the banister and got the rest of the way down the stairs. "Selena's upstairs."

"You better have killed her this time," Devereaux said as he holstered his gun. He pressed two fat fingers against Labaye's neck, then reached under his armpits, letting me take the feet.

"Oh, yeah," I said. Labaye's head lolled against the older cop's chest, which gave me a better view of the wounds.

I leaned against the front doors, threw the deadbolt, and led us out into broad daylight.

This all really seemed like nightshift work.

Devereaux didn't shut the door behind him, just jerked a jowly chin toward his old Lincoln, parked beside the Chevy pick-up. The bruises Alec had given him reminded me of the light show in that room upstairs.

"When I found you," he said, already out of breath, "back then, you'd already stopped bleeding." He leaned on the side of the trunk and fumbled for the back door handle. "That mean anything?"

I yelled I didn't know as we got Labaye into the long back-seat, then I ran around the other side and slipped in under him. While I made the patient comfortable, Devereaux made a call.

"Got a badly wounded officer," he said, lighting a fresh smoke. His car already stank of it. "Right, Labaye. Yeah, and it's bleeding like hell." He tossed his cell skittering the length of the dashboard, bouncing down beside the passenger door.

I cradled Labaye's head in my lap as the engine roared to life and we peeled out across the old porcelain tiles.

We drove past Paul Beaulieu's parents' house, and for just a second I thought of Scarlett, thought of all her suitors, the way she collected husbands like so many bad habits, always sure she had no choice.

They were all choices.

"Must've fallen 'sleep," Labaye muttered, trying to blink himself lucid. "Thought he was Alec, and just, fuck it."

"Aww, you finally swore." I stroked a lock of black hair off his forehead. "But he's probably back in Maine killing our alpha. Or getting killed." Labaye closed his eyes in a pained expression. "Alec and Selena had a lot in common."

We passed the turn for the freeway, heading for the center of Vinton. "Which hospital …?" I started to ask.

Devereaux hadn't turned on the siren, wasn't even driving that fast.

Aaron winced again as the Lincoln bounced over a pair of railroad tracks, then slowed almost to a stop beside a playground and turned into a small parking lot.

Devereaux pulled into the only handicapped spot in front of the Calcasieu Parish Public Library. He shoved the gear shift on the steering column into park, and before I could put it all together he'd hopped out and opened my door. He hooked his hands under Labaye's shoulders and helped me get him out of the car. I met Devereaux's eyes for just a second, but I didn't have time to be surprised.

"Okay, Rookie, try to stay awake," I said as we carried Aaron feet first into the library past Mam Byrdie, who held open the door. "We both need to pay attention to this next part."

ABOUT THE AUTHORS

LINDY RYAN is an award-winning horror and dark fantasy editor and author. When she's not immersed in books, Ryan is an avid historical researcher, with specific interest in nautical and maritime history, cryptozoology, and ancient civilizations. She is represented by Gandolfo Helin & Fountain Literary Management. She also writes clean, seasonal romance under the name Lindy Miller, where several of her titles have been adapted for film. Ryan is a member of the Horror Writers Association, serves on the IBPA Board of Directors, and was a 2020 Publishers Weekly Star Watch Honoree. Find her on social media @LindyRyanWrites or at her website, www.GlitterAndGravedust.com.

CHRISTOPHER BROOKS writes and edits in the Pacific Northwest with his wife and children and a blurry sense of reality.